THE RINGWOOD TREE

by
M. S. Stanley

Visit
www.ringwoodtree.co.uk

First Published in Great Britain in 2008
by
Tigwip Press

Copyright © 2008 Mark Spain

Names, characters and related indicia are copyright and trademark
Copyright © 2008 Mark Spain

Mark Spain has asserted his moral rights
to be identified as the author

A CIP Catalogue of this book is available from
the British Library

ISBN 978-0-9560768-0-9

Printed by the MPG Books Group
in the UK

For Sharon, my DDLL forever,
and for my Tom, with love

The Black Forest
Southern Germany 1784

The horsemen passed warily through the forest, each rider sitting low and leaning forwards in his saddle. Their horses were darkly coloured thoroughbreds, powerful and magnificent, but in this part of the forest at night they were ill at ease.

The captain of the guard suddenly left the forest trail, suspecting that the element of surprise would be his only real weapon during what was to follow.

"Halt!" he shouted. "Dismount!"

His men obeyed the order and began leading their horses on foot, the way ahead now dense with trees.

A single torch was lit, its flame casting a fragile pool of light against the blackness of the forest floor. Just as it was becoming almost too close to navigate, the bristling foliage thinned to reveal a clearing in which a house stood.

For many nights, the beauty of a full moon had shone upon the vastness of the Black Forest. That lunar cycle had now come to an end, and to both the farmer and the townsfolk, the following nights of darkness filled the land with an unpleasant and brooding menace. Many longed for the return of the moonlight but there were others for whom the darkness was a busy time; three dark nights in which to gather new ingredients; three dark nights in which to practise their sinister magic.

It was their time, their "dark of the moon", and not a minute of it was to be wasted.

The house was tall, and at each of its four corners rose stout timber supports that were as weathered and as twisted as the ancient woodland that surrounded them. Upper storeys bulged outwards, the tiny leaded windows slanted and dark. The roof was a steep-sided bank of razor-edged tiles with a tall, crooked chimney twisting up from its centre from which ribbons of filthy, ember-flecked smoke rolled into the air. Downstairs, the greasy flame of a single candle shone feebly through a ground-floor window and here, within its sour-eyed glow, sat the owner of the house - a small, bearded figure who feverishly mixed, poured and crushed his newly collected material.

His three dark nights of work had begun.

Five of the horsemen crept forwards, carrying small, wooden barrels, the contents of which they poured around the base of the house. They returned swiftly to the shadows of the tree line, and the entire company re-mounted. A torch was passed down the line, each man lighting the pitch on the end of his wooden staff. With fire blazing, the soldiers advanced and formed a circle around the dark and silent house.

"Forwards!" shouted the captain of the guard, and the circle began to close.

The little figure paused in his work, thinking he had heard the whinnying of a horse. But now there was only silence.

With a dismissive nod, he returned to his tools but dropped them again when a second noise reached him. Peering through the window, he stared in surprise at several dark shapes that were approaching on horseback. He withdrew into the shadows, trembling in the excited hope that they were travellers lost in this deep and difficult part of the Black Forest. He had helped many lost souls over the years and always enjoyed watching their relief as they arrived – and their horror when they tried to leave. His quick little hands tugged one another in excitement, and with a smile he threw open the door of his house and stepped outside.

Torches spiralled noisily onto the pitch-splattered earth and a sheet of fire sprang into the air.

"For the emperor!" shouted the men on horseback. "For the emperor!" they shouted in unison, the little figure suddenly realising who they were and what they had come to do.

The little man tried to remember an ancient summoning spell, a spell to raise a fierce rainstorm that would douse the flames and bring heavy thunderbolts to scatter his tormentors, but the rising smoke was foul and acrid and its heat burned the back of his throat.

"I am summoning spirits from the west!" he cried. "I am summoning spirits from the east! Rains, rains… give from your… skies. Burst water up… on…" but the heat forced him inside. With a scream he fled towards a trapdoor and disappeared.

The flames leapt higher and skittered excitedly across sun-dried woodwork. Ancient plaster fell in huge, brittle chunks. Giant, hand-carved timbers groaned as they were twisted and split apart by hungry fingers of flame. Tiny panes of glass popped and shattered in the rising heat, their lead frames bending slowly into the fire. In the owner's little workshop, bottles, vials and beakers grew hot, their strange, living contents exploding from confinement.

The warping roof and upper floors collapsed with a cavernous rumble and a triumphant cone of light leapt towards the stars. Below it, the fire feasted hungrily on ribs of blackened timbers.

A figure suddenly burst from the core of the building, its back bright with flame. "It is wooden!" yelled an astonished soldier, slashing at the figure with his sword. "It is a living thing of cloth, wood and metal!"

Other figures appeared, each as tattered and inhuman as the first, and four-legged beasts ran with them, bellowing and squealing in fear.

The entire company galloped forwards, slashing at the creatures until they lay broken and scattered. The soldiers regrouped, silent and watchful and keen to end their uncanny night's work.

Eventually, the order was given to dismount and the soldiers stepped forwards.

The captain of the guard nodded, relieved to have fulfilled the emperor's secret orders and satisfied that nobody, not even a person rumoured to have been in possession of many dark powers, could have survived such a blaze.

He stared in satisfaction at the mound of pulsing ash.

CHAPTER I

THE NOTE

The Present Day

It was mid-December in England and piercing winds were chilling the bones of anyone whose business took them outside. A heavy drape of violet-grey sky flashed orange along the horizon to the west, and birds gathered and called to one another across treetops. Another pale winter afternoon was drawing to a close, and as the town clock struck quarter past the hour, so too was another school day.

Waiting groups of parents held the tight-lipped conversations of the freezing, their mouths kept small against the dead winter air. Screams, whoops and last-minute battles came sweeping towards them as the children appeared, ready for home.

In the tumble of the playground stood a boy and a girl. The girl was the elder of the two and her straight blonde hair framed a suspicious expression. She was listening impatiently to her brother, whose tangled hair and crumpled school uniform suggested he had spent the entire day rolling around on the floor.

"*Where* did you say you were going?" she asked him for the third time.

"Jack's house," replied the boy. "It's been arranged for ages."

"Where is Jack? I can't see him."

"I-I'm meeting him at his house," stammered the boy. "I promise I won't be late. Just tell Aunt Betty where I'm going."

The boy cast a nervous glance towards the school gates and saw their aunt looking for them anxiously. She was moving closer but had not yet seen them.

The boy stared pleadingly at his sister, willing her to agree, but the girl remained unhurried and undecided.

"You know we're supposed to stay together," she reminded him. "Aunt Betty'll go nuts if I tell her you went off on your own. She's so twitchy at the moment and still thinks there are kidnappers in every alley…"

The girl paused and stared at the ground, her eyes filling with tears.

The boy knew only too well what Aunt Betty would say to them and could recite every one of her recent lectures, even mimicking their aunt's pleading tones if asked to. But he insisted he would be careful.

Cold and fed up, the girl finally agreed, and with a weary sigh she pushed her way over to the school gates where she was smothered by her aunt's hugs and kisses.

The boy ran quickly to the other side of the playground, flitting skilfully between legs, bags and pushchairs. He ran at full speed, whooping wildly and not quite believing that neither the endless suspicions of his sister nor the sweeping gaze of his watchful aunt had prevented him, Thomas Trenham, from beginning *the plan*.

Tom knew he'd be in trouble if his lie about visiting

Jack was ever discovered, but he also knew that he couldn't ignore the note. It had arrived mysteriously in the pocket of his school shirt as he had been changing after PE, and its message had been brief, simple and to the point. It read:

My Dear Tom,
Please visit me this Friday after school. I have news of your missing parents; good news! Tell no one you are coming. There will be tea and cake.
Courage, my boy,

Your grandfather
P.S. Would you be so kind as to bring some bananas? Splendid!

Tom hardly needed reminding that his parents were missing or that they had been gone for two weeks. For some reason Aunt Betty, who had arrived to look after him and his sister Cassie, blamed their disappearance on Tom's grandfather.

"*Whose* house were your parents walking to the day they disappeared?" Aunt Betty had asked them. "That's right: *his* house!" and she had vacuumed the carpet a little harder, muttering, "That mad old devil knows more than he's saying!"

It now looked as if Aunt Betty was right.

Tom reached the pedestrian crossing and suddenly decided to take the shortcut through the park, hoping it would stay light long enough for him to finish his journey in safety. He felt the comforting weight of his sister's mobile phone in his pocket and prayed that Cassie wouldn't notice that it was missing.

The park's double gates stood tall and open, their heavy ironwork a sinewy pattern of roses and snakes. As Tom drew closer to them, he gradually became aware of the stillness of the path beyond, and he jumped when a row of park lamp-posts suddenly blinked into life, one by one. Tom caught his breath and stepped forwards.

The normally busy playground was quiet and empty, and long winter shadows revealed the swings and the climbing frames in unfamiliar, bony outline. Tom stared anxiously and scurried on.

Moments later, he noticed a figure sitting on a park bench just ahead of him. The figure was hidden behind a large newspaper, its legs sticking straight out in front of it, too short to reach the ground. *If he's a grown up he must be small!* thought Tom, trying not to stare.

Then something strange happened.

The little figure kept the newspaper in front of him, using it like a shield to remain hidden when Tom passed by. Tom quickened his pace, aware that it was much too cold and dark to be reading outside. He stopped suddenly and stared in disbelief.

A second little figure sat on another park bench, holding another large newspaper. Tom spun round and saw that the bench he had just passed was now empty!

Tom ran at full speed and saw that this little figure also remained hidden behind its newspaper in the same secretive way.

Tom ran and ran, and soon reached the far side of the park where he stood panting in front of a wide bank of rhododendron bushes. The bushes provided excellent cover for him and his friends during the summer, but now they looked dark and forbidding and filled with danger. Tom realised that he had forgotten his torch and he pushed forwards anxiously, hoping that nobody was following him.

The waxy foliage swallowed what little remained of the fading light, and the view ahead of him became a dark and featureless haze. Tom crept through the undergrowth and felt as if he had been transformed into a boy-sized shadow that could pass, undetected, over anything. He smiled and closed his eyes, and marvelled at the powerful silence when all of a sudden a voice, just behind him, said,

"Three and a half steps to your left, young man, and you will find yourself falling into an old, collapsed drain."

Tom froze, too terrified to move.

CHAPTER 2

At Your Service

The figure stepped forwards and trod on a stick that was brittle with ice. The noise of it snapping spurred Tom into action. He crouched low and fumbled for his sister's mobile phone, but suddenly found himself off-balance. He tottered backwards and landed on his bottom with a bump.

The stranger stepped closer.

"S-stop or I'll call the police!" cried Tom, pointing the phone like a weapon.

The figure chuckled.

"Thomas Trenham!" it said. "I give you my word as a…" It paused, as if searching for the right word. "I give you my word as a *gentleman* that you will not be harmed."

"How do you know my name?" gasped Tom. "Who are you?"

The figure ignored Tom's questions and remained in the shadows.

"Were you to use that portable telephonic device," the

figure continued, "not only would it ruin your grandpapa's plan, but I, too, would be greatly inconvenienced, for your grandpapa has sent me to escort you to him. Evening draws near and there is much to explain. Come. Follow me."

The stranger turned and waited.

Tom struggled to his feet, one hand gripping Cassie's phone while the other brushed leaves and twigs from his coat. He studied the stranger carefully and saw that his trousers and coat were much too large for his small body. A woollen scarf and a wide-brimmed hat kept the stranger's features in shadow and a carefully folded newspaper stuck out from his pocket. It seemed that the little man *had* been watching Tom from the park bench after all.

The stranger cleared his throat and held back some branches, expecting Tom to follow. As he seemed rather small and claimed to know his grandfather, Tom decided to trust the stranger, and he stepped forwards cautiously. The little man nodded and moved deeper into the undergrowth.

"That note in my school shirt," asked Tom. "Did *you* put it there?"

The stranger nodded and said,

"Your grandpapa's description of your classroom and your school bag and your belongings was extremely accurate. My secretive escape, however, was hindered by having to disguise myself in one of your modern-day school uniforms. Most uncouth! In my day a stiff collar, jacket and a pair of breeches gave one backbone at school, but now…"

The well-mannered voice tailed away as the stranger reached the iron railings at the edge of the park. He squeezed between them easily but Tom was forced to scramble over them, and he jumped from the wall. Tom found himself standing on a wide and empty road where large houses nestled within high-hedged gardens. There were no cars and no people, and the only light came from a row of old-fashioned lamp-posts that shone feebly in the gloom.

"Now, child," said the little man, "we are approaching your grandpapa's residence. Do you see the light from his porch?"

Tom looked across to where the little man was pointing, but saw only the unchecked tangle of his grandfather's overgrown garden. He was about to reply that he couldn't see anything *and* that he preferred being called "Tom" to "child", when he suddenly caught sight of a speck of brightness shining through the trees.

"Yes, I can see it!" said Tom. "That's Grandfather's porch."

"Then know that I mean you no harm and will take you straight to him."

Tom nodded and accepted the stranger's help, but he kept a firm grip on Cassie's mobile phone. "Before we continue," the little stranger added, "I feel I must warn you of recent aberrations in your grandpapa's behaviour."

"Has he gone mad like Aunt Betty says he has?"

"Mad? Indeed not! He has the most brilliant mind I have ever had the pleasure of working with. It is almost the equal of mine! No, I speak of certain... perturbations in his temperament."

"Per-tur what?" asked Tom, not understanding the man's long words.

"Small constitutional imbalances," explained the little man, as if it were now clear.

Tom frowned again and the stranger gasped in frustration.

"He... is... a... changed... man," the stranger said. "I am sure his recent discovery is the cause of it. But I have said enough. Let us talk in more pleasant surroundings."

The stranger scurried across the deserted road, and Tom trailed after him.

In the pale, wintry twilight, the overhanging trees and

the overgrown bushes had turned the driveway to Tom's grandfather's house into a long and forbidding tunnel. The little man strode forwards but Tom hesitated, convinced that the roots, branches and twigs surrounding them all possessed a sly breath of life.

He jumped when the mysterious stranger suddenly began to murmur,

> *"Lead, kindly Light amid the encircling gloom,*
> *Lead Thou me on;*
> *The night is dark, and I am far from Home;*
> *Lead Thou me on.*
> *Keep Thou my feet;*
> *I do not ask to see*
> *The distant scene – one step enough for me."*

This may have comforted the little man but it scared Tom half to death. Between the heavy crunch of the frosted gravel and the peculiar chanting of his guide, Tom began to wonder whether he had made the right decision in coming after all.

CHAPTER 3

Grandfather and Friend

Tom was relieved when the dark silhouette of his grandfather's house loomed into view. He resisted the urge to run ahead of his "guide" to the welcoming hug he knew would be waiting for him.

The house projected its usual air of faded grandeur; its old, peeling shutters were closed as if in sleep. As they drew nearer, Tom suddenly noticed that the porch light was illuminating a rather curious object hanging at the centre of the front door. It was round and flat and appeared to be made out of metal, and it was large, much larger than a dinner plate, and Tom was certain that it hadn't been there during his last visit. He wondered if the object was an old shield from his grandfather's collection, but quickly decided that it looked too delicate for battle. Then he wondered if it was some strange kind of doorknocker.

Suddenly, and with no recollection of either approaching the steps or stepping into the light, Tom found himself standing in front of the curious object.

"Do not stare at it so!" shouted the little man, fumbling awkwardly for the keys. But Tom was transfixed by a pair of eyes that stared out at him from the centre of the disc.

The eyes belonged to a face that had been carved into the metal, a face whose features resembled hundreds of overlapping leaves. The eye-sockets were dark and empty and sat above a wide and horribly grinning mouth, and the face itself was filled with a sinister watchfulness.

An engraving of a forest filled the rest of the disc's surface, and just as Tom leant forwards to study it in detail, the door was flung open and Tom was bustled inside.

Tom stared unsteadily as the little man fastened the bolts and the locks behind him, his gloved hands trembling as they worked.

"Safe and sound!" said the little man, stepping into the hallway. "Kindly remove your coat and your bag and leave them on the bench over there. I will fetch us some hot fortification."

The man padded down the passageway still wearing his baggy hat, coat, scarf and gloves.

"Er... thank you!" called Tom, feeling light-headed and dizzy. "Thank you very much, Mr...?"

"Perkins!" shouted the figure, closing the door behind him. "*Professor* Perkins!"

Tom felt, as he always did, that he had wandered inside a cross between a very old museum and a very old library. The familiar scent of floor-wax, furniture polish and home-cooked meals surrounded him, and Tom gazed at the artefacts that his grandfather had spent a lifetime collecting.

He studied the books: row upon row of dusty old tomes that stood in towering piles from floor to ceiling. Most of the books were stacked neatly, but some had collapsed in on themselves and now looked like one of the ancient settlements that his grandfather had excavated. Small amber-jewelled lights sat amongst leather-bound volumes, the length of one wall resembling a bizarre Christmas tree of books that had been laid on its side, lights twinkling deep within papery branches.

Tom placed his coat and his rucksack on the bench, and caught his scared-looking reflection staring back at him from a mirror. He jumped in surprise, then jumped again when a voice from upstairs suddenly boomed, "Forgive me Tom! I will be with you shortly! *Blast!*"

There was a crash and a thud and a worrying silence. Tom ran to the foot of the staircase.

"Grandfather?" he called. "Grandfather, are you all right? Have you fallen?"

There was no reply.

Tom remembered the worried conversations his parents had been having about his grandfather's age and the possibility of him coming to live with them, an idea he knew his grandfather – who was a proud and independent man – would never agree to.

"Don't worry, Tom! Merely another book fall!" his grandfather replied, his voice tinged with embarrassment. "Please… go into the study. There's a good fire lit and several of the chairs are quite serviceable. Blast!"

More books thudded to the floor as Tom reluctantly did as he was told.

The study was filled with more dusty artefacts, but Tom didn't feel like inspecting any of these. Suddenly tired, he sank into a deep armchair and let the soothing warmth of the well-banked fire spread over him.

He sighed and trembled as he thought of his eventful journey through the park, and didn't notice when a figure slipped into the room. The gentle rattle of teacups alerted Tom to the stranger's presence, and when Tom looked he leapt from his armchair and crouched behind it.

Walking upright across the carpet was a monkey. Its fur was a pale shade of caramel and its face was light brown. It was carrying a tea tray upon which a teapot, teacups, a large and succulent ginger cake, and slices and slices of hot buttered toast had been carefully arranged. The monkey's eyes flashed with a quick intelligence, and Tom watched, open-mouthed, as the creature placed the tray on a footstool near the fire. It was concentrating very hard and didn't seem to know, or care, that Tom was there.

It paused for a moment, then settled into an armchair and pulled a thick, tartan shawl across its shoulders. It gazed into the fire with a sad, far-away expression and sighed.

Tom blinked in astonishment and crept forwards slowly, assuming the monkey was tame enough to stroke. The monkey saw Tom approaching and scowled.

"N-nice monkey!" stammered Tom, patting the creature's head. "Who's a clever monkey?" he cooed. "Who's a clever monkey?"

The monkey, clearly annoyed, sat up straight and said, "Given that I have won awards for my outstanding literature, I suppose it is *I* who is a clever monkey. Now kindly stop petting my head!"

CHAPTER 4

Strange News

or the second time that afternoon, Tom was too frightened to speak. He leapt behind his armchair and peered around its side, staring at the creature that had just spoken to him.

The monkey returned to its fire-gazing.

Just then, the tall and imposing figure of Tom's grandfather burst into the room, a pile of books under one arm, the other supporting himself on a walking stick.

"Your grandfather is here, quite well and in one piece!" he boomed. When he saw Tom crouching on the floor he dropped what he was carrying and limped over to his grandson.

"Tom! Tom, my boy! Are you all right?"

Tom tried to make the words to explain what had just happened.

"It... he... the monkey... it *spoke* to me!"

"Ah!" said Tom's grandfather quietly. "I see you've just met Perkins."

"Perkins?" said Tom. "No, Professor Perkins went downstairs to make some drinks. He must have sent up this monkey who *talks*, Grandfather! It's incredible!"

"Ah," said Tom's grandfather again. "I had hoped Perkins would have explained all this to you by now." He glared angrily at the hairy figure in the armchair, but the monkey shrugged dismissively. "Tom, this *is* Professor Perkins!" Tom's grandfather added dramatically. "The little 'man' I sent to watch over you in the park and the little 'boy' who delivered my note to your shirt pocket at your school – both were Professor Perkins!" The old man turned to the monkey. "Perkins! Why the devil didn't you warn the boy before you removed your disguise? Answer me, sir!"

The monkey bristled indignantly and replied, "Nature has given us *two* ears, *two* eyes and *one* tongue. We should therefore *hear* and *see* more than we speak. It seemed the wisest thing to do!"

"So wise as to have scared my grandson half to death! Now pour the refreshments while I assist poor Tom."

Professor Trenham took Tom's arm and led his grandson back to his chair.

Tom found it impossible not to stare at the peculiar little creature as it poured drinks and sliced the cake, still wearing its tartan shawl. It hummed a little tune as Tom's grandfather sank gratefully into his own battered armchair, propping his walking stick against its side.

"Now, Tom, as you know," the old man explained, "I have devoted my life to the study of the ancient world. I became a professor of antiquities many, many years before you were born and was lucky enough to have been present at a number of important archaeological digs. Ah, tea! Splendid!"

Professor Trenham took a cup and set it down next to him. The monkey approached Tom and held out a steaming mug.

"I have taken the liberty of preparing a hot beverage

derived from the seeds of a certain South American plant, *Theobroma cacao*, the qualities of which, I believe, small children have an insatiable appetite for."

Tom stared blankly, not understanding the monkey's long words.

"Oh for heaven's sake Perkins, speak English!" Tom's grandfather exclaimed. "He's saying that he's made you a mug of hot chocolate, Tom. Please, drink up!"

The monkey looked upset.

"May I remind the professor of whom he demands to 'speak English'? I am Professor Augustus Perkins. Classicist! Scholar! Man of science!"

The monkey raised an arm and the tartan shawl slipped to the floor.

A talking monkey who thinks it's some sort of professor? thought Tom, deciding to wait, watch and run if he had to.

Tom's grandfather sighed and said, "Forgive me, Perkins, forgive me. It has been an extremely stressful two weeks. Your command of English is exemplary."

"I have won awards for it," said the monkey.

"As you are so often kind enough to remind me. But now I think it best if you leave us alone for a while, as we agreed, hmmm? So that I may begin my explanation?"

The little monkey thought for a moment, then nodded and left the room, the shawl now draped over its arm.

Once they were alone, Tom blurted out, "Mum and Dad, in your note, you said you had news of them. Where are they, Grandfather? Have you seen them?"

The old man sighed and glanced towards the door.

"Yes… and no. Oh dear. I really ought to start from the beginning. Do help yourself to refreshment, Tom. I particularly recommend Perkins' hot buttered toast."

Professor Trenham settled back into his armchair and took a deep breath, then suddenly leant forwards and stared intensely. In quick, hurried tones, he said, "I imagine you noticed a large metallic disc hanging on my front door just now?"

"Er, y-yes. Yes I did," said Tom, taken aback by his grandfather's expression. "It was strange… and beautiful. Did you find it on a dig?"

"Beautiful!" cried his grandfather. "Well, I suppose it does possess a certain beauty, though one worthy of Hecate herself!" He flashed an odd smile before continuing, "Yes, my boy, I did uncover the object on a dig, but it was no ordinary dig. Oh, I have travelled the world discovering many ancient and beautiful relics, yet fate decided that I was to find my most extraordinary and troublesome one buried in my own garden!"

Tom sipped his hot chocolate nervously.

"As you can tell," said Tom's grandfather, "I have no time or talent for gardening but do keep a small patch of grass clear at the back of the house. Here I bury nails and coins and test my old metal-detector. One afternoon, two weeks ago, I wandered from this test patch and ended up in a wild part of the garden. I was daydreaming, you see, but was soon jarred to my senses when the old detector let out a piercing shriek!"

"It'd found the disc?" asked Tom, enjoying his hot chocolate.

"Yes, it'd found the disc. After retrieving it, cleaning it and undertaking some research, I discovered that the object was the work of a talented toymaker, a gentleman by the name of Hans Von Rippenbaum whose workshop once stood in the Black Forest of what is now southern Germany. To find one of his pieces so thoroughly intact really was quite a find, for Von Rippenbaum lived over two hundred years ago!"

"What was an old toy doing buried in your–"

"Oh, the disc is no toy!" cried Professor Trenham, almost

leaping from his armchair.

Tom was suddenly aware how tired his grandfather looked, how sunken his cheeks were and how strangely his skin shone. He grew uncomfortable under the old man's gaze and looked away into the fire. "Forgive me Tom, I… I didn't mean to startle you. I simply meant that the disc has certain powers that elevate it beyond those of a mere toy."

"Can it make animals talk?" said Tom. "Is that why the monkey sounds human?"

"No, Professor Perkins sounds human because he once *was* human. He found the disc and used it many years ago but became trapped inside it, only escaping after it became… re-activated."

Tom sat, open-mouthed, uncertain what to say. Eventually, he stammered, "If he was trapped inside the disc I… I suppose he was lucky you re-activated it for him."

"I didn't," replied Professor Trenham softly. "Your parents were the ones who did that, I am sorry to say."

CHAPTER 5

Professor Perkins

om was offered several triangles of hot buttered toast, but he remained too upset to eat any. He stared miserably at the carpet and wondered whether he was part of some elaborate, and not very funny, joke.

"All is not lost, my boy!" said his grandfather, trying to cheer him up. "Professor Perkins is alive and well and I'm sure your parents are both–"

"Professor Perkins is a *monkey*!" cried Tom, suddenly scared and angry. "Are Mum and Dad monkeys too?"

"No, of course they're not! At least, I don't think so. But please, Tom, hear the rest of my story then decide what you think of your old grandfather, hmm?"

"Sorry," mumbled Tom, suddenly feeling confused and embarrassed.

The old man smiled kindly.

"This is what happened. Your parents came to visit me two Saturdays ago to discuss some shards of Roman pottery that had been discovered locally. All talk of pottery was quickly forgotten the moment they saw the disc hanging on my front door. I had put it there to clean it, you see, and as you may imagine, your parents were most intrigued by it. While I was in the kitchen preparing tea, I felt the entire house rumble. Cups rattled, windows shook, and though alarming, I merely assumed that an aeroplane was passing low overhead. Returning through the hallway, however, I realised that the rumbling had, in fact, come from the disc itself. The door was wide open, little wisps of smoke were rising from the disc's leafy surface and, most peculiar of all, the hairy figure of a monkey now sat upon my doorstep! Alas, your parents were nowhere to be seen. You may then imagine my surprise when the monkey suddenly turned to me and asked, 'Do you possess a soothing tincture? I appear to have grazed my scalp!' The teapot I was carrying crashed to the floor."

"The monkey was Professor Perkins?" asked Tom in astonishment.

"Yes, and he had tumbled out of the disc with quite a bump."

"And Mum and Dad…?"

"As the professor fell out of the disc, I'm afraid your parents were drawn into it. After I had left them to make tea, and despite my warnings not to do so, your parents must have… re-activated it."

"What do you mean? What did they do?"

"From what Professor Perkins has told me, that innocent-looking disc is some sort of… Oh dear, how to explain it? It is some sort of travelling device. Those wishing to use it are meant to place their hand inside the open mouth of the grinning face or 'Spirit of the Trees' as he is known. They then recite the verse written at the centre and then *pop* off they go!"

"What do you mean, 'off they go'? *Where* do they go? Where have Mum and Dad gone?"

"I think it best if Professor Perkins explains that side of things to you now, Tom. He has, after all, journeyed through the disc."

Professor Trenham rang a small hand bell, and the monkey re-appeared and walked solemnly over to its armchair.

"Am I to understand that the boy is ready for my account, Professor Trenham?" it asked, gravely.

"He is, Professor Perkins," replied Tom's grandfather, nodding politely. Professor Perkins cleared his throat and began, "I am one hundred and seventy-three years old, young man! What have you to say to that?"

Tom stared at the grinning monkey-face, and opened and closed his mouth in astonishment. The monkey cackled with glee and continued, "Furthermore, I am the original owner of this house! What say you now, sir?" and he cackled again. Tom's grandfather interrupted.

"Perhaps you could explain yourself a little more clearly, professor?" he said irritably. The monkey nodded and calmed itself.

"Oh, forgive me, forgive me! I am still overjoyed that I have returned home after all these years, despite my appearance."

"How long were you inside the disc?" asked Tom, finding it hard to believe that he was talking to a monkey.

"I entered it in the year 1898 and emerged some two weeks ago! I have lived to see the future and the times you live in, young man! Such marvels! Such wonders! Such horrors!" The little monkey's smile faded.

"1898?" exclaimed Tom. "1898!" he repeated in amazement. "But that makes you some kind of... time travelling... Victorian... monkey-man!" He sprang out of his armchair again.

"I prefer 'gentleman scholar', but time-travelling Victorian is not without its charm. Now kindly be seated. You are looming horribly."

Tom fell back into his armchair, numb with disbelief, and asked, "Where did *you* find the disc, professor?"

"I discovered the accursed object in the summer of 1898. I was a seventy-two-year-old professor of science, quite human, who was enjoying the delights of a walking holiday in the Black Forest region of southern Germany. As I strolled amongst those mighty trees, I tripped and fell, and after examining the ground for what I imagined would be the protruding root of a tree or the wretched excavations of a burrowing mammal, I saw that I had, in fact, fallen over the rim of disc; a beautiful, half-buried disc! I unearthed the curious object and set off for England the following day, indeed to this very house, which is, or was, mine, bringing the treasure with me. I was fascinated by it but my housekeeper, Mrs Hardimann, and my dogs, were not. Mrs Hardimann would often complain of headaches in its presence and even threatened to bury the disc in the garden!"

"She must have done just that," interrupted Tom's grandfather, "because that's just where *I* found it over a hundred years later!"

"After I was swallowed up by it," continued Professor Perkins, "I must have become a 'missing person'. My house and its entire contents were sold as one lot, for I am surrounded by much of my old furniture!"

"This house was bought by my father," interrupted Tom's grandfather. "He's your great grandfather, Tom, and when he died, he left this house and everything in it to me!"

"I see," said Tom, scratching his head, "but where did the disc send you, Professor Perkins, and how did it draw you inside, and how did it turn you into a monkey, and how can my parents…?"

Professor Perkins raised his paw and closed his eyes.

"Patience! I shall endeavour to answer all your questions in full, young man, but first, tell me: did you remember those bananas – the ones you were instructed to bring?"

CHAPTER 6

The Request

Tom retrieved the bananas from his rucksack and handed them to Professor Perkins in something of a daze. His head was spinning with every incredible thing he had heard, and he tried very hard to accept the truth of it. His parents were still missing, Tom knew *that* was real enough, and as this was the last place anyone had seen them, he thought it best to wait and see where it would all end.

He returned to his armchair and watched the little monkey carefully.

"Mm, most welcome, most welcome! Thank you!" said Professor Perkins, dabbing his mouth with a napkin after eating all the bananas.

"Pleasure," said Tom gloomily.

"I fear I am costing your grandpapa a king's ransom in fresh produce but at least I no longer feel the aches and pains of the old man I once was. I can now swing amongst the trees for many hours – a most useful talent as it happens, for it enabled me to escape from the Ringwood."

"The Ringwood? Is that the place where the disc sends you? Is that where my parents have gone?" asked Tom, hoping to hurry the professor onto the next part of his story. But the little monkey would not be hurried, and he delicately folded the napkin on his lap and settled back in his armchair.

"The Ringwood is a forest," he eventually said, "a vast, arboreal realm whose likeness is etched upon the surface of the disc."

Tom nodded as he remembered his own quick look at the engraving.

"Once there, you discover a place like no other. The darkness itself is alive; its green, silent depths whisper to you at night and its creatures beguile and scheme as humans do. I fell into the hands of a woodland hag who thought it amusing to transform me into a monkey and keep me in her cage as a pet. Naturally, I escaped, and discovered the exit back into this world, but the same may not be true of your mama and your papa, I fear, for not everyone is as resourceful as I."

The little monkey fell silent and gazed into the fire.

"It's probably best if I continue," Tom's grandfather interrupted, "in somewhat less *dramatic* terms," and he stared at the monkey sternly. "Hans Von Rippenbaum lived and died in the Black Forest during the 1700s, and history records him as a simple toymaker. But it seems that he had other, somewhat darker talents, for he managed to create a secret realm that was *his* version of the real Black Forest. Entry into this world was through the disc, the disc that now hangs upon my front door. Are you all right?"

Tom nodded and stared miserably into his hot chocolate.

"It seems that Von Rippenbaum filled this secret forest with mechanical devices: people, animals and other, more unusual, things. Every one of them was a living, moving, *thinking* being, Tom. That toymaker must have possessed some very unusual powers indeed."

The old professor shifted uncomfortably in his chair.

"Is it dangerous?" asked Tom. "The disc, I mean. Can it hurt you?"

"Well, it certainly proved dangerous for Von Rippenbaum. History records that the emperor of the time ordered his soldiers to surround the toymaker in his Black Forest workshop one night and burn both it and him to the ground. It is always unwise to upset an emperor, Tom, and whatever Von Rippenbaum did to anger his royal patron, he made himself a deadly enemy."

"That's horrible!" whispered Tom, staring into the fire.

"Yes, quite horrible, but it seems that not everything was destroyed that night."

"What do you mean?"

"Consider the facts. Professor Perkins here takes a walking holiday in the Black Forest in 1898, some hundred years after the death of Von Rippenbaum. During his walk, he trips over a disc made by Von Rippenbaum. One can only conclude that the professor wandered across the very site where the toymaker's old workshop once stood and that the disc, being stored in a cellar or buried beneath the house, survived the blaze."

"So Mum and Dad are in this other Black Forest right now?"

"Yes and they will stay there unless–"

Professor Trenham was suddenly interrupted by the sound of a bottle knocking against the side of a glass. He turned and saw Professor Perkins pouring himself a large drink.

After remembering his own time spent inside the Ringwood, the little monkey decided he needed something to steady his nerves.

"A clear head, professor. A clear head if you please.

Remember the plan." Tom's grandfather glared at the brandy bottle in the monkey's paw.

The little monkey scowled and snapped, "Well, I don't much care for your plan, sir! I don't much care for it at all!" He tried to click his fingers at Professor Trenham, but the alcohol had already taken effect. "He who aspires to be a hero must drink brandy!" the monkey shouted. "Ha! What say you now, sir? A *hero*! You feeling like a hero, Tom?" he asked, getting giddier. "Your grandpapa… my dear, esteemed colleague… wants you and I to enter the disc and rescue your parents! *Through the disc* if you please! A monkey and a child! In the Ringwood! Alone! Together! *Ha!* You feeling heroic, Tom… dear, brave Tom?"

The little monkey's head lolled to one side, his glass tumbled to the floor and he was soon fast asleep.

Tom's grandfather stood up and wrapped the tartan shawl around the sleeping figure. He gestured for Tom to follow him outside. Once in the hallway, he whispered, "He'll be all right in a little while. He's only had a small amount of brandy. He has a fondness for cigars, too, and made himself quite sick with them the other night. I think it's his monkey blood – it's changed his tolerance to such things."

"But is it true what he said?" asked Tom impatiently. "Do you really want me to go through the disc and look for my parents?"

Professor Trenham poked at a threadbare patch of rug with his walking stick, and sighed.

"Yes, Tom. I have a plan and I need your help. Oh, I would go through myself in an instant, but old age and this wretched leg of mine…" He tapped his foot in frustration. "I cannot send the professor back on his own for I doubt your parents would believe the word of a talking monkey, let alone follow one. I therefore need you to accompany him and help him all you can. Will you do it, Tom? Will you journey to the Ringwood and rescue your parents?"

Tom's heart pounded. His mind raced uncontrollably and all he could hear was the sound of loud, rattling snores coming from the room he had just left.

CHAPTER 7

A Peculiar Demonstration

"Are you all right?" asked Professor Trenham gravely.

Tom didn't know. He had just experienced the strangest hour of his life, and wasn't sure how he felt. "I think so," he replied quietly. Professor Trenham smiled.

"All is not lost. I have been working night and day for the past two weeks in my efforts to formulate a plan. My first thought was to race through into the Ringwood myself but Professor Perkins' sensible advice stopped me from doing that."

"What about the police? Can't *they* do something?" wondered Tom.

"The police?! I would be taken for a madman the moment I began to explain what has happened here."

Tom supposed that this was true, and he imagined the police putting his grandfather in jail and Professor Perkins into some kind of zoo for talking animals, leaving his parents alone and trapped forever. Casting his doubt and fear aside,

Tom suddenly knew what he had to do.

"I'll do it!" he shouted. "Of course I'll do it! I'll go through the disc and find them!"

"Bravo!" cried Professor Trenham. "Oh, I *knew* you'd help! That's real Trenham blood in those veins of yours!"

Tom hoped that was where his blood would be staying, but he smiled bravely and tried to forget the look of fear on the monkey's face.

"Now I must go and prepare everything for tonight's journey," muttered Tom's grandfather, wandering down the hallway.

"*Tonight's* journey?!" cried Tom. "But I can't go tonight! I'm expected home! Aunt Betty'll go nuts if I'm late!"

"Please," the old man called over his shoulder. "Follow me into the dining room, Tom. There is something I want to show you, something you must see."

He threw open a pair of old wooden doors and disappeared inside.

The air that spilled from the room was heavy with age, and Tom expected to see another book-cluttered space. He was therefore surprised to see that the dining room had been transformed into a neat, tidy and very well-ordered laboratory. A large oak dining table was covered in wire and test tubes. Shiny glass bottles and beakers caught the light of a low-hanging chandelier, and a second table at the far end of the room supported three or four very thick and very old-looking volumes. In the centre of the room was an object that had been covered with an old sheet. Professor Trenham limped over to it.

"I can't go through the disc tonight," repeated Tom quietly. "Aunt Betty'll go nuts if I'm…"

He stopped when his grandfather suddenly revealed the object beneath the sheet.

"There!" he announced proudly, as if everything was

suddenly clear. Tom remained in the doorway, blinking in surprise and wondering how a blackboard full of strange writing could begin to explain what he had heard.

"Come in, come in!" urged Professor Trenham excitedly. Tom stepped forwards, his footsteps echoing loudly over the wood-blocked floor.

"Will this help get Mum and Dad back?" he said, squinting at the writing on the blackboard.

"In a way, yes it will."

Tom studied the chalk marks carefully, and recognised only some of the strange markings. He had seen something like them in books about magic and astrology, but there were many other symbols he had never seen before. The drawings sat within circles, each circle sitting within another until finally, at the centre, sat the smallest circle of all in which a tree had been drawn.

"This is a drawing of the controls set into the *back* of the disc," explained Tom's grandfather. "Let me begin by explaining the outer ring…or perhaps I should start with the inner ring… no, best to begin with…"

Suddenly, he cried, "Oh, a demonstration! Why not? Just a quick one! Perfectly safe!" and he limped from the room and headed for the front door.

Tom followed cautiously, not wanting to get too close to the object that had swallowed his parents.

He stood with his back against the wall and held his breath as Professor Trenham moved his hand up, around and then under the disc, feeling for something behind it. "There!" he whispered, setting the circle back against the door.

A sudden pulse of energy erupted from the disc and passed through Tom's chest, rippling unpleasantly through his entire body. Tom was reminded of all the bone-thudding explosions he had enjoyed at fireworks displays, only *this* burst of energy had been invisible, silent and, for some strange reason, quite repulsive. Tom bent forwards to catch his breath, and when he straightened up he saw that the two empty eye-sockets of the leafy-faced man were now *glowing with light*.

Tom's grandfather called to him.

"Follow me. We shan't go far," he announced casually. "We'll stay within the porch light."

Tom stumbled onto the driveway, his eyes watering in the cold night air. He stared along the path, wondering whether to make a quick dash for home, but saw how dark and forbidding the driveway had become.

"This should be far enough," announced Professor Trenham, turning to face the house. "Now pick up a stone, Tom. There are plenty lying about."

Tom's ears rang with Aunt Betty's warnings about the "mad old devil". But his curiosity made him obey his grandfather's strange request and he picked up a lump of stone. "Now throw it as far as you can!" shouted his grandfather. "Go on! Turn around and pitch it into the air, away from the house!"

Tom hesitated.

"What're you waiting for?" cried the professor.

"N-nothing," said Tom nervously.

He steadied his aim and flung the frosty stone as far he could, watching as it spun away into the night. Suddenly it stopped, as if caught by an invisible hand, and Professor Trenham cheered with delight. Tom ran forwards, wondering how a perfectly ordinary little rock could hang, unsupported and unmoving, inches above his head. He jumped up and tried to grab it, but the stone remained out of reach. Tom gazed up at it, mute with disbelief.

"It is vital that you do not step any further down the driveway," called his grandfather, who had returned to the disc. "Prepare yourself for switch-off. And keep your eye on that stone!"

A second burst of energy passed unpleasantly through Tom's body – its direction this time *towards* the disc. The stone quivered and fell with a muffled thud, and Tom stared at it in amazement. He looked at his grandfather then at the stone, then turned and ran inside the house.

Chapter 8

Preparation

om burst into the study and saw that Professor Perkins was still sleeping. He fell into the nearest armchair and shivered.

"Well!" said Tom's grandfather, entering the room after him. "What did you make of that?"

"It was horrible," said Tom.

Professor Trenham raised an eyebrow.

"Oh, I forgot," he said. "That was your first proper encounter with the disc, was it not? Forgive me. That sudden pulse of energy at the beginning *can* be a little ticklish."

"Ticklish?! It felt like a bag of snakes," said Tom, shivering at the memory of it.

"Hmm, very descriptive, but please accept my apologies for any discomfort you may have felt. I merely wanted to show you why you mustn't worry about getting home on time this evening."

Tom watched as his grandfather poured a cup of tea.

"Here," he said, "Drink this. Hot and sweet. Just the thing for shock."

Tom gripped the teacup and warmed his hands against its sides as his grandfather poured himself a second cup, despite having left his first cup untouched.

"That stone stopped in mid-air!" said Tom.

"Yes, it was grabbed by the hand of time," answered Professor Trenham, "or rather, the power of the disc." Tom supposed that he must be getting used to this very strange evening, for his only reaction was to sit and wait for the explanation that he knew was sure to follow. "I discovered," continued his grandfather, falling into an armchair, "that on being activated, the disc surrounds itself in a large sort of energy bubble. That was what you felt passing through your body."

Tom gulped his tea.

"Within this bubble, time passes quite normally and one notices nothing out of the ordinary. Yet beyond its boundaries, Tom, *beyond its boundaries*, can you imagine, this marvel actually *slows down* the rate at which time passes!"

Tom began to feel, with increasing unease, that there was part of his grandfather that actually admired this sinister object. Was it such a new and exciting discovery that he was unable – or unwilling – to recognise its dangers? "So," concluded his grandfather, "as our stone left the protective dome of the disc's energy, it entered slow time and although it appeared frozen in mid-air, it was, in fact, falling to the ground and would, I believe, have taken one hundred years to complete its journey!"

"But why?" asked Tom. "What's the point of slowing down time?"

"Because its creator, Von Rippenbaum, could travel to the Ringwood in the knowledge that a week spent in there meant that only an hour or two had passed in the real world."

Tom stared at the sleeping monkey.

"But the disc didn't slow down time for him. One hundred years have passed since Victorian times."

"The price of impetuousness, I fear. Professor Perkins rushed through without setting any of the dials on the back of the disc. Even if he *had*, once his superstitious housekeeper had buried the disc in his garden, he was well and truly trapped, for nothing can escape the Ringwood if the disc is buried in the ground."

"But it isn't buried now," said Tom. "Couldn't something *escape* from it?"

"I've switched it off."

"But what if Mum and Dad are trying to—"

"Tom," interrupted his grandfather gently. "I have been activating the disc for the last two weeks. Your parents have not appeared."

Tom leant forwards and placed his teacup on the table.

"So I really *can* go through tonight?" he said, startled by the idea.

"And be quite safe from Aunt Betty's timekeeping, yes. And once you find your parents, you will return to discover that only a few minutes have passed here in the real world. I will make sure of it."

Tom smiled and stood up, feeling better after the tea. Professor Trenham rose and limped towards the door.

"Now, if there's nothing else, I really must go and re-position the settings *and* check my calculations for your journey. Stay in the warmth, Tom, and gather your thoughts, and please, wake Professor Perkins in ten minutes. He needs to prepare himself." Tom's grandfather glared at the brandy bottle.

Tom nodded and stood in front of the fireplace. The warmth from the settled coals felt luxurious against his legs, and he turned and let its heat spread across his back.

He assured himself that everything would be just as his grandfather had described, but with every wheezing breath from the sleeping monkey, Tom's uneasiness increased. He simply had too many questions to stand alone and in silence for ten minutes, so he decided to wake Professor Perkins straightaway.

He cleared his throat as loudly as he dared, and the little monkey coughed and croaked, "Uhnn… be gone, foul hag!"

"*Professor*," whispered Tom, tugging his paw. "Professor Perkins, wake up! It's time to go!"

Professor Perkins leapt into the air and shouted, "Who the devil are you, sir? And where the devil am I, sir? And what the devil… Oooo!"

He fell into the armchair and clasped his forehead and groaned. Tom fetched a jug of water from the sideboard.

"It's me, Thomas Trenham. Drink this."

The professor gulped the water down and held his glass out for more.

"Trenham?" he gasped, squinting up at Tom. "Oh, the boy. Forgive me. For one moment I fancied I was back in…"

He paused and gulped a second glass of water. "Doubtless the, ahh, damp chill of twilight has, ahh, permeated the deeper regions of my cerebra, inducing my present, ahh, headache."

The little monkey skilfully knocked the brandy bottle under the armchair.

"I don't want to sound ungrateful, professor, and I do appreciate your help and everything, but why are you going back into the Ringwood?"

Professor Perkins got to his feet unsteadily and held out his arms, letting Tom see all of his furry body.

"To undo the indignity unleashed upon my person," he replied, "*and* to destroy that wretched place if I am able to."

The dinner gong sounded in the hallway. "The dismal knell of the tolling bell calling us to arms," sighed the monkey. "Let us proceed, but *quietly*, I beg of you," and he led Tom out of the room.

♦ ♦ ♦   ♦ ♦ ♦   ♦ ♦ ♦

A figure stood within the shadows.

It had run quickly through the night and had reached the driveway to the house but now it paused, suddenly aware that it would have to enter the wild and overgrown tunnel alone. The beam from its torch was a pale little dot against the tangled garden but it was anger that drove the figure on, and it stepped forwards confidently and sprinted across the gravel.

"Just you wait, Thomas Trenham!" it muttered. "Just you wait!"

CHAPTER 9

Those Seeking Nature's Pleasure

om's grandfather took the little monkey to one side, Tom noticing how grave they looked during their brief and intense conversation. A large canvas bag was handed to Professor Perkins who, after a quick struggle, hoisted the strap over his furry shoulder. Both professors shook hands and bowed politely.

"What's in the shoulder-bag?" whispered Tom.

"It is *not* your place to ask!" snapped the little monkey. Professor Perkins paused and added, less harshly, "Forgive me. The bag contains items of potential usefulness."

Tom offered to carry it, but Professor Perkins insisted that he could manage. "Let us grasp one another's hand," said the monkey, holding up a slender, black-fingered paw. Tom grasped it and was surprised at how soft and velvety it felt. "Your grandpapa informs me that children need inordinate amounts of... *reassurance*. Let me therefore say that I believe that the outcome of our journey will be, as the people of your century are so fond of saying, both 'O' and 'K'."

The little monkey bared its teeth in what Tom hoped was a smile.

Professor Trenham, meanwhile, paced up and down in front of the disc, muttering darkly and peering at a clutch of dog-eared papers. He chewed absent-mindedly on the end of a pencil and scowled at his calculations.

"Well here we are!" he said. "Two gallant pilgrims off into the New World! Kindly place your hand inside the mouth of the Spirit of the Trees, professor, and recite the ancient verse written at its centre."

"Yes, yes, I am well aware of the wretched procedure," muttered Professor Perkins. "I will even translate the ridiculous rhyme into English in honour of our guest."

He stood on tip-toe and slid his paw inside the leafy-man's mouth. Tom stared anxiously and doubted whether he could be so brave.

"Well, goodbye," said Professor Trenham airily, stepping back onto the driveway. "Listen to Professor Perkins at all times, Tom, and stay on the path!"

Tom nodded, surprised and upset that he had received neither a hug nor a handshake from his grandfather.

As Professor Perkins began translating the circle of words that ringed the leafy face, Tom looked directly into the eyes of the carving. They were filled with a greedy impatience that almost made Tom run in terror. Suddenly, Tom became aware of a peculiar drop in the weight of everything around him and a familiar pulse of energy burst from the disc. To his surprise and relief, the squirming ripples were less horrible this time; they were slower and gentler and almost welcoming, and they were filled with an unexpected feeling of peace. The eyes of the face blazed fiercely down at him, but Tom felt secure in its sinister gaze.

The mysterious words of the rhyme echoed around him

as Professor Perkins read,

> *"Those seeking Nature's pleasure,*
> *Joy and pain in equal measure,*
> *Place your hand within me,*
> *The Ringwood Tree,*
> *For now we journey together."*

Tom imagined that he was about to be hurled into a violent whirlpool or would be sucked into an enormous black hole, and was therefore surprised by what happened next.

Slowly, the world around him began to slide sideways while he, Professor Perkins and the disc remained perfectly still. The door and the walls of the house and even his grandfather slid smoothly to the left, like scenery in a theatre on a revolving platform.

As the professor's words faded into silence, Tom sensed a terrible pressure building in his ears. The ground trembled, the professor's grip tightened and Tom knew that he couldn't escape. Footsteps suddenly came thumping towards him, and Tom turned and gasped when a figure sprang out of the darkness.

"Got you!" the figure shouted, grabbing Tom's arm, but in the strange atmosphere of the disc, the figure's words were a ridiculous growl of slow-motion. Tom tried to answer but suddenly found himself pulled, stretched and unexpectedly dropped, and he found himself plunging, headlong, into an intense and terrifying darkness.

CHAPTER 10

Arrival

Although he sensed that his journey through the disc was now over, Tom wasn't certain, for he found himself sitting alone in a silent darkness. He remembered the running figure that had grabbed his arm and wondered if it was anywhere near him. Tom breathed deeply and reached out his hand.

The ground felt soft and gritty beneath his fingertips, and the air smelt damp and cold. Two dim shapes appeared just ahead of him and Tom stared nervously until he realised that they were the ghostly outlines of his trainers. As his eyes grew accustomed to the light, Tom saw a dim shape and called out to it, "Hello?"

"I am here," replied a voice.

Tom recognised its refined tones at once but before he could answer, Professor Perkins continued, saying, "Grasp my hand and I will assist you to your feet. Good. Now stand up."

Tom, whose hands were still in his lap, wondered who the professor was talking to, and he jumped in terror when a sudden blaze of light revealed his surroundings: the inside of a cave.

Standing to his left was Cassie, Tom's sister, and she had taken hold of Professor Perkins' soft paws. An equally astonished Professor Perkins was staring back at her until Cassie screamed and they both jumped apart.

Cassie swung at the professor with her torch. Professor Perkins ducked skilfully and dashed for the mouth of the cave.

"No!" shouted Tom. "No, Cassie! Don't! He's a friend!"

Tom leapt to his feet and grabbed his sister's arm.

"Tom?" cried Cassie. "Tom, is that you? Th-there was some kind of animal! It touched my hand! It helped me to my feet! It *spoke* to me!"

Tom looked round but there was no sign of the professor.

"What are you doing here?!" he cried. "You weren't supposed to–"

"You sneak!" shouted Cassie, remembering that she was angry. "Just look what I found! Look what I found!" and she thrust a crumpled piece of paper into Tom's hand.

Tom took it warily, but didn't have to read it to know that she had found Grandfather's note inviting Tom to his house.

"'I'm just going to Jack's house'," said Cassie, mimicking Tom's voice. "You miserable *liar!* Oh, and I don't suppose you know anything about my mobile disappearing, do you?"

Tom felt inside his pocket.

"I'm sorry," he said, handing her the phone. "I only meant to borrow it. It was Grandfather. He said he had news about Mum and Dad. Good news. I had to go and see."

"Mum and Dad? Have you seen them? Where are they? And where's Grandfather? And why's it gone all dark?"

Cassie paused, suddenly aware of her new surroundings. "*What just happened?*" she gasped.

"Cassie, there are some things I need to explain to you; weird things about Grandfather and Mum and Dad."

Tom led his bewildered sister over to a soft patch of earth and sat down, planting the torch in the ground between them like a flower.

Cassie remained silent during most of the ten minutes it took Tom to recount, with as much optimism as he could manage, the details of his journey through the park, his meeting with Professor Perkins, his encounter with the disc and all of its strange history. Cassie sat, open-mouthed, staring in disbelief, and it was only when Tom told her about their parents, how they had been drawn into the disc to a place called the Ringwood, that she sprang to her feet.

"Toys that *move? Talking* monkeys? Slowing down *time?* It's Grandfather! He's having a joke! He must be… *isn't he?*" She stared pleadingly at her brother.

Tom suggested that perhaps it was time that they both stepped outside.

After cradling his freshly pounding head, Professor Perkins eventually felt well enough to return to the cave. But his temper was shorter and his mood was considerably blacker. Out of his canvas shoulder-bag he withdrew a large and well-oiled army service revolver and he held it out in front of him.

Convinced that the figure who had attacked him in the cave had been one of Von Rippenbaum's "living" toys, he held the gun steady and crept towards the entrance. Tom and Cassie stepped into the light.

"Don't shoot!" spluttered Tom, his eyes fixed upon the gun. "Th-this is Cassie, Cassie Trenham, my sister. She found Grandfather's note and followed me to the house. She grabbed my arm as we passed through the disc and was drawn through with us. I'm sorry, professor! Don't shoot!"

"I see," snapped the monkey, lowering the weapon and scowling suspiciously at Cassie, who stared back at him.

"You were right, Tom. He *is* a talking monkey!" and Cassie smiled nervously.

Professor Perkins snorted.

"Young lady, I am Professor Augustus Perkins. Scholar! Classicist! Man of science! Furthermore, I now find myself in mortal danger with the welfare of *two* unwanted charges to consider. This has been a *most disagreeable* day! Pah!"

He stepped aside and jammed the gun back inside his shoulder-bag.

Tom and Cassie gasped in amazement, for the view beyond the professor was one of astonishing beauty.

The cave from which they had emerged was set into a high bank of rock that overlooked a huge and ancient forest. From their vantage point they were able to stare across the tops of thousands of trees that stretched away in all directions for many miles. They saw that they had emerged at the very edge of the forest – the Ringwood, as Professor Trenham had called it – and Tom now understood the reason for the name. The forest was a circle – a broad ring of trees – whose edges were sharply defined by the sky. Tom laughed at the billowing treetops that rose and fell with the ponderous movement of an ocean current. He marvelled at rich bands of green, red, copper and gold that spread from the centre in a widening circle, but it wasn't long before Cassie noticed something unusual.

"Here at the edge of the forest, it's all wintry and dead," she said, "but further in it looks like autumn then summer and right in the centre it looks like spring. But you can't get four seasons in one forest. That's not possible."

Professor Perkins laughed grimly.

"Both the possible and the impossible have little meaning

here, young lady," he said. "Each season lies within in its own band; four concentric rings."

"But how are we going to find Mum and Dad down there?" snapped Cassie. "And how are we going to get back to Grandfather's house?"

The professor gestured towards the centre.

"One leaves the Ringwood through its blackened heart, and, like the veins of some vast, almighty body, every forest trail leads to it. As to finding your parents, I am confident of making their acquaintance *somewhere* along the way."

"That's it?!" spluttered Cassie. "We're just going to walk and hope we bump into them?!"

The little monkey shrugged and looked away.

"And how long does this walk to the centre take?" asked Cassie, flicking the hair off her shoulder in a gesture Tom recognised only too well as a sign of increasing impatience.

"Our journey will take some four to five days – longer if we are inconvenienced." Professor Perkins patted the canvas bag into which he had thrust the revolver. "But we have tarried in the open too long. Come. We must enter the forest and hide."

He turned and scampered towards the tree line.

"What was Grandfather thinking, sending you here?" snapped Cassie. "*What was he thinking?!*"

"He didn't want to," mumbled Tom. "Not at first, anyway. He nearly came through himself – he'd done all the research and everything – but then he changed his mind at the last minute. That's when he sent me the note asking for my help."

"And what about things like food and shelter? What did he say about those?"

Tom looked startled and stared at the ground, suddenly aware that in the strange excitement of the afternoon, he had forgotten to ask.

"You didn't ask him, did you?" said Cassie.

"Yes!" blurted Tom.

"*Tom!*"

"No," said Tom miserably. "Grandfather looked ill. I didn't want to bother him."

"That's so typical of you! Never wanting to bother anyone! Always taking care! Always too scared to do anything! Well you've got bother now! *A whole weird forest full of it!*" Cassie sprang into the cave and disappeared inside.

Tom ran after her, shouting for her to be careful.

Professor Perkins heard the commotion and fumbled for his revolver. He ran to the cave and saw torchlight weaving crazily around inside it.

"What is this disturbance?" he called, stepping backwards as a figure loomed out at him. It was Tom and he was upset. "Thomas Trenham, what is the meaning of this noise? Where is your sister? Answer me!"

"She's going home, professor. She isn't very happy. She's going to tell Aunt Betty what's happened and Aunt Betty'll probably call the police. Then the police will arrest us."

Tom stepped aside, fully expecting the professor to dash past him to stop Cassie, but to his surprise, the little monkey laughed.

"Foolish girl! Did I not say that there is but one exit from the Ringwood? To go back, we must move forwards and pass through the tree at the centre."

He tutted impatiently and put his gun away.

Eventually, Cassie reappeared, breathless and sweating, her face and coat streaky with dirt. She had searched every inch of the cave, but had found no doorway or entry point that had given her a clue as to how she had arrived.

"This doesn't make sense," she said quietly, trying very hard not to cry. Tom became anxious that he might have to hug her, and sighed with relief when Professor Perkins suddenly interrupted, saying, "I see that words of reassurance are required. Let me therefore repeat the counsel I offered your brother, young lady, and state that throughout our forthcoming endeavours, I am of the firm opinion that we shall be both 'O' and 'K'. Now show some alacrity and end this foolish nonsense."

He turned and scampered back towards the forest while Cassie stood, unmoving and silent, watching him go.

"You sort of get used to him," said Tom, nodding after the professor, but Cassie's expression remained unchanged and Tom began to worry that he really would have to hug his sister.

Suddenly, Cassie sprang into action and said, "Come on. Let's follow it. With any luck that monkey'll bite me and I'll wake up from this stupid nightmare."

She darted forwards, leaving Tom wondering what "alacrity" was and whether his sister had any of it to show.

· · ·   · · ·   · · ·

Tom and Professor Perkins had faded, by degrees, into nothingness, and in spite of the disturbance of the leaping figure, everything appeared to have gone according to plan.

A curiously expressionless Professor Trenham approached the disc and waited for the little wisps of smoke to clear from its surface before moving a switch on its underside. He replaced the disc against the wide front door and watched as the grinning face of the Spirit of the Trees became dull and lifeless.

He returned to his study, his limping shuffle replaced by long and confident strides. He threw his walking stick to the ground and smiled fiercely at it before slamming the door behind him.

Grabbing the jug of water Tom had used to revive

Professor Perkins, he tossed its contents onto the smouldering fire before moving from light switch to light switch, snapping each one off angrily until a ghostly sliver of moonlight was all that illuminated the room. Dragging an armchair over to it, the old man sat in the moon's sickly light and stared into the garden.

As night claimed the room and the temperature tumbled to zero, a single tear ran down the professor's cheek. His jaw trembled violently and, like a man struggling for breath, he leant forwards and gasped, "Tom! *Tom!* Keep away from the lanterns! Keep away from the path!"

The fire spat, the embers faded, and Professor Trenham slumped lifelessly in his armchair.

Chapter 11

Figures on the Path

Tom and Cassie soon found themselves deep within the forest's outer edge, and were thankful for their winter coats and scarves. Despite three long tracks leading down into the forest, it quickly became apparent that only one of them remained clear.

"Annoying arboreal excesses!" spluttered the professor. "Unfavourable forest fecundity!" he added, staring at the left-hand path and the right-hand path, both of which were a tangle of gorse and bramble.

"The path ahead's clear," said Tom helpfully.

"That is what concerns me," replied the professor. "*All* these paths were clear when I first journeyed this way."

"Oh, what does it matter?" snapped Cassie, "Forests grow. Keep moving. I'm freezing," and she bumped Tom forwards with her crossed arms.

"Whatever we decide, the forest will know of it," muttered the professor, stepping onto the clear trail. Tom and Cassie

56

followed closely.

The path was slippery with ice and strewn with rocks and pebbles. Towering spruce trees, snow-dusted and magnificent, crowded in on either side of them, blocking what little light reached the forest floor. As they walked, Tom felt as though he had wandered into the belly of some enormous beast, and he quickly decided that the Ringwood was a forest best observed from the outside.

The path suddenly broadened and its twists and turns became less frequent until, with a final arcing bend, it opened up and ran in a needle-straight line ahead of them.

The three travellers stared in amazement.

The giant spruces had gone, replaced by yew trees that stretched into the distance. Each yew stood an equal distance from its neighbour, and every twisted branch bent over the path as if holding it in a protective clutch. The path itself had a swept and curiously cultivated feel to it, and reminded Tom of the long, straight avenue in his local park.

Between each yew tree grew huge brambles that were high and wild, their scribbled depths like great cathedrals of thorns, their twisting lengths like blackened shark's teeth. Tom quickly realised that once they were on the straight path, they would not be able to leave it.

Professor Perkins stepped forwards cautiously, his fur bristling with tension, and he held up his paw in a silent gesture of "halt" and sniffed the air for danger. He set off again, only to repeat the procedure every few yards.

Cassie's patience quickly grew thin, and she was about to stride forwards and overtake him when the professor suddenly stopped and pointed at something.

A large gourd dangled above them. Other gourds could be seen far in the distance. It quickly became apparent that the over-sized vegetables were growing upon every seventh yew tree.

Professor Perkins removed his shoulder-bag and scrambled into the branches of the tree holding a pocket-knife. A miniature shower of ice crystals covered Tom and Cassie as the gourd came crashing onto the path next to them. It broke apart like the segments of an orange, and Cassie ran over and held up a piece.

"Unhand that specimen!" shouted Professor Perkins above her. Cassie ignored him.

"Look!" she marvelled, holding the segment up to Tom. "Look, its sides are so *thick* and it feels like glass. Wait, what's it doing? *Why's it glowing like that? Tom, what's it doing?*"

The fragment had started to shine with a deep, pulsating light, and Cassie was about to let go of it when the image of a path appeared. It was the same forest path on which Tom and Cassie were standing, but the path in the fragment was filled with scuttling creatures.

"Phantoms!" cried Professor Perkins, scrambling to the ground. "Put that object down. Put it down this instant!"

"They're only pictures," said Cassie. "Like TV. Look!" and she turned the glowing image towards him.

The professor recoiled in terror.

"He doesn't know what TV is," whispered Tom. "Grandfather hasn't got one and they certainly didn't have them in Victorian times."

"Its very essence exudes devilry," snapped the professor, edging nearer.

Suddenly, Tom shouted when an image of their parents appeared. They were walking along the path, clinging to one another nervously, but as quickly as their image came, it faded away. Cassie shook the fragment, hoping to see more, while Tom ran to the gourd, looking for a segment that would show them the scene again.

"Ergh!" he cried. "The gourd's filled with slime! And it's moving!"

"Luciferic oleaginations!" muttered the professor. "You are right. The gourds *do* appear to be filled with some sort of living liquid. Enough! Night draws near and we have yet to find shelter. Leave the wretched vegetable where it lies and let us continue."

He scampered forwards, gun at the ready.

"At least we know we're on the right path," said Tom. "Mum and Dad really did come this way."

"Huh! That monkey-thing could be leading us anywhere," muttered Cassie.

"He's not a thing, he's a man," said Tom.

"Tom, it's a *talking monkey!*"

"Who used to be human."

"How do you know what it is?! That mad toymaker you told me about, Herbert Von Rippen Pants…"

"Hans Von Rippen*baum*."

"Whoever. That monkey could be one of *his* mad creations. It certainly acts like one."

Tom stared at her in astonishment, the idea new and horribly surprising.

"Professor Perkins isn't a toy," he said uncertainly. "He's real. He's flesh and blood. I know he is."

"But how do you know?" said Cassie.

"Because he helped me in the park."

Cassie laughed.

"He made me hot chocolate," said Tom. "And toast. Anyway, he's been helping Grandfather and now he's helping me. I trust him, that's all, and you should too."

Cassie couldn't decide whether to feel admiration for her brother's trusting nature or anger over his willingness to believe anything he was told, however fantastic. He was the same at school, she realised, and remembered how he believed ridiculous "facts" that the older boys often invented for him at school.

An impatient little cough interrupted their discussion. Professor Perkins stood waiting for them further along the path. He was scowling fiercely.

"Well *I* don't trust him," hissed Cassie. "And neither should you."

She stalked forwards angrily and returned the monkey's scowl.

CHAPTER 12

Voices

A creeping mist filled the edge of the forest, fooling the eye into seeing the half-glimpsed outlines of people and animals that were not there. Shadows lengthened too and covered the path with spider-like traces of darkness and light.

As evening fell, Professor Perkins was about to suggest that they should, perhaps, scramble up and sleep amongst the twisting branches of the yew trees, when his keen monkey ears detected a sound.

"*Thommmaaassss!*" cried two distant voices, echoing eerily. The professor held up his gun.

The voices sounded again and this time Tom and Cassie heard them. They froze for a moment then raced along the path, Professor Perkins chasing after them. He only caught up with them after Tom and Cassie skidded to a halt in front of a pair of old forest wells that squatted defiantly in the middle of the path.

"We've found them!" cried Tom. "Mum and Dad – they're down these wells!"

The professor raised his gun and peered over the stone wall.

"What are you doing?!" cried Tom. "You don't need a gun! It's Mum and Dad! They've fallen down the wells. Don't shoot them!"

"*Am I addressing the parents of Thomas and Cassandra Trenham?*" cried the professor, his question echoing strangely into the deep, circular shafts.

There was no reply until a cold blast of air suddenly swept along the path.

"*Thommaaassss!*" wailed the voices again. The professor gestured impatiently for Cassie's torch.

"It's no use," said Cassie. "I've already tried the torch. You can't see anything. It's too deep." She stared at the wooden buckets that dangled over each well.

"There will be *no* subterranean reconnaissance, young lady," snapped the professor, catching her look. "Not until I have decided it is safe to do so."

He turned away and paced along the path, trying to block the sound of the voices and the expectant faces of Tom and Cassie. He needed time to think, time to formulate a plan, and was all too aware of the dangers of the forest.

When the professor's back was turned, Cassie gestured for Tom to follow her. She scrambled onto the wall, jumped inside a bucket, and pointed to the big turning handle. It was obvious what she wanted Tom to do, but Tom could only stare, wondering whose temper was going to be the worst to deal with.

Cassie scowled and pointed angrily so Tom grabbed the handle, hoping the mechanism would be too rusted to move. But the handle turned easily. The wooden posts creaked, the rope unwound and the bucket dropped into the earth.

"I believe I have formulated a plan," announced Professor Perkins, turning just in time to see the determined features of Cassie Trenham descending into the darkness.

"*Thommaaassss!*" wailed the voices for the fourth time.

They were louder now, and somehow more insistent.

Chapter 13

Into the Well

assie stared over the rim of the bucket and tried to pierce the darkness with the beam of her torch. But the light revealed nothing to her except her own chilled breath, which vaporised in quick little clouds before her eyes.

She heard Professor Perkins' voice echoing angrily above her and realised that even here, far below the ground, the little monkey was still able to irritate her.

She concentrated harder, staring into the darkness into which she was falling, tense and alert to the slightest sign of movement or danger.

The bucket dropped steadily and turned in lazy revolutions as it fell, the ice-dusted brickwork sparkling magically all around her. Cassie kept calling into the darkness but the voices remained silent.

The bucket suddenly jolted, creaked and then stopped, and a profound and unsettling silence surrounded her. Cassie shone the beam of her torch straight down and illuminated a pale circle. It was water, frozen solid into a smooth disc of ice, but with no sign of anyone or any*thing* standing upon it.

Cassie looked up and was shocked to see that the world she had left was now a pale dot of light around which two small heads bobbed excitedly. She waggled the torchlight up at them and shouted, "I'm all right! I've reached the bottom but there's no one here!"

An icy blast of wind suddenly roared down the well shaft, sending the bucket spinning wildly. Cassie rolled into a ball as the wooden container smashed against the walls, and cried out when her parents' voices echoed up the shaft once again, repeating their cry for Thomas.

As suddenly as it had risen, the wind and the voices fell silent and the bucket slowed to a stop. Cassie shone her torch over the ice but saw that it was still empty.

She suddenly noticed a small, narrow archway carved into the wall of the shaft. It was shaped like a large mouse hole and appeared to be the entrance to a narrow tunnel.

"What's happening?" rang down Tom's voice.

"There's an archway," shouted Cassie, rubbing a bruised arm. "There's some sort of tunnel going sideways, I think. Mum and Dad must be in there. I'm going to take a look."

She clambered out of the bucket and ignored a howl of protest from Professor Perkins, who was peering down at her through his spyglass. Cassie rested one foot on the ice and tested it carefully. It felt thick and immovable so she hopped out and stood on both feet, ready to pull herself up at the first sound of cracking.

The ice remained firm so Cassie shuffled forwards.

"Return to your bucket this instant!" shouted Professor Perkins. "Foolish girl! Never walk across ice!" But Cassie had already reached the side of the well.

She crouched and studied the entranceway, and saw a curious marking etched into the keystone of the arch.

Similar to an Egyptian hieroglyph, tangled lines suggested interconnecting letters, but Cassie hurried on and peered inside the tunnel.

"Mum! Dad! Are you in there? It's Cassie!"

A long and uncomfortable silence followed, the torchlight revealing nothing except an icy floor and more curved brickwork. Cassie chewed on her thumbnail then lay on her stomach and pulled herself forwards like a seal across ice. She had only slid a little way when she noticed something deep inside the tunnel.

The object was black and fat with round, bulging sides that were covered in levers and dials. An odd set of sails, like miniature windmills, ran along the top of the device, and leading up from them was a series of metal tubes. The tubes rose like organ pipes and touched the curved ceiling where they glistened with ice.

Cassie raised herself up onto her knees and shone the torch between the pipes, wondering whether her parents had become trapped behind them. But there was only a long, empty tunnel leading off into the darkness. Cassie slid backwards out of the tunnel.

"Tom!" she called. "Tom, there's a tunnel connecting each well but it's blocked by some sort of machine. Mum and Dad must be in the other well. Hurry down it!"

She waved her torch at him.

"Has your sister always been so... so... so *wilfully disobedient?*" cried Professor Perkins, hopping angrily at the surface.

"I think so," said Tom, uncertain what "wilfully disobedient" meant.

"This is intolerable! *She* is intolerable! She leaves me no choice. I will record her every transgression in this notebook. I will call it her book of shame!"

Professor Perkins scribbled furiously for a moment then

paced along the path, wondering what to do next. Tom had already decided.

He jumped inside the second bucket, tugging the turning-handle as he went. At the first squeak of the handle, Professor Perkins spun around and stared in disbelief as Tom vanished from sight.

"I'm sorry! I'm sorry!" cried Tom as Professor Perkins jumped into the bucket after him.

"Sorry are you?" snapped the monkey. "Pray that your actions do not drop us into greater sorrow."

Cassie returned to the icy tunnel and crouched in front of the peculiar machine. She shone her torch between the metal pipes and waited to guide Tom towards her. She called into the darkness and angled the torchlight lower, then screamed and fell backwards when a hairy face suddenly loomed up at her.

"*You!*" she panted, picking up her torch. "What are *you* doing down here?"

"I rather think," snapped Professor Perkins testily, "that *I* should be asking that question of *you.*"

"I came down to find Mum and Dad. They were calling for help."

"They were calling for Thomas. And neither you nor I know that the voices belong to your parents."

"Of course I'm certain! Who else could they belong to? Anyway, where's Tom?"

"I'm here, Cassie. I'm all right."

Professor Perkins gasped in exasperation when Tom appeared at his side.

"I told you to remain inside the bucket!" he snapped.

"I know," said Tom. "But when Cassie screamed I had to come and see what was happening."

He waved at Cassie and she waggled the torch at him. Professor Perkins sighed again and decided to deliver a stern lecture once they returned to the surface. He turned his attention to the machine.

"Are Mum and Dad on your side?" asked Cassie, staring through the pipes.

"No," said Tom. "There's just an empty tunnel and whatever this thing is."

Tom spun one of the canvas sails, and deep within the device, cogwheels turned, bellows opened and membranes stretched across tubes.

The tunnel rang with noise.

"Thommmaassss!" wailed the voices, and Tom, Cassie and Professor Perkins jumped back in surprise.

"Mimicry!" shouted the professor. "Marvellous mechanical mimicry!"

Suddenly, he paused and cried in alarm, "Return to the surface, children! Immediately!"

He ran past Tom and raced towards the bucket.

"What's up with him?" wondered Cassie.

"Oh no!" whispered Tom, staring in terror. "Please, Cassie, do as he says. The ice underneath us. It's breaking apart!"

CHAPTER 14

A Change of Plan

Something hard rubbed against Tom's cheek and he woke with a start and saw that he was leaning against the low, stony wall of the well. A large woollen blanket had been wrapped around him and a familiar voice was urging him to eat. The concerned-looking features of a monkey swam into focus.

"Uhnn… thanks," Tom murmured, struggling to sit upright and staring as Professor Perkins offered him a small wooden bowl.

"Restorative broth," he explained, seeing Tom's expression. "Eat it up then try to stand. We really *must* be on our way."

Tom nodded as enthusiastically as his aching head would allow, then suddenly remembered his journey down the well. "The ice," he murmured, "it was breaking apart. There was water all around us. It was freezing cold. I saw Cassie. Where is she, professor? Is she…?"

"I'm here, Tom. I'm all right."

Cassie crouched next to him and placed a hand on his shoulder. Tom stared in confusion.

"It's the clothes, isn't it?" said Cassie. "I know, I know." She stepped backwards so Tom could see her more clearly.

Instead of jeans, Cassie was wearing old-fashioned breeches that reached her knees. Beneath them was a pair of cream-coloured stockings. A fine linen shirt and an embroidered waistcoat had replaced her sweatshirt, and a woollen green frockcoat hung from her shoulders. Even Cassie's well-worn trainers had gone, replaced by square-toed shoes that were fastened with square buckles.

"You look like a... like a highway robber or something," croaked Tom.

"It's all there was," grumbled Cassie. "I even lost my torch *and* my mobile when the ice broke apart."

"This broth and the antique clothing were waiting for us after we returned to the surface," explained Professor Perkins. "Someone has been observing us, Thomas, for there were enough provisions for both of you."

He pulled Tom's blanket aside, and Tom was astonished to see that he was also dressed in the same old-fashioned clothing.

"What happened?!" gasped Tom.

"Our clothes were frozen solid," explained Cassie. "We were lucky to survive. It was so cold you actually passed out."

Tom stared at the ground miserably.

"It is time to remind you," interrupted Professor Perkins, "to remind *both* of you," he added, glaring at Cassie, "that we are alone in the midst of mysterious things. Science and reason no longer prevail and we may perish at any moment." He glanced up at one of the lantern-gourds that dangled over the path and whispered, "*It is time for us to leave the path.*"

"Leave it?! We can't!" cried Cassie. "Mum and Dad came this way, we know they did. We saw them in the gourd!"

The professor shook his head.

"I doubt whether your parents are nearby, young lady. Recent developments have convinced me of that. Now let us be on our way and look for an exit."

He went to move forwards but Cassie blocked his way.

"What do you mean, 'recent developments'?" she asked. "What do you know?"

"I-I would rather not say," the professor stammered, trying to avoid her gaze.

"Well I would rather you *did* say!" Cassie insisted.

"Step aside!" the professor spluttered. Cassie didn't move.

The little monkey glanced left and right, then came to a decision.

"Very well. *Very well!* I *will* share my conclusions with you, only do not seek the comforting hand of Professor Perkins when next dark nightmares visit you."

He cleared his throat.

"I now understand the true nature of this path and the significance of our encounter with the wells. They are part of a cleansing ritual involving water."

"Cleansing ritual?" cried Cassie. "We nearly *drowned!*"

"No, no, no!" replied the professor. "That wasn't the intention at all. From what I learned of forest folklore when studying the subject with your grandpapa, those whose journeys took them along ceremonial paths were meant to survive these watery encounters. That is why warm clothing and food were provided upon your return to the surface. Someone has built a ceremonial path, children, filled with ancient rituals. That is why we must leave it immediately and escape into the forest."

"Why did that machine sound like Mum and Dad?" asked Tom.

"To lure you into the water."

"I'm not leaving the path," insisted Cassie. "Mum and Dad came this way and I intend to find them."

"But we are being driven to the centre like sheep!" cried the professor. "Who knows what other ceremonies await us?"

"How do you know this even *is* a ceremonial path?" said Cassie. "Just because of some stupid wells, a horrible machine and a weird inscription, you think—"

"Inscription?" said the professor. "*I* saw no inscription! Why did you not speak of this earlier?"

"It was just a few lines. More of a squiggle, really. It was written over the entranceway to that stupid tunnel."

Professor Perkins searched the path.

"Here!" he said, handing Cassie a stick. "Scratch what you saw into the dirt and try to be as accurate as your feminine mind will allow."

Cassie's cheeks flamed a particular shade of red that Tom had never seen before, and for a moment he thought she was going to use the stick for a different purpose. But Cassie turned away and drew what she had seen.

"There!" she said, tossing the stick aside. The professor stared in terror.

"That cannot be," he whispered softly, staring at the squiggle. "That simply cannot be."

Tom moved closer and peered at the ground. Cassie was right. The lines *did* look like a meaningless squiggle until Tom realised that he was viewing them from upside down. He turned his head from side to side and began to see the familiar shapes of letters.

"H," he said. "And is that an R?"

"It is H *V* R," corrected the professor miserably, jumping forwards and scraping the drawing into the dirt. "He has escaped the flames of justice, children, and lives to create new abominations!"

He whirled around and pointed his revolver into the brambles between the yew trees.

"What's the matter?" asked Cassie. "Who's survived?"

"Our shepherd is the wolf and we are his prey!" sang the little monkey, hopping from paw to paw.

"*I don't understand!*" said Cassie.

"HVR," answered Tom quietly. "Hans Von Rippenbaum, the toymaker, the one they burned to death over two hundred years ago. He must have escaped into the disc and he knows we're in the forest."

"Stay close if you wish to live," hissed the professor, slinging his shoulder-bag onto his back and bounding along the path.

•••   •••   •••

A shambling figure moved beyond the yew trees, its keen forest eyes fixed upon the strangers as they sped along the path. It snorted quietly, and filtered the night air through its deep and sensitive nostrils and smelt that danger lay close. With long, powerful strides, it matched the hurried pace of the running figures and knew that it had to be careful.

CHAPTER 15

"I thought you said you'd been here before?" panted Cassie, struggling to run in her old-fashioned clothing.

"What of it?" snapped the professor, looking for a way to leave the path.

"If you've been here before, surely you knew Von Rippenbaum was still alive."

The professor stopped to catch his breath.

"Young lady," he wheezed, "following the grievous indignity unleashed upon my person," he pointed to his furry body, "the mechanical hag who perpetrated this outrage upon me thought it amusing to keep me in a cage and parade me through an assortment of taverns and fairgrounds. I was therefore unaware of who was in charge of the Ringwood nor did I encounter Von Rippenbaum."

Cassie stared at him suspiciously.

"I'm not just going to leave this place," she said. "I've still got to find Mum and Dad."

"Impossible! We will be lucky to escape with our own lives."

"They're dead, aren't they?" said Tom quietly. "Mum and Dad, I mean. If Von Rippenbaum's got them, then they're dead. And he must have got them because he knew what their voices sounded like."

Cassie whirled round.

"Don't say that!" she cried. "They're not dead. They can't be! I'll find them and I'll prove it to you!"

Her eyes glistened with tears.

"Actually, Thomas, on this occasion I find myself in agreement with your sister," said Professor Perkins. "Von Rippenbaum will not wish to harm your parents, for they are the lure he will use to draw you along this path. What disturbs me more is how he knew of our arrival. No one but yourselves and your grandpapa were aware of our plan to enter the forest, yet here we stand upon a fully prepared ceremonial path. There is the mystery of it." He stared into the distance. "We *must* hold fast to reason, children, and find a way home. Once there, we will formulate a new plan."

He turned and trotted up the path.

"What about Mum and Dad?" cried Cassie, but the little monkey didn't answer.

"Don't get cross, Cassie. He's only trying to help," said Tom.

"*Help?!* So after nearly freezing to death, losing all our clothes *and* the torch *and* my mobile, and with monkey-brains not even aware that Von Nutter was still alive, you still think his help's worth *having?!*"

"*Please*, Cassie, try and stay calm. The professor might be the only chance we get to find Mum and Dad. Try not to upset him."

Cassie groaned in frustration.

"All right," she muttered angrily. "All right. I'll try and be *nice* to him but I just wish he wasn't so… so…"

"Tarry-long brings little home!" shouted the professor.

"… *annoying!*" she said, and she stormed up the path.

Tom was about to run and catch up with her when Professor Perkins suddenly raised his paw.

"Remain here!" he ordered, staring at Cassie. "There is something glistening on the path far ahead of us. *I* will investigate this matter."

He scurried forwards and Cassie slumped against a yew tree, pulling her coat around her. Tom remained on his feet, watching as the professor's fur changed colour beneath the multi-coloured lantern-gourds.

A familiar scampering sound made Cassie jump with a start, and she realised that she had drifted off to sleep. Professor Perkins stood over her and he seemed to be in high spirits.

"Food!" he panted. "And drink and shelter where we may spend the rest of the evening!"

"Is it safe?" wondered Cassie, struggling to her feet. But the professor had already turned and was running back along the path.

A golden table stood before them, its curved legs decorated with vines and creepers. Three high-backed chairs stood around it, framing an impressive feast that sat upon large, golden platters. A teetering spiral of cakes and pastries rose from the centre of the table, and dotted amongst them were forest creatures sculpted out of chocolate.

Dangling above the table was an amber gourd that hung at the end of a golden chain. The gourd blazed as fiercely as a tiger's eye, and Tom and Cassie studied it nervously.

"Do you think someone's watching us right now?" whispered Tom as they stepped into its light.

"Roast quail!" cried the professor, staring at the feast.

"You're not going to *eat* this stuff are you?!" said Cassie. "What if it's poisoned or something?"

The professor shook his head.

"Those clothes you are wearing and the restorative broth that was left for you means that Von Rippenbaum wishes to keep you alive... for the moment. Travellers on ceremonial paths were often given food and shelter so that they could complete the rigours of the following day. Now, if you will excuse me..."

The little monkey hopped onto a chair, tied a white napkin around his neck and started filling his plate with food. Tom went to step forwards but Cassie grabbed his arm.

"Wait," she said nervously. "I want to see what happens."

"I'm hungry!"

"Wait!" hissed Cassie.

The professor remained in high spirits throughout his meal and made his pleasure known to Tom and Cassie with grand, sweeping gestures of his knife and fork.

"Exquisite!" he marvelled. "It tastes quite exquisite! Oh, I have dined at the tables of the great Parisian chefs, but even those fine dishes cannot compare to these."

"Look, he's all right," said Tom as the professor finished his meal. He was staring at the display of chocolate animals.

"I am better than all right!" cried the professor. "I am 'O' and 'K'!" and he waved merrily.

Tom rushed forwards.

The professor filled their goblets with a sweet berry juice he had tasted during his first visit. He drank to their health. It was during his third helping of a particularly sweet and sticky gateau that an unusual escape plan formed in the professor's mind. He set his fork to one side, sat back in his chair and smiled at his own cleverness.

"It is a curious fact," he pondered quietly, "that any object I upset at table will fall into the open mouth of my shoulder-bag. Most unfortunate! Most unfortunate indeed!"

He raised his glass to the illuminated gourd.

CHAPTER 16

Escape from the Path

After they had eaten, Professor Perkins walked over to three golden hammocks that had been tied between the branches of the yew trees. The hammocks had been arranged like the rungs on a ladder, and after struggling with a heavier-than-usual shoulder-bag, Professor Perkins jumped into the lowest bunk. Cassie scrambled into the highest, leaving Tom staring at the hammock that dangled between them. He brushed away rose petals and flower heads that decorated his pillow, and wriggled gratefully under a thick and fleecy blanket.

"The smell!" he gasped. "Cassie, those petals smell like Mum's perfume! Can you smell it?" He prodded the bulge of his sister's back that dangled above him.

"I know," said Cassie miserably. "It's probably meant to keep us on the path. Just ignore it, Tom, and go to sleep."

Tom could tell that Cassie had been crying.

"Yes, sleep, my boy," whispered Professor Perkins. "But

remember: darkest is the night before dawn." He chuckled slyly to himself.

The light from the gourds faded slowly and Tom was soon fast asleep. But Cassie remained awake, anxious and determined to catch the little monkey doing *something* suspicious. She rolled onto her side and stared along the path, listening carefully for the slightest sound of treachery, when she suddenly found herself running through the forest, alone and in terror. Cassie stumbled forwards and fell, headlong, into a ditch where sinister shadows rippled towards her. She felt their hatred and sensed that every one of them meant to kill her.

Suddenly, something large stepped in front of them and the shadows slithered to a halt.

It was a magnificent white stag, whose powerful features glowed as brightly as moonlight. Its mate appeared, a hind of pure white, and both deer turned their faces towards Cassie.

"Run," the deer urged her, their voices echoing in Cassie's mind. "Run and know that you are safe at our side."

Cassie leapt to her feet and fell against their soft flanks, and immediately felt safe and loved. She buried her face in their soft, white skin and whispered, "Please. Please help me. I'm lost in this forest and I don't know where to go. Please help me."

A different voice answered,

"I *am* trying to help you! Now kindly release my arm!"

Cassie sat upright and realised that it wasn't the neck of two white deer she had been clutching but the hairy forearm of Professor Perkins. "Ach! You have moistened my fur!" the monkey complained. He was sitting on the edge of Cassie's hammock.

"The deer," Cassie mumbled, blinking sleepily. "There were two white deer…"

"That have doubtless galloped back into your dreams,"

snapped the professor. "Now wake up, wake up, and creep to the ground."

The monkey scrambled down to wake up Tom.

Cassie peered over the edge of the hammock, longing for a glimpse of the deer and not quite believing that she had fallen asleep. The path remained silent and empty, and Cassie slid to the ground and stared into the brambles. Tom appeared and was about to ask her what she was looking for, when Professor Perkins gestured impatiently for them both to join him at the edge of the path.

"Behold the industry of a single night's work!" he whispered, pointing to a trench he had dug beneath the brambles. "Would you care to know how I, Professor Augustus Perkins, accomplished such a marvel?"

"No," said Cassie.

"Yes!" whispered Tom.

"By the clever use of a fish slice, a silver tray and a stout pair of poultry shears, items I 'borrowed' from the feast! Would not Brunel himself have marvelled at my ingenuity?"

"Famous Victorian engineer," yawned Cassie, seeing her brother's frown at the name Brunel. "It's only a shallow ditch, Tom," she added.

Cassie lay in the ditch and slid under the thorns. Tom scrambled after her and it wasn't long before they stood side by side amongst the leaves and the trees and the shadows and the moonlight of the mysterious Ringwood Forest.

"The air!" whispered Tom. "Can you feel it? It's tingling like electricity. *What is it, professor?*"

"It is the spirit of the forest," answered Professor Perkins gravely. "Its strange influences are rushing upon us, its crepuscular light feeling to see who we are."

The little monkey paused and realised that perhaps this wasn't the best way to calm nervous children. "However," he added quickly, "the peculiar sensation is like indigestion.

Eventually, it passes. Now let us be on our way. The night is almost over and we must seek shelter before sunrise."

He hitched up his shoulder-bag and scampered into the trees.

"Great," said Cassie. "Even the light wants to kill us."

They ran and rested and ran again until morning, as dawn brought depth and colour to their new surroundings. But the welcoming light only made Professor Perkins even more nervous.

"No shelter!" he twittered. "We must find shelter!"

He came to a wide bank of earth that was topped with gorse and tree roots, and saw that it was filled with the abandoned burrows of forest animals. The professor approached the largest and cleanest-looking, and smiled with relief. He whirled round and instructed Tom and Cassie to help him cover the opening with sticks and branches.

They worked quickly and were soon scrambling inside their makeshift shelter.

"So now we just *lie* here," groaned Cassie.

"And rest, yes, making certain that we have not been followed," said the professor.

"Are we safe?" wondered Tom.

"Safe enough, doubting Thomas. Besides, there is always your grandpapa's Webley to protect us," and the professor patted the revolver.

The little monkey settled back against the earthen wall and opened his shoulder-bag. He removed some fruit and some biscuits he had "accidentally" dropped at the feasting table and shared them with Tom and Cassie.

"After breakfast, you must sleep," he said. "We have many miles to travel and I cannot always guarantee such luxurious accommodation. I will take the first watch and will guard the opening assiduously. Now sleep, both of you, sleep."

Tom removed his woollen jacket and used it like a pillow,

and it wasn't long before he was fast asleep. But Cassie leant against the wall, watching the professor closely and still determined to catch him doing *something* suspicious. As the minutes passed, however, and the wind rustled gently in the trees, Cassie was lulled to sleep.

Slowly, carefully, and as silently as he could manage, Professor Perkins withdrew a small wooden box from his shoulder-bag. He opened the box cautiously and reached inside for a small scrap of paper he had hidden beneath a pile of loose-leaf tea. He angled the paper towards the light and whispered gleefully, "Ever nearer, here I tread. Reclaim that which I thought dead!"

He studied a map scrawled upon the paper's surface and smiled.

•••   •••   •••

The creature had watched jealously as Tom, Cassie and Professor Perkins had feasted at the golden table. It had watched them as they had slept in their hammocks, staring in surprise when they had scrambled beneath the thorny barrier to stand close to where it lurked in the shadows of the Ringwood. It had followed them until morning and had smiled as they had hidden themselves in a burrow that any forest gatherer, good or bad, would have had no difficulty in finding.

Now it nodded slowly to itself and knew that its moment had come.

CHAPTER 17

Into the Forest

E ven before she had opened her eyes, Cassie sensed that something was wrong. Half the camouflage screen was missing and Tom was no longer lying next to her.

"Tom!" she shouted. "Tom! *Where are you?!*"

The pale ball of fur lying on the shoulder-bag mumbled, "Quell your fulminatory tones, Mrs Hardimann. I will be down for breakfast *whenever I please*."

Cassie snatched one of the upright sticks that covered the shelter and prodded the monkey in the back.

"What have you done with Tom, you ridiculous little... *thing?!*" Cassie jabbed him again.

"Lower that stick or it will have my eye out!" gasped the professor.

"It'll have *both* your eyes out if you don't tell me what you've done!" said Cassie, and she swooped the stick nearer.

The professor shuffled back against the wall and decided it was futile to confront this hot-tempered girl. She seemed so irrational, so suspicious and – worst of all – so terribly impolite. He nodded towards the opening and said, as calmly as his own temper would allow, "Perhaps your brother has ventured outside?"

Cassie dashed outside but the forest was still and empty, and Cassie knew that Tom was no longer near them.

The professor appeared, revolver at the ready, but lowered his weapon when he noticed a peculiar set of footprints near the entrance of their shelter.

"Ursine!" he muttered, crouching to the ground. "And yet, and yet…" He started following the trail. "Here!" he exclaimed, tapping each footprint as he went. "And *here!*"

"What are you doing?" snapped Cassie, irritated by his odd behaviour.

"And *here*… and *here*. Here it ends." The professor sat on his haunches and stared sadly into the forest.

"*What are you doing?!*" shouted Cassie, her voice echoing noisily.

"Silence!" hissed the professor, running back to her. "Do you wish to attract every one of Von Rippenbaum's creatures?"

"Haven't I done that already?" said Cassie, glaring at him.

"Why do you insist that I am not human? I am an Englishman, proud and honest, who does not go about inconveniencing children. Your brother accepted me as such. Why cannot you?"

"Because I'm not Tom!"

"You most certainly are not, young lady, you most certainly are not," and the professor returned to the footprints.

"He's been taken, hasn't he," said Cassie. Professor Perkins stared at her in surprise.

"I fear that is so, but how did you know?"

"Because I'm his sister and I know Tom. He never wanders off on his own. He's much too careful." She paused

84

for a moment. "What sort of creature's taken him? Tell me the truth. And no funny business! " She raised her stick and the professor scowled at her.

"As you may observe," he snapped, pointing to the footprints, "large, mammalian imprints, family Ursidae, yet exclusively bipedal, appear to have–"

"In English!" Cassie demanded.

The professor sighed and shook his head.

"A *bear,* young lady, a peculiar species of man-bear has come and has taken your brother from us."

Cassie's knees buckled under her and she crumpled to the ground. Professor Perkins ignored her and continued in his best lecture-hall manner, "The creature appears to have walked upon its hindmost legs. Observe the curious discrepancies, in particular the elongated metatarsals. 'But surely those are the metatarsals of a hominid, professor!' I hear you exclaim. Quite so, quite so, though the ursine characteristics remain dominant."

"What *are* you *talking* about?" demanded Cassie.

"To the talented amateur, such as myself, whatever took Thomas appears to have exhibited an alarming mixture of man and beast; neither fully man nor fully beast, rather a grotesque hybrid of both."

The professor paused.

"Sadly," he mumbled, "we will not be able to follow it, for the creature appears to have possessed enough low cunning to have covered its tracks."

Cassie struggled to her feet and walked away. Professor Perkins watched in alarm as she wandered into the trees.

"Where are you going?" he demanded.

"Back the way we came," said Cassie. "At least when that toymaker catches me I'll be able to see Tom again."

"Von Rippenbaum had nothing to do with this!" the professor shouted. "There are no indications of a struggle or any pools of blood one would normally associate with one of *his* misdeeds. And why were *we* left undisturbed?"

Cassie paused as the professor continued, "By all means, dispose of yourself in any way you see fit, but know that I, Professor Perkins, will never falter in my quest to find your brother or your parents! Goodbye, young lady! Goodbye!" and he waved her an enthusiastic farewell.

Cassie spun round.

"*Your* quest?!" she shouted. "Of all the arrogant…!" She sprinted back towards him. "*Who was asleep on lookout?*" she demanded.

"Ahh. An unfortunate lapse," mumbled the professor. "I do apologise."

"If *anyone's* going to find my parents it'll be *me*, not you!"

"As you wish," sighed the professor.

He was about to return to the shelter and retrieve his shoulder-bag when a booming rumble sounded in the distance. The professor ran to the nearest tree and scrambled into its uppermost branches, and scanned the forest with his spyglass.

What he saw made him cry out in terror.

Far away, in the direction of the path, hovered a large and peculiar hot-air balloon. Its rounded sides trailed propellers and ropes but it was the balloon's elaborate undercarriage that held the professor's attention. It was large and wooden and had been carved to resemble an enormous boar's head. Hundreds of leaded windows glittered brightly along its sides, and flags and banners fluttered majestically behind it. Evil-coloured smoke belched from the boar's nostrils, and far above it a tight knot of birds wheeled angrily.

"*Corvi corax!*" gasped Professor Perkins, studying the angry flock of ravens. He started to scramble back the way he had come when a rotten branch broke underneath him. The professor bounced to the ground and landed with a thump at Cassie's feet.

"*Corvi corax!*" he gasped, the air knocked out of him. "*Boar's head… Von Rippenbaum… Danger…Must flee!*"

Cassie folded her arms and glared at him suspiciously.

♦ ♦ ♦   ♦ ♦ ♦   ♦ ♦ ♦

The birds swirled around a golden throne that stood on a raised platform at the top of the wooden boar's head. Their master, Hans Von Rippenbaum, raised his arms and waited for the biggest and the blackest of the ravens to land. The raven appeared and sensed its master's fury.

The creature bowed, cogwheels whirring deep inside its metal casing. Its sculpted head cocked left and right and its bright little eyes blinked ice-blue.

"Risratch," sighed the emperor, using the strange, brittle language of the Ringwood. "Risratch, I have been disappointed. Those who serve me, failed me."

He stared at a rope that secured the balloon to the forest below. Halfway down it, a thick-necked man-beast pleaded for its life. "Those honoured with the nightwatch fell asleep," continued the toymaker. "Its *eyes* failed me, allowing the bloodlings to escape into the forest. I therefore offer you those eyes. Your army may take the creature's remains."

Risratch cawed and fell upon the figure on the rope, who screamed in horrified surprise.

Beaks pecked through the rope's wiry strands until, thread by thread, it sheared the lifeline in two. The balloon leapt free of its tether while the man-beast plummeted to the ground below, smashing onto the table where Tom and his companions had feasted hours earlier.

A new and more terrible feast began.

CHAPTER 18

The Messenger

The little boat rocked gently on a swell of ocean currents that made Tom feel as if he was being carried out to sea. He smiled contentedly and nestled deeper into a furry blanket that lay beneath him, wishing that this journey would last forever.

Something jolted him awake, and Tom jumped with a start and raised his head.

"Cassie?" he croaked, seeing that he was alone. "*Cassie, where are you?*"

The forest was sliding past him at a peculiar angle and Tom tried to sit upright but saw that he was lying on his stomach with his arms tied around a shaggy boulder. The boulder turned slowly, left and right, and when it moved again, Tom realised that it was, in fact, the broad, living head of an enormous animal that had slung him across its back.

Tom thrashed up and down in terror and tried to wriggle free but the creature growled at him menacingly.

"W-who are you?" cried Tom, hardly able to speak.

The creature didn't reply.

"Are you going to eat me?" he asked.

A curious bark, like a sudden burst of laughter, came from the creature, but it said no more. "Wh-where's my sister and my friend?" asked Tom breathlessly. "My sister's a girl but my friend's a monkey who's really human, except my sister doesn't think he is—"

"*Enuff!*" growled the creature.

Tom stared in amazement. It had sounded almost human.

A sharp, stabbing pain suddenly flashed through his arms and Tom cried out,

"I-I need to get down. My arms, they're hurting me." He squirmed uncomfortably.

Tom felt the ties on his wrists being loosened and he suddenly felt himself hurtling down the slope of the creature's long back. Just when he expected to feel the blunt edge of a root or the sharp edge of a stone strike him as he fell, the creature's massive paws lowered him gently the rest of the way. Tom stood on the ground, weak-eyed and wobbling, and saw the massive paws return to their owner's sides.

The creature turned and faced him.

It was an eight-foot tower of fur, its massive frame supported by column-thick legs that ended in a fearsome set of claws. A dark swag of burgundy cloth draped across its broad chest, giving the creature a curiously gallant air. The creature was a bear and it bent forwards and stared at him quizzically.

Tom would have turned and fled had it not been for the creature's eyes. They were bright and shiny, like newly opened conkers, but they were not the hungry eyes of the wild forest predator Tom had expected to see. They were filled with a kindly intelligence that was studying Tom intently.

The creature straightened and leant upon a wooden staff that was as tall and as broad as the apple trees Tom clambered about in at home.

"*You're half-human!*" whispered Tom, suddenly realising what it was he was looking at. The giant bear-man stiffened and pointed for Tom to sit down, then it paced about and gathered kindling for a fire.

Tom watched in silence as the creature scattered chestnuts next to the flames. He edged backwards when it sat opposite him and produced a long pipe from its sash and settled back against the side of a broad tree. The creature closed its eyes and growled with what Tom hoped was contentment.

Only the snap of the fire-splitting wood broke the silence between them, and Tom glanced nervously at the shadows of the forest and the bear-man's face. Gradually, the giant's breathing became deep and regular, and Tom realised that it had fallen asleep.

Tom crept from the firelight and fled into the night, fear feeding his flight. He ran as fast and as far as he could and saw branches and hollows and rises and dips all flash before him in a blur of terror. He eventually stood, doubled over and gasping for air, when a familiar set of claws stepped into view.

The bear, it seemed, hadn't been sleeping after all, and it towered over Tom like a shaggy cliff. It raised its paw and Tom shrank back against the blow he expected to feel. But the bear reached inside its sash and produced a small scrap of paper, and gestured for Tom to read it.

Tom took the paper nervously, and before the words or the sense or the meaning of the message even reached him, Tom knew who the note was from. He slid to the ground in astonishment.

The bear-man lifted Tom onto his shoulders and lumbered back towards the fire.

The chestnuts it had scattered were ready to be eaten, and the creature licked its lips and wondered if the small bag of bones it was carrying would like to join him for supper.

CHAPTER 19

The Furnace

"It doesn't feel right leaving Tom behind," said Cassie, leaning against a tree.

She had spent the afternoon following a nervous Professor Perkins through the bleak, outer forest where they had seen no sign of either Tom or the creature that had taken him.

"Thomas is resourceful. I am sure he will be safe," said the professor. "We must continue towards autumn with its abundant foliage. These wintry branches provide little cover from the gaze of whoever is in that hot-air balloon."

"This isn't winter!" said Cassie. "There's no snow or ice. It isn't even cold any more. And why doesn't anything *smell* of anything? Everything's just grey and dead – look!"

Cassie grabbed a branch and crumbled it between her fingers. The professor stared in amazement and repeated the experiment, crying in surprise when a branch crumbled in the same peculiar manner.

Fear, he realised, had blinded him to his surroundings. Worse yet, it had taken a child – a female child – to tell him what he should have noticed.

"You are a most… observant young lady," he muttered grudgingly. "The winter forest *does* appear to be in the grip of some sort of disease. The subdued hues, the apparent absence of life, the curious desiccation of the timber; yes, yes, a creeping decay is feeding upon winter."

"I've observed something else, too," said Cassie.

"Oh?"

The professor walked on, pretending not to be interested.

"I've observed that you don't like children, especially girls. In fact, you probably think we should be seen and not heard."

"Seen and not heard! Well, I am glad that a seed of wisdom from my century has drifted into yours!"

"Wisdom?!" cried Cassie. "You Victorians were cruel to children."

"Cruel? Children knew their place. Indeed, rhubarb and soda were often administered to my younger self with a forcing-spoon whenever I transgressed the bounds of civilised behaviour."

"*A forcing-spoon?* See! Victorian cruelty!" said Cassie.

"Then you accept that I am from your past and was once human?"

"I-I never said that," stammered Cassie. "I don't know what you are. I don't even know why you're helping me."

The professor sighed and rubbed the bridge of his nose.

"I have bound my honour to a pledge, a pledge I made to your grandpapa in which I promised to bring about a successful conclusion to this sinister business. I do not intend to disappoint him. Believe me to be cruel if you wish. Believe me to loathe all children if you like. Believe that I sup with the Devil himself in the high-halls of hell! But what I cannot

– nay, *will* not – tolerate is your persistent belief that I am a product of this ghastly place and that I mean you harm, for I do not!"

The professor stalked to the top of a rise on which he intended to sulk, when he gave a startled cry and pointed at something.

Cassie joined him.

"Winter!" cried the professor, gesturing between the branches of the dead forest. "See what is left of winter, and beyond it, the colours of autumn!"

He scampered down the slope, and Cassie raced after him.

They plunged into the snow and were immediately engulfed by a bitter, gusting wind. Cassie gathered her frockcoat around her while the professor uncoiled his tail and wrapped it around himself like a scarf.

Snow speckled their faces and clumped around their feet, and between ice-crusted tree trunks and icicle-laden branches, the tantalising colours of autumn drew them on. They struggled forwards and eventually came to a great sheet of ice on which they skidded and slid before tumbling, head-first, into a deep bed of leaves.

After the decaying edges of the forest, Cassie felt as if she had fallen into an extravagantly decorated room. The forest was filled with colour and life, and it was all Cassie could do to stand in its midst.

"Conceal yourself!" cried Professor Perkins, shouting over a gusting wind. He was hiding in a clump of bracken and was gesturing frantically. But Cassie remained where she was, enjoying the furnace of sound and colour. "*Conceal yourself!*" the professor shouted. Cassie sighed and wandered over to him.

Professor Perkins studied the forest ahead of them and jumped with excitement.

"What fortune!" he cried, handing Cassie the telescope. "Look to the oak tree and the object dangling from it."

Cassie focused the lens and saw an oversized pinecone swaying at the end of a cord. The pinecone glittered brightly and appeared to be made out of gold.

"It's a nasty Christmas bauble. So what?" said Cassie.

"No, no, no! I know where I am!" cried the professor. "I have passed this way before!"

"So we'll reach the centre quicker and get help sooner?" said Cassie, suddenly excited.

"The centre?" exclaimed the professor, staring at her in surprise. "Oh, yes, the centre. Er, of course. Come. Let us proceed!"

He ran to the golden pinecone and struck it with a stick, and a clear note rang throughout the forest.

The rushing wind ceased for a moment and the Ringwood seemed to listen.

CHAPTER 20

A New Companion

The bear-creature held out its paw and offered Tom some chestnuts. Tom shook his head, too astonished to eat any.

He knew by the note's hurried scrawl that its author had been upset when he had written it. Tom even noticed teardrops staining the edge of the paper, and he wiped his own eyes dry and angled the paper back towards the firelight and re-read the message.

My dear Tom,

If you have passed through the disc and are walking through the Ringwood, I am afraid you have been tricked.
I am very, very sorry.
The 'grandfather' who lured you to my house was a device of wax and metal created by

Von Rippenbaum. It emerged from the disc late one evening and forced me, your real grandfather, into the Ringwood where creatures were waiting to take me to the forest centre. The fate of your parents remains unknown to me.

Please read the following very carefully, Tom, and do as I say.

The first path you will encounter will be long and straight. Leave it at once for it is a ceremonial path; Professor Perkins will know what to do. And please inform the professor that Von Rippenbaum lives! It is a difficult thing for me to write and an even more difficult thing for me to accept, but there is evidence of his handiwork all around me.

Stay close to Professor Perkins, Tom, AND to the creature who delivered this note to you. He is a sympathetic friend — in spite of his fearsome appearance.

Courage, my boy, and draw strength from the knowledge that we will soon be together. Then we will see what is what!

With much love,
Your Grandfather

"A mechanical!" gasped Tom. "That thing at grandfather's… it wasn't human. It was *a mechanical!*"

He remembered how the creature he had met at the house had neither eaten nor drunk the refreshments Professor Perkins had prepared for them, and Tom shivered to think how close he had come to hugging the glassy-eyed 'grandfather' goodbye. He suddenly realised that the creature could, if it wanted to, simply re-bury the disc in the garden and trap them all in the forest forever. He groaned miserably and slumped against a tree, and the bear-creature lowered its pipe.

"Eat," it rumbled, its voice a deep bass, and it offered Tom another pawful of chestnuts. Tom decided not to upset this new, "sympathetic friend", and he accepted the food gratefully. The bear nodded and returned to its pipe.

Between the warmth of the chestnuts and the glow of the fire, Tom started to feel a little braver and he asked, "Th-there were two others travelling with me: a girl and a monkey…"

He paused, uncertain whether the bear could understand him, but the creature nodded. "The girl was my sister," Tom added. "The monkey was my friend."

"Yer gran'father sed nothin' about a girl," replied the bear.

"But she's my sister!" said Tom.

"Cudder been a mechanical. That's why I left 'er wi' munkey."

Tom suddenly realised that his grandfather – his *real* grandfather – wouldn't be aware that Cassie had followed him to the house and had been drawn through into the Ringwood.

"But she isn't a mechanical!" cried Tom. "We *must* go back for her. And the professor. They'll both think I'm dead!"

"Rest yer firelock!" rumbled the bear. "Bristlebeard'll know you've left the path by now. His spies'll be everywhere. I'll go back an' fetch 'em after I've taken you to yer gran'father."

"But…"

The bear rose and kicked over the traces of the fire. It was clear that the conversation was over *and* that it was used to getting its own way.

"If they stay out o' sight an' avoid the unnaturals, they shud be safe," added the bear sympathetically. Tom nodded and got to his feet, and noticed a hefty-looking stick lying on the ground. Deciding he needed a useful weapon, Tom picked it up, whereupon the stick crumbled into pieces. "Forest's dyin'," grunted the bear. "It's Bristlebeard's fault. At least we're safe from 'is unnaturals. They can't survive in this dead, outer greyness. It kills 'em stone dead."

The bear studied the sky. "We'll walk through the night an' on into tomorrow an' follow the contours of the land. Are yer with me, lad, or do I need to tie you again?"

"I'm with you, I'm with you," said Tom, rubbing his wrists.

The bear turned and melted into the darkness and Tom stared after it, wondering how something so large could disappear so completely. He tried to follow it but was uncertain which way it had gone when the bear suddenly growled. Tom saw its eyes shining in the darkness, and he held out his arms and walked towards them.

▸ ▸ ▸   ▸ ▸ ▸   ▸ ▸ ▸

Risratch bobbed onto the windowsill and waited. The window was small and set into the neck of the wooden boar's head where Von Rippenbaum's living quarters were arranged.

The light from an ornamental lantern cast the raven in a sinister harlequin of colours, and it strutted forwards and bowed. Von Rippenbaum ignored it and continued eating his meal.

"You are here to inform me how well you and your brethren performed today," the toymaker said sarcastically, "how tirelessly you flew the length and breadth of my kingdom, never pausing in your quest to…" He circled his hand as if to say, "et cetera, et cetera."

Risratch hopped from claw to claw, alarmed by its master's tone. "You will continue by telling me how, in spite of several encouraging moments, you *failed* to catch the bloodlings."

The raven sank lower.

"You will then add that no effort will be spared to catch the bloodlings and that you will continue your search at first light. Have I left anything out?"

"Only that you are wise and glorious, master," croaked the bird.

Risratch suddenly found itself pinned to the floor by a ceremonial rod. Its mechanical innards ground noisily as it tried to pay even grander compliments to its master. But all it could manage was a feeble, "craww."

Von Rippenbaum kicked the bird across a floor that was an enormous circular window set into the base of the boar's neck. A haphazard weave of lead strips held hundreds of pieces of glass together, and through it the forest drifted far below.

"Crawww!" cried the raven, staggering to its feet.

"Fail me tomorrow, Risratch, and I will set your eyes into the glass you now stand upon. *Then* you may gaze upon the forest at your leisure! Now go and do as I commanded!"

Von Rippenbaum stormed from the chamber, kicking over his supper tray as he went.

The raven hopped miserably back the way it had come, and flapped into the night. It wheeled beneath a rising moon and cawed a harsh cry to its companions. But those birds were living creatures of flesh and feather, and Risratch knew that they would not rise again until morning.

The metal bird skimmed low and dived into the forest. It perched upon a branch and cocked its head, watching and waiting and listening to the night.

Chapter 21

Unwelcome Guests

"What's happening?" asked Cassie as the chimes of the golden pinecone faded.

"Watch!" said Professor Perkins, pointing into the trees.

Cassie grew impatient and was about to step from their hiding place when another bell sounded in the distance.

A large, wooden object came shambling out of the forest, scuttling like a crab on wooden legs that ended in carved lion's paws. The object was an antique cabinet decorated with carvings of animals, plants, flowers and fruit. A golden bell jingled on top of the cabinet's pyramid-shaped roof and only fell silent when the walking box stopped beneath the oak tree where it sat like an obedient dog. A door in the cabinet's side swung open and revealed an ornate chandelier, leather seats and an interior lined with fabric.

"*What is it?*" cried Cassie.

"A sedan chair!" cried the professor. "A railway

compartment! Call it an automobile if you wish!"

"But what does it do?"

"It perambulates throughout the Ringwood, making itself available to the weariest forest traveller. I used this very one during my first visit and happen to know that it will carry us close to shelter where we may rest for the night. Now hurry inside before we are seen. Quickly, young lady, quickly!"

Cassie placed her foot on the cabinet's polished step and felt the wood quiver under her as if it were alive. Cassie leapt forwards and heard the door slam behind her and felt the box adjust itself to its new passengers. The box stood and plodded forwards like an old cart horse. Cassie fell into a leather seat, listening nervously as timbers creaked and the chandelier swayed and tinkled overhead.

"Does it stop and let other people on?" she whispered, suddenly aware that they would be trapped if it did.

"It did not when I first used it," answered the professor, peering through a curtain he had drawn across the window.

"But what if Tom or Mum or Dad want to get on?"

"Then I will invite them to jump!" snapped the professor, trying to concentrate on the view outside.

Cassie scowled and crossed her arms.

"How long is this journey?" she wondered.

"Long enough to indulge in some *quiet* contemplation," murmured the professor.

Cassie thought of Tom and she started counting aloud. "Two days to the exit… then rest at Grandfather's house… then another two days' travel…"

She sat up in alarm. "By the time we get back here, five or six days will have passed. Tom could be anywhere by then!"

"We will find him," said the professor.

"How?"

"Many things will be different upon our return," smiled

the monkey mysteriously. "There is a little volume sitting in my… in your grandpapa's library. It is a book of arcane lore."

"Arcane?"

"From the Latin, 'arcanus', meaning 'secret' or 'hidden'. I trust you are not neglecting your Latin studies at school?"

"Er, no," lied Cassie, who only studied French.

"The secrets within the book are powerful," continued the professor, "for it is a genuine medieval grimoire!"

He paused, expecting to hear a cry of amazement, but Cassie said nothing. "It is a *sorcerer's spell book!*" he explained, and Cassie snorted dismissively.

"Not more mumbo-jumbo!" she said miserably. "Now I know I'll never see Tom again. Where is this stupid spell book, anyway?"

The professor frowned.

"Your grandpapa neglected to put it in my shoulder-bag as we agreed. If it weren't for this revolver, we would be quite defenceless."

"So that's your new plan, is it? More magic."

"I, too, once dismissed the supernatural as foolish nonsense. I even wrote a pamphlet entitled, 'Science, Reason and the Death of Superstition'. Perhaps you have read it?"

"No," said Cassie.

"It was well received, though it will need considerable revision given what has befallen me."

"I haven't read it."

"Have you read *any* of my work?" asked the monkey hopefully. "What of my writings concerning Greek vase inscriptions, the non-Attic schools?"

Cassie shook her head.

"'Perkins' Shilling Improver – A Guide to Proper English Usage'?"

"No!" insisted Cassie. "I haven't read *any* of your weird books. My family are missing and all you can do is talk about spells and magic! I just wish I could wake up from this *stupid, stupid nightmare!*"

"Oh! Nightmare is it? There are times when I envy you your youthful simple-mindedness."

The cabinet suddenly swayed and slowed, and Cassie and the professor stared at one another nervously.

"Mechanicals!" hissed the professor, peering out of the window. "We are about to be boarded! What will we do? What will we do?!"

"I thought you said this thing didn't stop?" hissed Cassie.

"I was unaware that it did!" squeaked the monkey, scrambling for the revolver.

"Fire a warning shot!" said Cassie, pointing at the door.

"I dare not. The loud retort would attract many others."

Professor Perkins padded back and forth across the carpeted floor. "We are caught like rats in a tastefully decorated trap!" he whispered. "What will become of us? What will *he* do to us?!"

Suddenly, Cassie sprang onto her seat.

"What are *you* doing?" gasped the professor.

"Using my youthful simple-mindedness," snapped Cassie, and with a quick little hop, she jumped into the air.

CHAPTER 22

Deadly Pursuit

itches, gullies and half-buried tree roots loomed from the darkness. The bear-creature stepped around them as if it was daylight.

The moon appeared as a delicate rim of ivory then brightened quickly and passed through its cycles until it became full and fat. It looked so large that Tom imagined he could hear it thundering skywards and he skidded to a halt and stood in its brilliance, caught like a rabbit in the beam of a poacher's lamp.

A giant arm drew him back into the shadows.

"Night march," the bear reminded him but Tom cried in amazement when splashes of colour suddenly spilled across the moon's mottled surface. The colours grew brighter and glowed like stained glass, and formed themselves into an image of several forest animals nestling at the feet of a bearded man.

"Who's that?" whispered Tom, staring at the image of the

stranger. The bear growled.

"'e is pain an' misery an' a thousand other reasons why there's not a creature in this forest 'oo wouldn't miss a chance to slice 'im, gizzard to chop!"

"You mean it's Von Rippenbaum?!" whispered Tom.

"Ay, Bristlebeard!" growled the bear, lumbering back into the night.

The image suddenly changed and showed the toymaker standing next to a waterfall that was framed by a rainbow. He was feeding grain to a flock of white doves that fluttered happily around him, and baby deer nestled at his feet. Tom shivered and turned away.

"What's *your* name?" asked Tom.

The tower of fur froze.

"Yer wish to call me *by name?!*" it said in surprise.

Tom nodded.

"'ere in the Ringwood I go as Bearskin the Hunter but most call me other names and shun me."

"Bearskin the Hunter," said Tom, liking how it sounded. "I'm Thomas. Thomas the Schoolboy. But you probably knew that already."

The bear grunted and walked on.

"How did you get Grandfather's note?" asked Tom. "Did you meet him? Was he all right?"

"Yer chatter worse than a peckin' yaffle!" grumbled Bearskin, leaning on his staff. "It were 'is cry for help that drew me to 'im. It'd been so long since I'd heard my native tongue spoken that I crept closer to see 'oo it were. Yer gran'father were on that blasted path – the straight one you were on – but were surrounded by unnaturals. They were takin' 'im to the centre of the forest. I bided my time and crept through the brambles an' spoke wi' 'im."

"Is that when he gave you the note?" asked Tom.

Bearskin nodded and set off again.

Tom decided to question the giant later, after they had stopped to rest. He stayed within the bear-man's shadow and didn't speak again until a pre-dawn murkiness lightened the path. At sunrise, Bearskin led Tom towards a fallen tree trunk and pointed for him to sit down. Tom collapsed gratefully and rubbed his aching feet.

"Snow bones," whispered Bearskin, nodding at a patch of half-melted snow that lay just ahead of them. "It's what's left o' winter," he added, shambling over to it.

"I thought we were going to rest," groaned Tom, struggling to his feet.

An icy wind swirled around him the moment Tom entered the frozen landscape. He had only taken a few footsteps when Bearskin drove his staff deep into the ground and reached inside his sash. He brought out a little bird that flew ahead of them, then Bearskin angled his staff like a plough blade and pushed dense tree branches aside. Meringue-shaped clusters of snow fell all around them, covering them both with a dusting of ice. Tom shivered and turned his collar up, avoiding the deeper snowdrifts by using Bearskin's footprints like stepping stones. He hopped from one print to the other like a flea, but when Bearskin came to a sudden halt, Tom crashed into him and fell backwards.

The little bird was chirruping an alarm and Bearskin turned and flung Tom onto his shoulders, before bounding back the way he had come.

Pinecones and needles whipped past his face, and Tom jumped in terror when the forest suddenly filled with a chorus of terrifying howls. A pack of wolves burst from the shadows and bounded towards them with an odd, stiff-legged gait.

"Mechanicals!" shouted Tom. "They're wooden mechanical wolves!"

Bearskin swung his staff like an enormous scythe and sent the first wolf crashing against a tree trunk where it shattered into pieces. Tom felt as if he was sitting on top of an exploding volcano, and he gripped Bearskin's fur and shouted encouragement. The giant swung his staff again and again and the wolves snapped angrily then fled into the forest. Bearskin ran back towards the grey wilderness.

"Why are we going back?" cried Tom. "The wolves have gone. You chased them away. We can head into the living forest."

Just then, a wolf stepped out in front of them.

It was larger than the others and its face was dark and sinister. Its eyes blazed with green fire, and it watched Tom and Bearskin closely before trotting away.

"You've frightened it away!" cried Tom.

"It's turnin' to attack us," said Bearskin.

"Fight it off, like you did all the others!"

"They were used to wear me out. This one's come to finish me off. Tek 'old, lad. Tek 'old!"

Bearskin continued running towards the wilderness, knowing they would be safe in the dead, outer fringes. The giant wolf sprang after him, howling as it ran.

The creature bounded nearer, its jaws snapping hungrily, then it launched itself high into the air. The wolf landed on Bearskin's back and Bearskin roared and struggled forwards, inches away from safety.

"Climb 'igher, lad!" shouted Bearskin. "Climb out of its reach!"

Tom stayed where he was, determined to help his struggling friend. He raised his foot and took careful aim and kicked at the wolf's snapping muzzle.

Tom's last conscious memory was of a hot, crushing pain, a deep and throaty growl, and a pair of green, blazing eyes looming over him.

. . .　　. . .　　. . .

"Where do you dogs fly?" cawed Risratch as a pair of mechanical wolves ran beneath the tree. The wolves hesitated, knowing it was unwise to ignore Von Rippenbaum's raven.

"We were summoned…" explained one.

"… by our leader," finished the other. "He called to us."

"For food or to hunt?" asked Risratch.

The wolves circled the tree.

"It was a cry for food!" answered one.

"It was a cry for blood!" corrected the other, snapping at his companion.

Risratch flapped lower, wondering if it was possible that the wolves had found the bloodlings before he or his ravens had had a chance to prove themselves.

"Show me," commanded the raven.

The wolves snapped and snarled and continued on their way.

CHAPTER 23

The Haus in the Woods

assie stood on a ledge that ran around the base of the pyramid-shaped ceiling, hidden behind swags of material that decorated the inside of the walking cabinet. Professor Perkins stood opposite her, peeping out through a fold in the fabric. They stared at one another through a link in the chandelier's chain before staring down to see who, or what, had entered the carriage.

At first, Cassie thought the passengers had carried twigs and bundles of twisted wood aboard, but quickly realised that the cracked and knotted forms were the bodies of the creatures themselves.

Shoots and tendrils formed sinewy veins around their tree-stump bodies, which were covered in leaf-mould and fungus. A powerful stench of rotten vegetables filled the carriage. Cassie covered her nose and almost screamed when one of the creatures started to speak in a series of wood-splitting cracks. Their language reminded Cassie of chittering insects, and both creatures talked rapidly and often at the same time. One of the creatures leant forwards and started to pick a hole in the leather seat, and its companion clicked loudly, as if it was laughing. All of a sudden, the walking cabinet shuddered to a halt, flung open its door and leaned over at such a steep angle that both creatures tumbled out. The carriage then righted itself and continued on its way.

Cassie and Professor Perkins jumped from their hiding place.

"A self-regulating vehicle!" marvelled the professor, brushing bits of wood from the seats. "Our little box does not tolerate misbehaviour!"

"Lucky it's not a school bus," muttered Cassie, sitting as sensibly as she could.

"Your choice of hiding place was inspired," said Professor Perkins, turning to face her. "Are all young females of your century as resourceful as you?"

"Only if you don't use forcing-spoons on them," said Cassie.

Professor Perkins frowned, uncertain whether Cassie was teasing him.

"You could understand what those things were saying," said Cassie.

Professor Perkins stared in surprise.

"Yes, I understand their foul tongue for I have a keen linguistic ear."

"What were they talking about?"

"They spoke of a hunt – a hunt for the 'bloodlings' as Von Rippenbaum appears to call you."

"Did they mention Tom? Did they say whether they'd caught Tom?"

The professor shook his head.

"They spoke of a wolf's cry heard at the edge of winter.

The creatures were arguing whether to go and investigate it."

Cassie sat up in alarm when the carriage started to slow.

"All is well," said the professor. "Our journey has almost ended. Prepare yourself and be ready to jump."

Professor Perkins leapt into the night and scuttled behind a pine tree. Cassie jumped after him and ran from shadow to shadow, watching sadly as the wooden cabinet ambled away, its cheery light and tinkling bell quickly swallowed up by the night.

The forest billowed restlessly around them as Professor Perkins turned in a wide circle. He nodded and set off towards a forbidding stand of trees through which he led Cassie. They emerged into a clearing where a small, elegant building stood illuminated in the moonlight.

The roof of the building was domed like a pineapple and supported an ornate little cupola. The building was octagonal with a window on every side, but the windows were shuttered and the building appeared dark and silent. Professor Perkins paused at the edge of the clearing and studied it carefully.

"Remain hidden while I investigate," he whispered. *Now where's he brought me?* Cassie wondered, trying to read a sign that hung above the building's entrance. Cassie had just made out the letters "T" and "H" when she felt something tap her on her shoulder. She spun round and saw a breathless Professor Perkins standing behind her.

"Don't *do* that!" she hissed, unnerved by the monkey's speed.

"All is well," panted the professor. "The building is deserted. We may shelter there in safety."

Cassie followed him into the clearing and saw the sign more clearly.

"What's a 'Teehaus'?" she asked.

"It means 'Tea House' of course. I trust you are not

neglecting your German studies at school."

"Er, no," lied Cassie, wondering if there was ever going to be some French for her to translate.

The professor threw open the double doors and gestured Cassie inside. The doors closed with a thud and Cassie stared in horror.

She was surrounded by dozens of seated mechanicals.

CHAPTER 24

Friendship

earskin's chest rose like a cliff, and the underneath of his muzzle thrust forwards like a rocky outcrop. Tom blinked in confusion, wondering why he was viewing it from such a peculiar angle, when he suddenly realised that he was being carried in Bearskin's sash.

He moved the cloth to one side and saw patches of snow marking the boundary line between the living forest and the grey, outer wilderness. He also saw the giant wolf running alongside them on its stiff legs, making certain that it didn't cross the deadly divide. Its jagged muzzle was speckled with Tom's blood.

Two more wolves burst from the undergrowth and fell in behind their leader. Above them flew a sinister raven.

The raven studied Bearskin and cawed dismissively. It was about to turn and flap away when it saw Tom's face peering up at it.

"Bloodling!" it cried. "Bloodling! I have found you! You!

Running creature. Give me the bloodling and I will spare your life."

Bearskin turned away from the snow line.

"You who run in the flesh of a bear!" cried Risratch. "Give me the bloodling and your curse will be lifted. You will live in the forest as a man!"

Bearskin stopped running, and the raven flapped to the ground. The wolves gathered behind it, their eyes fixed upon Bearskin's throat.

"Bearskin!" cried Tom. "Bearskin, what are you doing? Please don't hand me over! You promised you'd help me. *You promised!*"

Bearskin said nothing, and walked to the edge of the living forest.

"Lift my curse?" he said, staring at the raven. "Lift my curse in return fer the boy?"

Risratch nodded.

"All right, come tek 'im." Bearskin lifted his sash.

"Do not mock me, Master Longtooth!" snapped Risratch. "To cross this divide would result in my death, yet this you already know."

Risratch raised its beak and spoke to Tom. "Your family await you!" it cawed. "Your grandfather awaits you! Your sister and the ape-creature await you! Leave this stink-beast where it stands and I will take you to them."

Tom thrust his head out of the sash.

"You know where Cassie and my parents are?" he gasped. Bearskin pushed Tom back inside the sash.

"Rest yer firelock, lad!" he whispered angrily. "Greasy-beak hopes ter split us wi' lies but I fancy I've a better deal I can strike. Now lie still while I strike it."

Bearskin shambled closer and stared down at the raven, who hopped backwards nervously.

"Lift my curse?" he repeated, rubbing his chin.

"In return for the bloodling, yes," snapped the raven impatiently.

Bearskin nodded.

"All right then, tek 'im!" Bearskin moved, as if handing Tom over.

Tom suddenly felt himself lurching forwards and almost tumbled from the sash when Bearskin lifted his staff and brought it crashing down. A glittering plume of snow exploded into the air and something black and ragged whirled into the trees, screeching with fury.

The wolves were enraged by the attack and they pounced forwards as a howling mob. Their mechanical innards whirred noisily for a moment before crashing to the ground, dead at Bearskin's feet.

"Legions of creatures now stand against you, tree-scraper!" screamed Risratch from a tree. "You will wander the edge of the Ringwood as a dung-sniffer, a squirrel-chaser, a root-grubber! *Give me the bloodling! Give me the bloodling!*"

Its taunts grew fainter as Bearskin turned back into the wilderness, but the raven's words echoed in Tom's mind.

"It said it had Cassie and my parents and Professor Perkins. Maybe I should go back and surrender."

"It called me a dung-sniffer," grunted Bearskin. "Dun't make it true, though."

"You mean it was lying?" said Tom.

Bearskin grunted and rolled his eyes.

"Sorry," said Tom. "I really thought you were going to hand me over, Bearskin. I should have trusted you."

"An' I'm sorry I'm stuck wi' a boy 'oo thinks 'e can fend off a wolf wi' 'is foot!"

Tom studied his ankle and saw a ring of teeth marks bleeding through a tear in his stocking. The wound burned painfully.

Bearskin lifted Tom onto a tree trunk, reached inside

his sash and produced a leather pouch filled with leaves. He scooped some rainwater from a hollow and worked the leaves into a dark and sticky paste.

"What's that?" asked Tom, hoping he wouldn't have to eat it.

"Mustard seed. Nettle leaf. Fire toad," grunted Bearskin. "Lie still."

Tom winced as Bearskin dabbed the sticky mixture around his wound. The bite grew hot.

"Lie still!" grunted Bearskin. "It's drawin' the badness out."

The pain gradually weakened, and Bearskin released Tom's leg. He sat down next to him and withdrew his pipe and tobacco. It wasn't long before clinging wreaths of smoke enveloped the bear-man's head.

Grey mist drifted between dead tree branches, and Tom picked up a clump of moss and threw it at the ground. He had so many questions about his grandfather and his parents that he found it difficult to sit still, yet knew that his friend was not to be disturbed.

Deep in the map of his hunter's mind, Bearskin was running along gullies and trackways and half-remembered paths in the hope of finding a safe passage back into the living forest. But he could think of no pathway secret enough or hidden gully safe enough that he would risk using now, and he began to fear that they would be forced to wander the edge of the forest forever.

Bearskin's thoughts eventually settled on an encounter he had once had many years earlier, in which a favour had been granted and a promise made. Bearskin remembered that he still carried a souvenir of that day.

"Gnomen!" he rumbled. "Must find the gnomen."

He picked up his staff and jumped off the log.

• • •   • • •   • • •

116

The boar's-head undercarriage turned slowly as the ravens guided the hot-air balloon closer to the place where Bearskin had been sighted. The ravens screamed with excitement.

"If you are as successful in finding the bloodling as you are in your rabble-rousing, Risratch, then you will have redeemed yourself well," shouted Von Rippenbaum, throwing a chunk of meat, coated in the oily, life-giving essence, into the air.

The mechanical raven devoured it greedily.

CHAPTER 25

A Useful Change of Clothing

The mechanicals were lit by a curious weave of moonlight and shadow, and their eyes glittered eerily. They remained seated and silent.

Cassie edged towards the door, hardly daring to breathe, when an unexpected howl filled the room.

"You have stepped on my toe!" whimpered Professor Perkins, hopping over to a chair.

"Serves you right!" snapped Cassie. "Serves you right for betraying me! Is this where you hand me over to these weird little creatures?!"

"Hand you over? What the devil do you...? Oh, the mechanicals. Did I neglect to inform you of their presence?"

"You *neglected* to tell me anything!" cried Cassie.

"Then let me assure you that they are all quite harmless. Ow! I think you have bruised my hallus."

"You mean this isn't a trap?"

"Of course it isn't. Now do you think you could lock the

inner doors without causing me further injury?"

Cassie kept her eyes fixed on her silent audience as she closed and bolted the doors.

"Are you sure we're safe?" she whispered.

"Yes," snapped the professor, rubbing his toe and gazing around the tea house. He smiled as he remembered his first visit. "What a pandemonium of noise once filled this little room, for the mechanical owner really was the kindest and most attentive host. Both he and his customers appear to have been silenced, however. I wonder why?"

"I thought you said mechanicals were evil."

"There are good and bad throughout the forest. The traveller must choose his path – and the company he keeps upon it – with care."

Curiosity eventually overcame fear, and Cassie approached the wooden figure of a man sitting at a table. An axe dangled from his belt and Cassie wondered whether he used it as a weapon or a tool. She prodded the man's arm but the figure didn't move, so she stepped closer and admired the fine detail of his wooden face

Cassie approached a group of ladies whose eyes glittered menacingly out of chalk-white faces. Tiny pin joints creaked as Cassie lifted their fingers, their "skin" as cold as the marble-topped table they were resting upon. Cassie shivered and backed away.

"How do they move?" she wondered. "How do they *think?* These things are just wood and metal."

"Shall we find out?" said the professor.

Professor Perkins jumped from his chair and lifted the small figure of a boy onto a table. He stood over it, lost in thought, and picked up a knife and fork. "I fear I am without my dissection kit but I do not intend to make a meal of it." He laughed at his joke, but Cassie was horrified.

"You're not going to *operate* on it, are you?" she gasped,

but the professor had already jabbed the prongs of the fork into a slot in the boy's chest. A door sprang open and a faint hiss of air escaped into the night.

"What if it wakes up?!" cried Cassie.

"I have a calming bedside manner. Now do not disturb me. I am close to discovering Von Rippenbaum's secret."

The boy's hair was almost the same colour as Tom's, and Cassie found herself holding its wooden hand.

"Fascinating!" muttered the professor, holding a candle and prodding inside the chest with a knife. "There are two small pumps placed left and right but there are no apparent atria or valves... Wait, what is this?"

He emerged holding a glass jar that glistened with a familiar sheen. "Look!" he said. "The mysterious oil. It is transparent and viscous. There is very little of it left."

"Put it back!" cried Cassie. "The boy might die or something."

"The oil resembles the fluid we encountered in the lantern-gourds on the ceremonial path. See how it undulates!"

"Put it back! Put it back!" cried Cassie. "That jar could be its heart."

"Do you mean to suggest a link between this oil and human blood?"

"*I don't mean to suggest anything!*" cried Cassie. "Just put it back!"

"Ichor!" cried the professor suddenly.

"What?"

"Perhaps Von Rippenbaum has created ichor: the ethereal fluid that flowed in the veins of the Greek Gods. But if he has forged reality from myth, by what dark distillation has he created it? Oh, to have my laboratory equipment for one quarter of an hour!"

Cassie sighed with relief when the professor returned the jar to its owner. She rushed forwards and covered the boy with a tablecloth.

"I can't stay here," she said. "This place is a tomb."

"There is a parlour behind the counter, away from these creatures. We may rest in there. And rest we must if we are to continue in safety. And might I suggest a change of costume? Those unpleasant creatures we encountered in the carriage knew of your appearance and could describe your clothing in detail. There are plenty of dresses you could take from one of those elegant ladies."

But Cassie had already seen the outfit she wanted and she ran to the back of the tea house and stood over a figure that lay slumped against a pillar.

Cassie shivered as she undressed the mechanical, and was pleased to discover that its long leather boots, its floor-length jacket, shirt and waistcoat, which bristled with hooks, fitted her well. She removed the mechanical's headgear – a strange, leather helmet attached to a pair of tinted goggles – and pulled it over her head. Two tufts of leather gave the impression that the helmet-wearer had horns or ears, and Cassie smiled at her reflection before stepping into the moonlight.

Professor Perkins jumped from his chair.

"I… I have a revolver!" he gasped, backing away from her in terror.

"I know you do," said Cassie.

"Oh, it is you. I was expecting feminine charm, but once again you confound me. What costume is that?"

"I don't know, but these goggles are amazing. I can see in the dark."

Cassie stepped between the tables without stumbling.

"Kindly remove it!" snapped the professor. "It is ghoulish and unsettling."

Cassie tucked the helmet inside her pocket and followed the monkey over to an ornamental tea urn that stood on the counter. The professor lit a match, and a bright ring of flame sputtered into life beneath it.

"Do you know what the great poets say about the best-quality tea?" he asked, gathering teacups and saucers.

"I think I'm about to find out," muttered Cassie.

"They say the finest-quality tea should crease like the leather boot of Tartar horsemen, should curl like the dewlap of a mighty bullock, should rise like mist from a ravine and should be wet and soft like the finest earth. Such tea may be found here."

"We *are* heading straight to the centre, aren't we?" wondered Cassie, suddenly concerned that the professor was becoming distracted by the pleasures of the forest.

"The centre?" he exclaimed. "Of course, of course. Oh, dear. We have no milk."

"I'll drink my tea clear," said Cassie. "*Crystal* clear."

The monkey's paws started to tremble.

CHAPTER 26

Descent

The muddy paste Bearskin had smeared around Tom's wound had hardened into a thick crust, and Tom tapped it cautiously and got to his feet. He paced up and down, watching Bearskin closely.

"No other way. No other way," the giant muttered anxiously, worrying a hole in the ground with his staff.

Bearskin's guide, a little bird Bearskin called Chiffchaff, appeared and flapped around his master's head, chirruping loudly. Bearskin leapt off the log and ran at Tom at full speed, who ducked and covered his head. In one swift movement, Bearskin lifted Tom by the scruff of his coat and bundled him back inside his sash.

Tom curled into a ball.

An ear-splitting screech rang through the forest, and hundreds of dots filled the sky.

"I thought you said mechanicals couldn't live in the wilderness!" shouted Tom.

"Those're birds! Real flesh an' blood ravens sent to fetch us!" roared Bearskin. "Stay down, lad. Stay 'idden!"

Bearskin bounded along a ridge then half-scrambled and half-fell into the forest below. Tom peered from his sash and saw that Bearskin was heading towards a cluster of rocks that sat at the bottom of a gully. He recognised the rocky shape at once: it was a dolmen, something his grandfather once explained to him as a structure built over the entrance to an ancient burial chamber.

It was obvious that Bearskin meant to hide there.

The ravens started their attack and swooped down viciously. Bearskin raised his staff and Tom yelped when a beak suddenly burst through the fabric of the sash. It was quickly joined by another and another and then several more, and Tom started kicking at the thrusting dagger-shapes.

Bearskin ran on all fours now, aware that if he tripped, he would crush Tom instantly.

"Tek 'old!" he shouted, tipping Tom onto a cold and gritty surface. Tom wobbled to his feet and saw that he was standing beneath the slanted rocks of the dolmen. The ravens circled outside, their wing-beats creating a whirlwind of noise.

"*Stand guard!*" shouted Bearskin, throwing Tom his wooden staff, which almost knocked Tom backwards. "Strike any 'oo fly in," added the giant. "An' don't let 'em near yer eyes, lad. It's the first thing they go for."

Bearskin started scrabbling at the earth, while Tom wondered how he was going to stop even one of the angry ravens from entering. Four black shapes suddenly swept past him and perched on a ledge.

"Shoo!" shouted Tom, unable to lift the staff. "*Shoo! Go away!*"

The ravens cawed mockingly, then flew at Tom, who staggered backwards over a stone. Behind him, Bearskin strained against the weight of a boulder.

"Move!" Bearskin growled furiously.

The ravens beaks pierced Tom's clothing.

"Help!" shouted Tom. "Bearskin, I can't…"

"*Moooove!*" roared Bearskin, pushing against the boulder.

More ravens appeared and joined the stabbing frenzy. Tom grabbed his head and rolled into a ball.

An ear-splitting crack filled the narrow dolmen and the ravens screeched in terror. The boulder rolled aside but revealed another slab of rock beneath it. Bearskin roared in frustration and raged against the new obstacle. More ravens appeared and formed a circle around Tom.

They started closing in.

Boom! Boom! Boom! echoed the dolmen as Bearskin stamped on the ground. An ominous rumble sounded far beneath him, and the walls and the ceiling trembled and shook. The rock at Bearskin's feet suddenly collapsed with a terrifying "*whoosh*" and the dolmen filled with clouds of dust. The ravens fled into the daylight, the dust rolling after them as if in pursuit. Tom struggled over to where he had last seen his friend and suddenly found himself falling into a hole. He threw out his arms, expecting a painful landing, when a familiar pair of arms caught him mid-fall.

"Bearskin!" cried Tom. "You did it! The ravens have gone!"

"They'll be back," muttered the giant. "Quickly, lad. 'Elp me block up this 'ole."

Tom saw that he was standing in a narrow tunnel that stretched away in both directions and ended in darkness. The walls of the tunnel were peppered with tree roots and stones, and the air smelt damp and musty.

"Wh-where are we?" Tom whispered, staring along the tunnel.

Bearskin grunted and gestured for Tom to help.

Chapter 27

A Message in the Tea-leaves

Early morning mist drifted eerily through the forest as Cassie and the professor continued their journey. The professor remained alert to the slightest sign of danger while Cassie studied the undergrowth through her magnifying goggles. She was nibbling on a biscuit she had taken from the tea house.

"I'm thirsty," she said, staring at the professor's shoulder-bag.

"There is a grassy bank in a secluded ridge with an accommodating cave. There we may rest in safety."

"Is there any tea in that flask of yours?"

"We shall take tea at the cave. We do not have far to go. Perhaps if you stopped consuming dry biscuits?"

Cassie pulled a face and groaned.

The morning sun filled the forest with warmth but the path remained dark and forbidding. A curious smell drifted through the trees, and though it was pleasant at first – it smelt sweet and minty – an underlying sourness quickly spoiled it. Cassie's eyes started to water and she coughed and spluttered and wafted her hand in front of her nose. She yelped when something hard bumped against the side of her head, and Cassie turned and found herself staring into the empty eye-sockets of a bird's skull that dangled from a tree branch. Hundreds more dangled over the path.

"*What are these for?*" Cassie demanded, chasing after the professor who was short enough to pass under them.

"They are without meaning," he replied casually.

"But they must mean *something!*" said Cassie.

"Perhaps they are charms hung for our protection."

"You just made that up!"

The professor sighed.

"The mind of man is like an enchanted glass, full of superstition and imposture. A few ossified avian skulls have you trembling in fear, a fear that prevents you from continuing. Ah, but perhaps you are right. Perhaps we should end our quest because of these gruesome trophies."

"I didn't say I was *frightened*," said Cassie. "They just startled me, that's all."

She strode forwards, the "ears" of her helmet making the skulls spin wildly.

"That smell's getting worse," said Cassie. "What is it?"

The professor ran ahead without answering, and Cassie picked up a stick and chased after him.

They hadn't gone very far when they came to a cave set into a ridge of dark stone, framed by a carpet of grass. The cave commanded a sweeping view of the forest while the ridge below it was peppered with the ruined battlements of an ancient fort. Cassie joined the professor in the cave and slumped against a rock, watching as Professor Perkins poured tea into china cups he had "borrowed" from the tea house.

"Why's the forest turning grey again?" asked Cassie,

noticing a line of withered tree branches. "I thought we were heading away from all that."

"Who can say how the mysterious decay ebbs and flows?" replied the professor nervously.

They drank their tea in silence and listened to the wind outside. The grass felt soft and welcoming, and Cassie untied her boots and stretched out her legs. She shuffled deeper inside her leather coat and forced herself to stay alert and awake…

Cassie blinked when the white deer appeared, running in tight circles around her. Their bodies were steaming with sweat.

"Stop!" shouted Cassie, terrified by the sound of their thundering hooves. "Stop! Please stop!"

But the deer ran on, mad with fear, their voices distorted as they struggled to warn her of an unseen danger. Cassie covered her ears and felt herself falling…

… she woke with a start and realised that she had fallen asleep again without meaning to.

The cave was now empty. The professor's shoulder-bag lay next to her, open and ransacked. Beside it lay a wooden box and a piece of paper that was sticking out from a pile of tea-leaves. Cassie took the paper carefully and saw a hand-drawn map of the forest with many familiar features on it, including the cave in which she now sat. A large "X" had been drawn near the ruins of the fortress and the words "My Dignity" had been written alongside them. It was clear that the professor had been leading Cassie *away* from the centre of the forest and home.

"I *knew* it!" hissed Cassie. "I *knew* you were up to something, you miserable little creature. Why did you lie to me?"

She grabbed the shoulder-bag and saw that the revolver was missing.

Cassie ran outside, intending to leave the cave and Professor Perkins far behind her, when she suddenly noticed something moving in the distance. She lay on her stomach and saw Professor Perkins creeping through the undergrowth far below her. Cassie adjusted the goggles on her helmet, and watched as the professor crept towards a ruined cottage that sat at the bottom of the dip. He was holding the revolver out in front of him and was trembling like a leaf.

Cassie froze when a peculiar mound of sticks gathered themselves up onto gnarled stumps and scuttled forwards like a spider, moving in horrible little jumps. It followed the professor as he entered the ruin.

Cassie hesitated, uncertain whether to shout a warning, when the silence was shattered by gunfire.

CHAPTER 28

The Tunnel

Bearskin squeezed between knob-knuckled tree roots and sharp-edged rocks that bulged from the walls of the tunnel, grumbling as he went.

"What're those?" cried Tom, pointing at a tree root that had been carved into a row of bearded faces.

"We've arrived then," grunted Bearskin, wedging a candle into the ground.

"Where?"

"Winter… or what's left of 'er." Bearskin pointed to the roof of the tunnel. "Up there in the forest lies the boundary between winter and autumn, the same boundary we tried to cross. These carvings are a signpost fer the under-dwellers 'oo live down 'ere. It tells 'em they're enterin' a new season."

"Something *lives* down here?" gasped Tom, staring along the tunnel.

"Gnomen," said Bearskin. "The winter gnomen are called Bluecaps. Autumn gnomen are called Yellowcaps. I know nothin' of spring or summer."

"Why haven't we met any?" asked Tom, uncertain whether he wanted to. Bearskin shrugged.

"P'raps the winter ones are dead; perished when their season died."

Bearskin paused and added awkwardly, "It's time yer went on alone, lad. I can travel wi' yer no further."

He reached inside his sash and handed Tom a silver object.

"*Alone?!*" cried Tom. "Why, Bearskin?"

"It's the tunnel, lad. Look at the tunnel. I'm like a musket ball in a vintner's pipe."

Tom didn't know what a vintner's pipe was but he could see that the tunnel was narrow – and it seemed to be getting narrower. It wouldn't be long before Bearskin would be stuck fast.

Tom held the silver object up to the candlelight and studied it carefully.

"It's a button," said Bearskin. "It were given to me by a creature I rescued from a bird- trap many years ago. The creature stood no bigger than a cockerel yet it were a fully grown man wi' a beard an' a cap an' a jacket an' leather shoes. I freed 'im an' 'e thanked me an' that's when 'e handed me that button, sayin', 'If you ever need help, show my people this token, for you have saved the life of Barrowstaff, son of the lord of the Yellowcaps.' Then 'e bowed like a gentleman an' took off down a rabbit 'ole!"

Tom admired the button's intricate pattern.

"I found out, many years later," continued Bearskin, "that the creature were a gnoman: small, secretive under-dwellers 'oo live an' die beneath the Ringwood. Luck it was that reminded me of rumours that spoke of 'idden ways into their kingdom."

"So the dolmen was an entrance?"

"Aye, an' there are other places like it: rare, secret places scattered throughout the forest."

"Are they friendly? The gnomen, I mean. Are you sure they'll want to help me?"

"You 'ave the button an' yer know my story. I'm sure they'll honour their promise. Ask to be taken to the Table of the Feasting Kings deep in the autumn forest. I'll meet yer there tomorrow."

"The Table of the Feasting Kings," murmured Tom, glad that Bearskin wasn't abandoning him completely.

"You've a brave heart, lad," said Bearskin, seeing Tom's worried expression, "an' a quick mind too. Don't let one out-flank the other."

"When you speak, you always sound like a soldier," said Tom, staring up into the bear's eyes. Bearskin turned away.

"Tek this," he mumbled, handing Tom the candle, "an' these," and he gave Tom his flint-stone and striker. He straightened up as far as he could and gestured for Tom to squeeze past him. Then he extended his claws and started digging through the roof of the tunnel.

"G-goodbye, then," said Tom nervously, not wanting to leave.

Bearskin nodded.

"I'll see you tomorrow," Tom added.

Bearskin nodded again.

"At the Table of the Feasting Kings," said Tom.

Bearskin's roar sent Tom scurrying down the tunnel, and after a few twists and turns Tom realised that he was alone.

More gnomen carvings appeared, the flickering candlelight giving them the illusion of movement and life. The faces looked like ill-tempered Father Christmases and Tom tried not to look at them.

The tunnel suddenly plunged deeper, sending Tom into a hobbling little run. A bend loomed out at him from the darkness and Tom took it at speed but tripped and fell. The button and the candle flew from his hands and the comforting circle of light snuffed out instantly.

Tom groped forwards, feeling for the candle and the gnomen's silver button, when his fingertips brushed against something soft and damp that was lying against the wall like a plump sack of flour. Whatever the object was, it appeared to be covered in cobwebs, until Tom suddenly realised that the cobwebs were neither fine nor sticky. Tom sprang backwards, aware that he was touching the beard of a small, lifeless body.

Tom leapt to his feet and saw a light glowing in the distance. He ran without stopping, his wolf bite flaring painfully, until he came to an illuminated doorway framed by a pair of stone columns. The columns were decorated with the carvings of birds whose eyes were precious jewels, and more gnomen faces peeped out at him from behind leafy stonework, their expressions as stern as ever. But it was the light beyond the entranceway that held Tom's attention for it shone so vividly that the grain of the wooden doors was transformed into slivers of fire. Tom opened the doors cautiously and found himself standing at the end of a leafy tunnel. Tree roots spread across the walls and the ceiling, each one decorated with precious metal that blazed with light. Tom stared in astonishment and was about to step forwards, when a pair of whip-like tendrils sprang up at him and dragged him to the ground.

All along the tunnel, the leaves began to stir.

Chapter 29

Witch Bottle

rofessor Perkins burst from the cottage firing the revolver. The bullets passed harmlessly through the jumble of "living" sticks that had followed him inside, and the peculiar creature wriggled and danced and seemed to be enjoying the terrifying game. The creature's head, Cassie noticed with disgust, was a large ball of fungus that looked like a rotten piece of popcorn, and she shivered when it suddenly croaked, "Shoot an old friend would you?!"

The creature grabbed the professor by his tail and threw him inside a wooden cage, which it hoisted onto its back. Professor Perkins dropped the revolver and an old glass bottle he had taken from the cottage.

"Sing our little song; something pretty for our customers!" laughed the creature. It twitched its claws and the bars of the cage sprang into life, squeezing the professor until he obeyed. "*Sing!*" insisted the creature.

The professor's voice rose from the clearing,

134

"Where once a man stood, now stand I,
A foolish monkey, nimble and spry.
And though my fate is well deserved,
My punishment here is not yet served."
The creature nodded with pleasure.

"So you returned to steal *this!*" it said, kicking the glass bottle.

"I cannot steal that which is mine," Professor Perkins shouted. The stick-creature spun around in angry circles.

"Off to market I'll take you!" it shrieked. "There you'll sing and dance as you once did. Now sing another song. Something pretty!"

Professor Perkins looked up the rise to where the trees grew thickest, and let his gaze stop near to where Cassie was hiding. He straightened up, as if he had just had an idea, then he cleared his throat and sang.

Cassie recognised the tune straightaway. It was "Daisy Bell", an old song she sometimes sang herself. But the professor had added new words to the familiar tune and he shouted as he sang the words,
"Cassie, Cassie,
Please forgive me do,
My loose tea,
Holds a map,
That's meant for you!"

"Instructions!" gasped Cassie, remembering the map she had found in the tea-leaves. "He's singing me instructions!" She leaned closer to hear the rest of his song.
"Journey to the Turk's Head,
Duman is dressed all in red,
You'll look sweet,
At thirty feet.
To the centre,
He'll send you!"

"Sing something prettier!" demanded the witch, not understanding, or liking, the new song. But Professor Perkins was laughing now and was making sweeping gestures with his arms as if telling Cassie to go. "Something *pretty!*" shrieked the witch as it turned and carried the professor deep into the forest.

Cassie lay in the grass, wondering why her deceitful little guide had risked so much to steal an old bottle. Part of her was glad that he had been captured, yet the sight of him being punished upset Cassie deeply.

She returned to the cave and scrawled the words of the professor's song onto the back of the map before she forgot them. Then she studied the map in detail. The Turk's Head lay many miles away and Cassie decided she would feel safer if she could use the revolver to defend herself. She stumbled down the slope and crept into the clearing.

The revolver was where the professor had dropped it and Cassie picked it up and tucked it inside the shoulder-bag, hoping she wouldn't have to use it. She was about to leave when she noticed the bottle, unbroken and sealed and apparently empty. Cassie picked it up and rubbed its muddy sides, and almost dropped it when the bottle began to glow.

The image of an elderly man rippled to the surface and shimmered mysteriously. The man wore an old-fashioned frockcoat and necktie, and stood in front of a pile of old books. His expression was stern and was made even sterner by a pair of half-moon spectacles that balanced on the end of his long and pointed nose. Mutton-chop whiskers completed the image of the Victorian gentleman that he appeared to be, and it was at that precise moment that Cassie realised who it was that she was looking at.

"Professor Perkins, I presume," she whispered sadly, remembering how he had labelled this part of the map, "My Dignity".

His story had been true, Cassie realised guiltily. He really *was* a human being who really *had* been transformed into a monkey by a "woodland hag".

The image faded and Cassie cradled the bottle, determined to keep it safe. She removed a roll of bandages from the shoulder-bag, wrapped the bottle in them, and tucked it away.

"I'm sorry," Cassie whispered. "I'll try to keep you safe, professor. I'll try to take you home."

Cassie turned and ran into the forest.

CHAPTER 30

The Gnomen

The leaves moved like quick little hands, tugging and pulling viciously. Tom tried to cry for help, but the leaves surged forwards and silenced him. A whirlpool formed underneath him, and Tom bucked and heaved and tried to wriggle free but felt the leaves quickly overpower him.

A commanding voice suddenly cut through the noise and the leaves blew apart as if caught in a wind.

Tom's ears rang from the attack. He sat up, coughing and spluttering, and saw two little figures standing over him. The gnomen were as short and as ill-tempered as their carvings had suggested, and Tom blinked in surprise and studied them. They wore pointed hats, woollen trousers and green tunics. White beards covered most of their bellies, and their eyes were quick and watchful. One of the gnomen stepped forwards and spoke gruffly in a language Tom didn't understand.

"Button!" said Tom. "I had a button but I dropped it."

He pointed through the open doorway.

The gnomen spoke to one another in hurried whispers before one of them scurried away. The other gnoman stayed where he was and glared at Tom suspiciously.

It wasn't long before other gnomen appeared, their scurrying footsteps filling the tunnel. They were dressed in the same colourful tunics, and none of them were smiling. Suddenly, the crowd parted and an elderly gnoman stepped forwards. He was small and crooked and he leant upon a stick, and he approached Tom slowly and wheezed, in perfect English, "Hello. Hello. Hello, hello, hello."

"Er... hello," said Tom.

"Did you know that there are over forty-four species of tree-root lining this tunnel? I counted them myself."

His beady eyes twinkled merrily but remained fixed on Tom.

"That's...nice," stammered Tom.

"It's better than nice! It's a sign that the creeping decay has not yet reached autumn. What do you make of that?!"

Tom smiled and nodded, and wondered if the old gnoman was a bit dotty.

"Oh, but you expect me to talk about minerals and gemstones and silver and gold and all manner of gnomen treasure, don't you! Well I won't, do you hear me? I won't!"

"All right," said Tom, backing against the wall.

The little man looked startled.

"I *could* talk about those things if I wanted to. We Yellowcaps aren't paupers, you know."

A shout went up from the back of the crowd, and the old gnoman sighed and shook his head. "In my capacity as official translator," he said, "my impatient brethren here have asked me to question you without mercy."

"Have they?" said Tom feebly.

The old gnoman cleared his throat.

"The question they ask is this: 'You! Uplander! What are you doing here and how did you arrive? Tell us now or we will kill you!'"

The old gnoman tutted and shook his head. "Oh dear, that's a bit harsh," he said. "Forgive them. They are not normally so bloodthirsty. These are fear-filled times and fear breeds suspicion, and suspicion leads to all manner of unpleasantness. Just tell me the truth and I will translate your words for them."

He smiled encouragingly.

"First of all, tell them not to kill me!" said Tom. "That bit's important. Tell them I come in peace then remind them not to kill me."

The old gnoman translated Tom's words as Tom explained about his missing parents, his journey through the disc and Bearskin's request to take him to a place called "The Table of the Feasting Kings".

The gnomen listened carefully, nodding and muttering amongst themselves. But when Tom mentioned the name "Barrowstaff" and told them Bearskin's story of the silver button, the gnomen stamped their feet and gestured with their beards in ways that looked insulting.

"W-what did I say?" asked Tom. "Don't they believe me?"

The old gnoman gestured for silence.

"They think you are a spy, sent by the winter Bluecaps to deceive us."

"I'm not!" said Tom. "I've never even *met* a winter Bluecap. It was Bearskin who gave me the button and it was Lord Barrowstaff who gave it to him. Why don't they believe me?"

"Because your friend must either be exceedingly old or exceedingly deceitful. You see, Lord Barrowstaff died over one hundred and twenty-eight years ago!"

Every accusing eye fell on Tom.

Chapter 31

Clockwork and Bones

assie re-traced her footsteps beneath the dangling bird skulls and found the path that would take her to the Turk's Head. She pulled the strange helmet over her eyes and gripped her shoulder-bag, praying that whoever or whatever Duman was, he would help her get home.

The path wandered aimlessly between tree stumps and bracken while a clinging mist made the forest damp and miserable. Cassie trudged through it wearily, relieved that the creature that had captured Professor Perkins did not appear to be following her.

She was about to check the map when she heard voices just ahead of her. Cassie ran into a clump of bushes and saw a clearing filled with mechanicals and market stalls. Suddenly aware that she would need food for the long journey ahead of her, Cassie lowered her goggles, tucked her hair inside her helmet, and stepped from her hiding place. The effect on the mechanicals was dramatic.

They stamped in all directions, hooting and bellowing and running into the trees. Cassie whirled around, assuming some terrible creature was behind her, but saw that she was all alone. She dashed forwards, hoping to do as much shopping as she could before the creatures returned. She ran from market stall to market stall, ignoring the mechanical stall-keepers who were attached to their pitches on poles, and who were snapping angrily at her.

Cassie grabbed a wedge of cheese, but saw that it was a carved and painted piece of wood. She picked up some bread and some fish and saw that these were wooden too. Frustrated and angry, Cassie ran to the final stall and saw that it sold real, usable cooking pots. She grabbed a small cauldron and a goat-skin bag, filled with what she assumed would be water, and offered the stall-keeper several hooks from her waistcoat as payment. The stall-keeper waved its claws at her in terror.

Cassie threw the hooks on the counter and returned to the forest, unaware that she was being followed.

She walked until evening, unnerved by her strange encounter and by her increasing hunger pains. The light had almost faded when Cassie stumbled into a circle of rocks that huddled around a forest pool. She sat at the water's edge and plunged her feet into the icy water, and decided to risk a little fire. Cassie filled the cooking pot at a trickling waterfall and threw what remained of Professor Perkins' tea-leaves into the pot. She lit a small fire, tucked her knees under her chin, and had just drawn her helmet lower over her ears for warmth, when the sound of a twig snapping made her sit up.

Something was standing at the edge of the firelight, watching Cassie closely. Cassie adjusted her goggles and saw a collection of bones shimmering in the heat.

It was the skeleton of a dog that Von Rippenbaum had re-jointed and re-assembled to make walk upright. The dog's head had been replaced with the skull of a pony, and its chisel-blunt teeth glinted menacingly in the firelight. The bizarre mix of bones stepped forwards and bowed.

"*I'm sitting here!*" Cassie blurted, too shocked to think of anything else to say.

"You speak language of our prey!" laughed the skeleton, hobbling closer. "I speak it too, wise gatherer. We speak bloodlings' tongue together!"

The grotesque creature was now close enough for Cassie to see that its eyes were empty sockets. She shrank back and shivered as the creature continued, "Wise forest gatherer. Sit I here?"

Its tone was sly and horribly servile and it filled Cassie with disgust. She wondered why it had called her "gatherer" then remembered her waistcoat, boots and jacket, and the sinister helmet that covered half her face.

"Sit!" Cassie commanded, suddenly aware that the creature was more frightened of her than she was of it.

The skeleton sat down at once.

"Bloodlings?" said Cassie, trying not to sound frightened.

"Where?" said the creature, peering round in excitement.

"No. I mean, tell me what you know about the bloodlings."

The creature bobbed up and down.

"You honour me with test!" it squealed. "I know much and will answer! Bloodlings are hu-man. One boy. One girl. One green coat. One blue coat. One fair hair. One…"

"Good!" said Cassie, realising that the creature had described the clothes she and Tom had been wearing after their encounter in the wells.

"I sent to catch bloodling boy," said the horse-headed thing, gesturing into the forest. "I sent to catch boy but ravens catch instead!"

"*The ravens have caught a boy?*" cried Cassie. "*Where is the boy? What have they done to him?*"

The creature poked a bony claw into the fire and watched it smoulder. It thought for a moment then shrugged, which made its shoulder-blades rattle like dinner plates.

"Ravens stupid," it said. "Ravens lose bloodling. Bear-man take boy under ground. Bear-man helping boy."

It sniffed the pot of bubbling tea.

So Tom *was* alive, thought Cassie, trying to hide her joy. And Tom's kidnapper really was some sort of bear-man. Cassie jumped to her feet and grabbed the shoulder-bag. The skeleton stood as well.

"Pass I test? Pass it good?" it croaked.

"Passed it good," said Cassie. "Passed it very, very good."

She gathered up her things and smiled.

CHAPTER 32

The Search Party

"I have ordered a search," announced the old gnoman.

"The button's near a bend in the tunnel," said Tom. "That's where I fell."

"If it is there to be found, they will find it."

The search party assembled and walked in single file, carrying lanterns, knives, pickaxes and rope. The gnoman bowed in front of the elderly figure then disappeared through the wooden doors.

"What if they don't find anything?" asked Tom, all too aware of the hundreds of eyes still fixed upon him.

"I think a thief would be more slippery, a spy more convincing, while a conjurer of illusions would have had the keys to our vaults by now," mused the old gnoman with a smile. "I have studied the Upperlands and most of the things in it and see none of *those* characteristics in you, young fellow. So come. Let us talk of more pleasant things."

Tom leaned against the wall, still waist-deep in leaves,

while the gnomen walked *upon* the leaves, as if the leaves chose to support them.

"This friend of yours, this Bearskin," said the old gnoman. "I am unaware of his presence in the forest."

"He used to be human," said Tom. "But I think he was cursed. He doesn't say very much but when he does, he talks like a soldier."

"A soldier, eh? Well, if he has been wandering the Ringwood for as long as you say he has, there may be a record of him in our royal archives."

The old gnoman's eyes narrowed and he stroked his beard.

"Could we see the royal archives?" asked Tom. "Would your king or your queen let us?"

"I think so," smiled the gnoman.

"Could we check them now?"

"Patience! The button first. Then we will see what is what."

The minutes passed slowly and the crowd continued to stare. A silver tray appeared and it was offered to the old gnoman. The tray was filled with twigs and bits of old tree root, and the peculiar selection was offered to Tom.

"Burgoroot!" smiled the gnoman. "You chew the fat end first then quickly chew the thin end. Try some."

Tom picked the smallest piece and bit it carefully. A dark liquid spurted from the root and dribbled down his chin.

"Eurgh!" cried Tom. "Oh, wait. It's quite nice."

"Quickly! Spin it round and chew the other end!" said the old gnoman.

The taste of the second liquid transformed the first and both juices blended together.

"*'S'delicious!*" dribbled Tom, taking a second, longer piece.

"Especially if you have no beard. Burgoroot gets so horribly sticky!"

Tom's stomach growled, reminding him how long it had been since he had last eaten, and he decided to ask the gnomen if they could spare him a little food – once he was certain they were going to help him.

Three heavy knocks signalled the return of the search party, and the wooden door swung open. The gnomen marched in, their lanterns shining brightly. The leader stepped forwards and placed a bundle of cloth at the feet of the old gnoman, who pulled the cloth aside and revealed a small, lifeless body. There were gasps of astonishment from the crowd then cries of amazement when the leader of the search party held a bright point of silver in the air.

"That's it!" cried Tom. "That's the button Bearskin gave me! And that must be the person I thought was covered in cobwebs."

"You spoke the truth and for that I am glad," sighed the old gnoman. Behind him, the crowd were becoming restless and it wasn't long before they were shouting again.

"What is it now?" asked Tom. "Don't they believe me?"

"The search party saw many bodies," explained the gnoman. "They were winter Bluecaps and they were all dead."

"Well I didn't kill them!" cried Tom.

"I know, but my fellow Yellowcaps think you may be carrying the creeping decay."

"I'm not!" said Tom.

"I know, I know. The creeping decay affects only the wood of the living forest. Besides, the person responsible for such terrible monstrosities is far from here."

"You mean Von Rippenbaum?"

At the mention of the toymaker's name, the tunnel exploded in noise.

CHAPTER 33

The Gathering in the Grove

"Will you honour my patrol with visit?" asked the horse-headed creature, tottering around the fire.

"Your *patrol?*" said Cassie, staring around in alarm. "You mean there are more of you?"

"More-of-you? Yes! Come see more-of-you!"

It ran forwards on its dog-legs, waiting for Cassie to follow.

"I-I'm going a different way," stammered Cassie, not wanting to see any more ghoulish creatures. "I'm going to the Turk's Head."

Cassie cursed herself the moment she had said it and hoped that the creature hadn't heard her. But the little skeleton barked, "Turk's Head? Take guards from patrol! Take more-of-you guards for safety! They will show you quickest way!"

"There's a quick way to the Turk's Head? Is it quicker than this?" Cassie showed the skeleton the professor's map.

The creature laughed and nodded.

Cassie stepped forwards and ordered the strange creature to take her to its patrol. The skeleton squealed with joy, and for the second time that day Cassie felt sick with fear.

Horse-head scuttled through the forest, holding back branches and bowing every time Cassie passed by. Cassie shivered with disgust.

They eventually came to a grove of tall pine trees where an oversized moon illuminated a terrible gathering. Ragged silhouettes glowed in Cassie's goggles and she paused for a moment and studied them.

There were cat skulls and dog skulls and pig skulls and bear skulls all set upon the skeletal frames of many different animals. Some creatures were covered in fur or were dressed in ragged frockcoats, and all of them were the half-finished experiments of the forest toymaker.

The pine grove buzzed with cogwheels and pistons and the clicking of metallic pincers, and a horrible wailing caught Cassie's attention. She stared towards the centre and saw something being roasted over an open fire. Whatever it was remained alive, and Cassie covered her mouth and stifled a scream.

She was about to turn and run into the forest when she became aware of the two white deer standing in the shadows.

"You're real!" Cassie whispered, knowing that she wasn't asleep and that she wasn't having another disturbing dream.

The deer nodded gracefully and vanished.

The skeleton stepped forwards and guided Cassie into a sea of grinning skulls. The mechanicals fell silent and parted as Horse-head led Cassie towards the bonfire. Whatever had been roasting there had finally expired, and Cassie kept her back to it.

The skeleton addressed the crowd in their own harsh language then cried out, in English, "Gatherer speaks bloodlings' tongue. Better to hunt them down!"

"Then we speak it too!" cheered the crowd.

"Gatherers shoot fire from their eyes!" shouted a figure. There was an excited murmur.

"Gatherers can turn invisible!" shrieked another. The skeletons rattled in amazement.

"Gatherers cannot be slain!" said a third, stepping from the shadows.

The creature was enormous, with a ribcage that would have easily accommodated Cassie for it had once belonged to a wild forest ox. The creature's skull was small and was one of the few that Von Rippenbaum had covered in dark and spiky fur.

The ox-creature strode forwards on massive bones and glared at Cassie through domed, rabbit-like eyes. Cassie forced herself to hold its gaze and watched in alarm when it started to unhook a club that dangled at its side.

"*Gatherers cannot be slain!*" the beast repeated slowly, and Cassie saw that it meant to challenge her. Whatever strange powers *real* forest gatherers had, Cassie knew that she would be quickly exposed if she simply turned and ran, so she stepped forwards and shouted, "Challenge me and you will die!"

The crowd gasped but the giant shambled nearer, forcing Cassie closer to the fire.

"S-stop or you will die!" Cassie shouted.

The creature laughed and raised its club.

CHAPTER 34

Doctor Albertus

"So you journey against Von Rippenbaum?!" asked the old gnoman.

Tom nodded.

"Then truly you are a friend to all Yellowcaps!" The little man grasped Tom's hand and led him down the tunnel.

The crowd parted as Tom passed beneath the decorated tree roots. Ahead of him stood a second set of doors on which elaborate hinges spread in leafy patterns. The doors opened at a touch from the gnoman's staff and revealed a circular room ringed on all sides by shelves of ancient parchment. A circular dais and a high-backed chair stood in the centre of the room, and both the chair and the chamber were illuminated by light that shone through a crystal ceiling.

"Our royal archives," announced the old gnoman proudly.

"It's… beautiful!" gasped Tom, studying the ceiling.

"We stand at the bottom of a deep, forest pool. The light

that shines through the water comes from the Ringwood itself. I find the effect quite relaxing."

A fish-shaped shadow swam overhead.

"Is it safe?" wondered Tom, touching the crystal.

"What a nervous fellow you are!" smiled the old gnoman.

More figures appeared and for the first time since his arrival, Tom saw what appeared to be female gnomen. They looked as formidable as their men-folk and were equally fascinated by Tom. They laughed and whispered when Tom sat on the floor, trying to blend in with the crowd.

"Are we waiting for someone?" whispered Tom as the room fell silent.

"Our ruler," replied the old gnoman, nodding towards the empty chair.

Three short blasts sounded on instruments that Tom couldn't identify, and the crowd lowered their heads. Tom did the same and stared at the ground, waiting for a signal to look up. When none came, he glanced to his left and saw that the old gnoman was no longer standing next to him. Tom raised his eyes and saw that the elderly figure was now sitting upon the throne, staff in one hand, button in the other. He was grinning broadly.

"I am Rowanbole!" the old gnoman laughed. "Lord of the Yellowcaps, Underseer of Autumn and a direct descendent of Barrowstaff, our celebrated former leader whose silver button you have kindly returned to us."

The room filled with applause and Tom gaped in astonishment.

"Um, th-thank you, your royal-ness," stammered Tom.

Rowanbole laughed again and gestured Tom nearer.

"And how should we address *you?*" he asked.

"I'm Thomas, Thomas Trenham. But Tom will do."

"Well, Thomas Tom-will-do, it seems you spoke the truth and acted bravely travelling through those tunnels alone and in darkness. Are you really as fearless as our bravest gnomen warriors?"

"No!" said Tom, blinking in surprise.

"We will repay our debt to your friend, Bearskin," continued the old gnoman, "and will help you all we can. Tonight, there will be a great feast in Bearskin's honour and *you* will be our guest. But first you must visit our physician. That wound of yours looks painful and you appear to be limping."

A pair of gnomen warriors escorted Tom back into the leafy tunnel where a long, wooden sleigh stood waiting for him. "I will meet with you later, Thomas, for there is much to discuss." Tom nodded as the large double doors closed behind him.

The sleigh was formed out of two saplings lashed together to form a long Y-shape. Strips of bark had been stretched between the saplings' arms, and Tom was instructed to lie on them and rest. Tom watched as two gnomen warriors strapped themselves into a harness before setting off, dragging Tom behind them as if he were weightless. The leaves of the tunnel spiralled colourfully behind them, and Tom watched them nervously.

The journey was filled with tantalising glimpses of the gnomen's life underground; there were illuminated markets filled with food, and singing and laughter echoing from taverns. Tunnels branched away in all directions and were filled with gemstone-laden carts, each cart pulled by birds whose beaks were bridled like a horse. Gnomen miners worked at glittering seams, their harvested treasure decorating every tree root and stone.

The sleigh came to rest in front of an impressive archway and the gnomen warriors gestured for Tom to stand up. Tom stood as upright as the narrow tunnel would allow, and was led towards a staircase that plunged into the earth. Fingers of light flickered up from below and a blast of warm air ruffled Tom's hair. The gnomen gestured Tom forwards.

Tom descended nervously until a spiralling turn brought him to the edge of a spectacular cavern. Glistening pillars of rock rose like half-melted wedding cakes, joining floor to ceiling. Hundreds of stalagmites ranged across the floor like a miniature forest. Between them, steaming pools of water bubbled and boiled. A misty vapour filled the cavern and it was scented by flowers and herbs that hung in great bunches from the ceiling.

A figure stepped out from behind a rock and flicked Tom on the leg with a birch twig.

"Ow!" said Tom, jumping backwards.

"I am Doctor Albertus, herbalist and healer," said an ancient-looking gnoman, bowing stiffly. He remained bent over, studying Tom's ankle. "Volf bite!" he snapped. "Not good. Follow me!"

Tom limped between the stalagmites, studying the gnoman carefully. The doctor's beard was plaited and forked and was filled with beads and strange amulets. His face was streaky with paint and his skin was as lined as the rocks he was scrambling over. Dangling from his tunic were several leather pouches crammed with herbs and powder. "Volf bite!" the doctor muttered. "Bath! Quickly!"

Tom was led to the edge of a bubbling pool where Doctor Albertus gestured for Tom to jump in. Tom removed his shoes and his stocking and lowered his foot into the water.

"Nein, nein! All of you, *in!*" cried the doctor, flicking his twig impatiently.

"But I haven't got my swimming trunks!"

"In, in!"

Doctor Albertus placed a towel on a rock and left Tom to his peculiar bath.

154

CHAPTER 35

A Fight to the Death

assie hunted for the revolver. Tea-leaves, string, a compass and Professor Perkins' bandaged bottle all tumbled uselessly between her fingers. Cassie threw herself to the ground when the creature's wooden club came sweeping over her. The club passed through the fire and was immediately transformed into a blazing torch.

Cassie lay in the mud, praying for a glimpse of the white deer, but saw that she was surrounded by skulls and empty eye-sockets. Something cold and metallic suddenly brushed against her fingertips and Cassie gripped the handle of the gun and leapt to her feet.

"Stop now or you will die!" she shouted, pointing at the giant skeleton. The skeleton lunged forwards.

With no time to aim or to even remove the weapon from the shoulder-bag, Cassie squeezed the trigger and was immediately thrown backwards by the force of the blast. She lay on her back, staring in terror as the giant skeleton towered over her. It shuddered and shook then sank to its knees and slammed into the mud next to her.

Through the tangle of its ribcage, Cassie saw that the bullet had shattered a glass bottle containing the creature's life-giving oil. The crowd edged backwards, convinced that a real forest gatherer now stood in their presence, and only Cassie's horse-headed guide dared approach her.

"You kill with finger!" it whispered, staring at Cassie's hand in amazement. Cassie frowned then suddenly realised that she had been pointing at the skeleton when she had fired the gun.

"Yes!" she shouted, determined to make the most of the misunderstanding. "Yes, I kill with my finger. Does anyone else challenge me?!"

She swept her "killing finger" over the crowd and the skeletons shrank backwards.

Cassie strode from the pine grove and collapsed against a tree-trunk while Horse-head asked for volunteers to accompany them to the Turk's Head. The skeletons didn't move and Horse-head returned to Cassie alone.

"Blast them with finger!" it urged her. "Make them help!"

"No!" said Cassie, staring at the finger that really *had* ended the ox-creature's life. The gun's trigger had left an angry imprint in her fingertip. "There'll be no more killing," she said quietly, horrified by what she had done.

Horse-head took Cassie's goat-skin pouch and offered her a drink. Cassie lifted it, expecting fresh water, but cried out in disgust when a bitter liquid filled her mouth.

"*What is it?*" she spluttered, wiping the taste away.

"Wine of Life… from Tree of Life. All gatherers know that." The little skeleton stared at her quizzically.

"Of course, of course," stammered Cassie, remembering that she was travelling in disguise. "Bad vintage, I suppose.

Now take me to the Turk's Head. I want to go there now."

Horse-head scurried into the trees and Cassie turned to follow it when the pine grove erupted in noise.

Von Rippenbaum's creatures were fighting over the remains of the fallen skeleton. Bones and wire flew through the air and the soil upon which the life-giving essence had spilled was being clawed at and devoured.

Cassie shuddered with horror and ran into the night.

CHAPTER 36

At the Feast

Doctor Albertus stood at the edge of the bubbling water and threw in a great armful of herbs. Tom thought the herbs looked like ingredients in a strange kind of soup and he edged away from them, staring as they dissolved. The little doctor turned away.

The herbs were sweet and Tom found their scent relaxing, and he lay on his back and closed his eyes. He thought of Bearskin and wondered how long the poor bear-man had been trapped in the forest, and he thought of the mechanical device that had tricked its way into his grandfather's house. He wondered if Cassie and Professor Perkins would find his parents first and if they would return home without him. Tom found the idea so alarming that he almost jumped from the water.

Doctor Albertus suddenly appeared and said,

"Out now and dry. Let the bite heal."

Tom grabbed the towel and followed the doctor to a cave

where a flat slab of rock rose from the ground. The slab was covered in leaves and downy feathers, and the doctor pointed to it and said,

"Here now you sleep and perhaps also dream, for do not dreams reveal hidden truths?"

"I don't know," said Tom. "I once had a dream that my nose could see round corners. Does that reveal anything?"

The doctor stared at him curiously, then walked away.

Tom hopped onto the slab and was surprised how comfortable his new "bed" felt. The lanterns dimmed and the water bubbled softly, and it wasn't long before Tom was fast asleep.

Tom woke with a start and sat up. Thinking he had only closed his eyes for a moment, he suddenly noticed that his old-fashioned clothing was sitting on a rock next to him. They had been washed, ironed and repaired. Tom jumped from his "bed" and dressed quickly.

"And did you glimpse any hidden truths?" asked a voice behind him.

Tom spun round and saw Rowanbole in the entrance of the cave, smiling warmly. Two gnomen warriors stood behind him holding spears.

"I didn't dream, if that's what you mean," said Tom.

"Pity," nodded Rowanbole. "Poor Albertus will be disappointed. He collects dreams, you know, like a naturalist gathers butterflies. He collects all our dreams and divines hidden meanings in them. Recent ones have troubled him greatly and have… Ah, but I am getting ahead of myself. Come, you must be hungry. We await our guest of honour!"

The old gnoman gestured towards the stairs.

Tom *was* hungry – extremely hungry – with an appetite he had never experienced before. He raced after the old gnoman.

"How long have I been asleep?" he asked, rubbing his eyes.

"Six, almost seven hours. I imagine you feel better?" Rowanbole tapped Tom's ankle with his walking stick, and Tom realised that the pain of his wolf bite had vanished. He hopped from foot to foot, laughing in amazement.

"Mineral waters," said Rowanbole. "They keep us all sprightly!"

The sleigh was where Tom had left it, and the gnomen warriors bowed deeply as Tom approached them. A second wooden sleigh stood in front of Tom's but this one was smaller and grander, and covered in exquisite carvings. Rowanbole eased himself into it and both sleighs took off at a much slower pace than before.

The ground rose steadily and entered a narrow passageway. Rowanbole raised a hand and ordered the sleighs to stop. He then invited Tom to walk with him.

Three short blasts sounded on instruments that Tom still couldn't identify, and when he stepped into the light Tom saw that he had been brought to the edge of an enormous pit. The pit was deep and circular, and was filled with colourful lanterns, and wild gnomish cheering filled the air. Rowanbole led Tom over to a steep, wooden ramp that spiralled all the way down to a long table where a grand feast had been set. As they descended, Tom saw hundreds of alcoves carved into the walls of the pit. Inside each one, gnomen families cheered and waved.

"I must apologise for the location," shouted Rowanbole.

"What do you mean?" said Tom. "It's amazing!"

"It is merely an old mine working, decorated in your honour. Our banqueting hall would not accommodate a fellow of your stature. Here you may stand tall!"

"They seem really happy about that button I returned," shouted Tom, embarrassed by all the attention. "If there's anything else I can do, let me know."

"Oh, but there is more that you *will* do; more that you are *destined* to do!"

Rowanbole smiled mysteriously and tottered down the ramp.

CHAPTER 37

One Hundred Surprising Things

he forest glowed under a ghostly moon as Cassie's guide led her scrambling over rocks and tree roots. They walked through the night, Cassie unaware that a mile or two behind her and deep underground, Tom lay fast asleep in the gnomen's cavern.

They stood on a rise and Horse-head scanned the forest below, clicking its teeth excitedly. "There. See. Come! Come!" It ran towards a something that lay in the shadows. Cassie followed it warily.

A huge tree trunk lay along the forest path, its bark and branches stripped away so that it resembled an enormous, blunt-ended pencil. Cassie jumped in surprise when two torches, fixed into metal brackets on the tree's circular end, suddenly sprang into life. Their light revealed a circular door on which text had been formed out of hundreds of iron nails. Cassie ran her finger across the bumpy list until she found a language that she could understand. The label read,

THE MUSEUM OF ONE HUNDRED SURPRISING THINGS. ENTER, WONDER THEN GO IN PEACE.

Horse-head kicked the door angrily and sat on the steps. It took a swig from the goat-skin bag and belched with pleasure.

"Where are we?" snapped Cassie. "What is this place?"

"Quick way through," the skeleton answered.

"You mean this tree trunk's hollow and we can walk through it?"

Before Horse-head could answer, the sound of pattering footsteps approached and a bizarre-looking creature stepped from the shadows.

It was a large man's head that was as wide and as tall as a garden shed. It had short, pointed whiskers and a high forehead with a long, sloping nose. Cassie backed away but the enormous head stepped closer, striding forwards on pencil-thin legs. It was only when it stepped into the torchlight that Cassie saw that the head was the body of an extremely tall bird whose own head and neck grew out of the top of the man's. The bizarre combination of man and bird towered over her.

The head muttered angrily in what sounded like German. The bird leant forwards and pinched the man on his nose, making him cry out with pain.

"I apologise for the rudeness of my body," said the bird. Cassie decided that the bird was a crane, for its sleek feathers and elegant movements were like the birds she had seen in a zoo. "I speak many languages and am familiar with yours. Do you wish to enter our museum?"

The crane spoke with a gentle civility that put Cassie at her ease, but before she could answer, Horse-head jumped to its feet and kicked the door.

"Open it! Open it! Open it!" it shrieked. The crane nodded obediently but the head of its body shouted, "Miserable ghoul! How would you like it if I were to kick *you*?!"

Again, the crane silenced its own body by pinching the man on his nose. It then produced a key from under its wing and opened the door.

Horse-head ran forwards, drinking from the goat-skin bag.

"I'm sorry," whispered Cassie. "I think it's drunk."

The crane bowed graciously but the head scowled at her.

Inside, the museum was as straight as a railway tunnel and the air smelled sweetly of wood sap. A string of lanterns illuminated a central path as well as dozens of alcoves that had been carved into the walls of the tree trunk.

Cassie peered into the nearest alcove and saw a label that read,

Enchanted Hen. In Life it Divined the Future.

A stuffed hen stood beneath a spotlight looking old and ragged. Cassie hoped it hadn't foreseen its own future and she walked over to the next alcove in which several strips of wood lay in an untidy pile. The objects were labelled as,

TOE & FINGER NAIL CLIPPINGS TAKEN FROM THE EXTREMITIES OF A GIANT. RETRIEVED AT GREAT COST.

Cassie wrinkled her nose.

The next alcove contained a wooden bowl, which was simply described as,

ENCHANTED.

A pile of oats swirled restlessly in the bowl before transforming themselves into a lump of steaming porridge. The porridge turned back into oats and the process started all over again.

The next alcove contained a cylindrical jar in which the body of a small, bearded man floated in an amber liquid. A label described it as,

YELLOWCAP GNOMEN.
ONLY SPECIMEN EVER
CAPTURED.

Cassie shivered and walked on, and noticed that the remaining exhibits were either damaged or missing.

"What happened?" she wondered aloud.

"Ask your bony friend and all his thieving kind!" snapped the head of the man-bird. The crane laughed nervously. "Please, forest gatherer," it said. "Ignore my bad-tempered body. He speaks nonsense."

"I speak truth!" blazed the head. The crane leant forwards and pinched the head on its nose.

"Please stop doing that!" said Cassie, alarmed how red the man's nose was becoming. "That skeleton isn't my friend. And what do you mean by 'all his thieving kind'?"

"That skeleton and its patrol passed through our museum a few days ago," said the head. "They stole what they wanted and destroyed what they didn't and reduced our collection to a mere forty-seven surprising things. They even threatened to roast us alive if we tried to stop them."

The crane flapped its wings at the memory of it.

"Damn all mechanicals!" blazed the head. "And damn their creator, too!"

The crane gasped in terror and tried to run away, but the head filled its cheeks with air, which made the crane stagger sideways and tumble to the floor.

"I thought *you* were a mechanical!" said Cassie, staring at the odd creature.

"Us? A mechanical? Indeed, we are not!" gasped the crane, struggling to its feet. "We are loyal subjects of his majestic highness, Von Rippenbaum. We are loyal, forest gatherer. We are loyal!"

The crane bowed awkwardly.

"Feathery fool!" laughed the head of its body. "She's no forest gatherer! She probably stole those clothes from a *real* forest gatherer while wandering through the forest. Perhaps she's the bloodling Von Rippenbaum is looking for. What a surprising thing that would be!"

The crane padded forwards and peered into Cassie's eyes.

CHAPTER 38

The Secret of the Essence

The merrymaking began the moment Tom took his place at the head of the table, with a boisterous display of beard-wrestling. The gnomen sport looked eye-wateringly painful and Tom was glad that he wasn't qualified to join in. He picked at his food, unnerved by Rowanbole's comment about him being "destined" to help. He looked along the table and saw Rowanbole watching him. The elderly gnoman smiled and gestured for Tom to follow him. Tom was led to a door in the side of a pit.

The beard-wrestling continued as Tom passed into a room that was cramped and dingy. He paused for a moment and let his eyes grow accustomed to the dim light.

A single lantern shone above a wooden table upon which several layers of parchment lay. Three gnomen were huddled over them, studying the sheets intently. They straightened and bowed the moment Rowanbole approached them.

"Dr Albertus, you already know," said Rowanbole. Tom

smiled as the little doctor stared at his ankle as if admiring his handiwork. "Captain Jussell, you have not met. Captain Jussell is in charge of our boundaries and defences."

Captain Jussell was young – his beard had not yet turned white – and his eyes glittered as brightly as the medals that decorated his tunic. He regarded Tom cautiously.

"And this is Holligold," said Rowanbole.

A female gnoman stepped forwards. Her hair was grey and was swept up into a loose knot, while her movements were quick and agile. The embroidered flowers on her dress swayed gently as she reached for Tom's hand.

"We honour you and welcome you," she said.

The gnoman stared at Tom in silent admiration, and Tom shuffled uncomfortably under their gaze.

"I'm not very strong," he said. "My sister thinks I'm an idiot so if there's anything dangerous you want me to do, perhaps you'd better ask Bearskin."

The gnomen smiled.

"This parchment was written by our ancestors," said Rowanbole. "It is a glimpse of their lives from long ago."

The parchment was filled with beautiful paintings of the forest.

"*This* parchment is new," continued Rowanbole. "It shows us which parts of the Ringwood now lie in ruin."

A black and sinister circle ringed the circle of trees.

"That's the dead forest! Bearskin and I walked through that bit," said Tom. "It used to be winter but it's crumbling away. Is Von Rippenbaum to blame?"

"*Yes!*" said Holligold, almost shouting. She lowered her head and apologised, but Rowanbole smiled and asked her to continue. "The roots of the mighty Ringwood Tree spread throughout the forest," she explained. "They spread and grow and fill our world with wonderful, life-giving essence. When *he* discovered the tree, he burrowed beneath it like a rat and extracted the vital essence. Now he uses it to power his devices, not caring that the world he stumbled into is dying."

"Stumbled into?!" gasped Tom. "But I was told Von Rippenbaum invented this place. And the disc."

"He did not!" said Rowanbole. "The Ringwood, the gnomen and all the creatures that live here have existed far longer than he."

"So Von Rippenbaum just *found* the disc, like Grandfather and Professor Perkins did?" asked Tom.

"Stole it, more likely," muttered Captain Jussell.

"However he came by it," said Rowanbole, "it wasn't long before Von Rippenbaum claimed the Ringwood for himself and ruled its seasons like an emperor, hovering over us in his sinister balloon where none can reach him." The old gnoman let out a weary sigh. "And now," he added miserably, "you must hear the worst of it."

The other gnomen shuffled uncomfortably.

"Many outsiders once entered the Ringwood and travelled along the ceremonial path. They were lured here by Von Rippenbaum, little knowing what lay ahead of them. One day, the outsiders stopped arriving. It was as if the passage to your world had become blocked."

"It had," said Tom. "Von Rippenbaum's workshop was burned to the ground. The disc got buried underneath it. My friend, Professor Perkins, found it years later but the disc got buried again – in my grandfather's garden. My parents activated it and–"

"And signalled to Von Rippenbaum that a fresh supply of victims was available once more," sighed Rowanbole.

Tom nodded miserably.

"There remains one other substance," continued Rowanbole, "a substance that, when mixed with the living essence of the tree, breathes life into things that should not have it. It is the reason Von Rippenbaum lures so many to their deaths. It is…"

"Blood," said Tom, quietly. "It *is* blood, isn't it? He needs blood to power those devices."

Rowanbole nodded.

"Mum! Dad!" gasped Tom. Holligold gripped his hand.

"Even now it may not be too late to save them," she whispered.

"And Cassie!" said Tom. "She's out there in the forest and doesn't know any of this!"

"Does she not have the companionship of your friend to guide her?" asked Holligold. "I am sure he will protect her."

Or drive her crazy, thought Tom, remembering how Cassie and the professor argued.

"What can I do?" asked Tom suddenly. "How can I stop Von Rippenbaum?"

Captain Jussell unrolled a length of ragged parchment.

On it was a remarkable drawing.

CHAPTER 39

Asleep in the Storeroom

Horse-head's voice echoed eerily through the wooden gallery. Drunkenly it sang,
"I hunt for birds,
An' wild game too,
An' mix 'em up in a tasty stew,
Now I hunt,
For different prey,
The bloodlings' lives
I'll steal away!"

It laughed at its own cleverness then tumbled head-first into a display case filled with mechanical butterflies. The butterflies flew in all directions as the little skeleton lay on the broken glass and went to sleep.

Cassie heard the noise but didn't move. The man-bird was studying her suspiciously. Remembering how hostile it had sounded towards Von Rippenbaum, Cassie decided to trust the bizarre creature, and she whispered,

"You're right! I'm not a forest gatherer. I took these clothes from a creature in a tea house. I don't even belong here. I'm trying to get home. Please, will you help me? Will you help me get home?"

The head laughed triumphantly.

"I knew it!" it cried. "I *knew* you were an impostor! Oh, I've quite the nose for trickery, quite the nose... when it isn't being pecked."

"You wander the forest in the company of ghouls?!" gasped the crane. "Do you value your life so lightly?"

"The skeleton said it knew a shortcut to a place called the Turk's Head. There's someone there who'll help me... I think."

"So you walk with mechanicals, yet you go undetected!" laughed the head. "What a surprising thing you are! If only we could display *you*!"

The crane continued to stare at Cassie in amazement.

"You are an out-dweller!" it whispered. "An other-worlder from beyond the forest!"

"Well I don't live here if that's what you mean," said Cassie.

"Tell me, is it true that in your world, a million surprising things surround you every day?"

"Yes... I suppose they do," said Cassie, picturing half a million of them cluttering up her bedroom.

The crane lowered its beak and whispered excitedly in the head's ear. The head nodded in approval and the crane turned back to Cassie.

"We offer you our assistance, our loyalty and our friendship," it said, "providing you send us twenty–"

"Thirty!" said the head.

"... *thirty* surprising things after you return home. Your land is a place of myth and fable to us, and to display some of *your* surprising things in our museum would be most surprising."

"All right!" said Cassie, trembling with relief. "I'll send you lots of surprising things! Lots and lots of them! Now have you heard of someone called Duman? I was told he would help me."

"We know Duman," groaned the head, "and all his ways. He is a trader who has grown wealthy from his wanderings. But he is also a mechanical."

"A mechanical!" gasped Cassie. "Well that's no good. He'll be loyal to Von Rippenbaum."

"Duman's loyalty lies with those who have the fattest purses," said the crane. "You do *have* a fat purse with which to trade?"

Cassie shook her head.

"No? You really are a lost leaf, tumbling through the forest. We will show you to our storeroom. There are trinkets in there to tempt the greediest magpie."

The man-bird led Cassie to a tapestry that hung against the wall. It pulled a tasselled cord and the cloth parted to reveal a wide door. The crane strode through it but Cassie hesitated and stared along the gallery.

"Guard the tunnel!" she ordered, pointing her "killing" finger at Horse-head. The little skeleton didn't move and remained fast asleep on its bed of glass.

The storeroom was filled with hundreds of cardboard boxes that were neatly stacked on wooden shelving. The crane extended its neck and peered along the highest shelf, but the head insisted that it should start lower down. It wasn't long before the man-bird was arguing with itself.

Cassie groaned and flopped into an armchair built to accommodate the bird's wide body. She removed her gatherer's helmet and yawned, and wrapped the gatherer's coat around herself. Cassie leant upon a cushion and frowned when the crane started pinching the man's nose.

"Please," she mumbled sleepily. "Stop doing that. It looks really painful…"

CHAPTER 40

A Strange Prophecy

Gnomish writing covered the parchment. Gaps had been left between the text creating the illusion of paths meandering through a forest of paragraphs. Tom traced the longest "path" with his finger and came to a drawing of a tree growing upon a mound. The mound was guarded by a ring of mechanicals.

"Is that the Ringwood Tree?" he asked.

The gnomen nodded.

"And what are those?" asked Tom, noticing some peculiar flecks of ink.

Rowanbole slid a lens towards him and through its magnifying curve, the flecks were transformed into a drawing of a girl, a boy and a monkey.

"That's us!" cried Tom. "We're standing next to two forest wells! Have you been watching our journey?"

"No indeed," said Rowanbole. "But it seems that your visit was not entirely unexpected. This parchment contains the writings of Theocrastus, our most revered seer."

"Seer?"

"Theocrastus was Doctor Albertus's great, great, great... Oh dear, it continues for some time. He was a remarkable prophet who predicted your arrival many hundreds of years ago. He drew his visions on parchment but unfortunately for us, this particular parchment has only recently been discovered. We really must sort out those royal archives."

Tom stared at the creatures guarding the mound and saw that they were far more terrifying than any he had encountered. He had just begun to despair of ever returning home, when Rowanbole placed the lens over the sinister shapes and revealed a second drawing.

"It's us again!" gasped Tom. "We're together at the centre, surrounded by those creatures. Is this really going to happen?"

"Of course," snapped Doctor Albertus.

"Are Mum and Dad's drawings on here?" Tom searched the parchment with the lens.

"This vos the last, great prophecy of Theocrastus," sighed Doctor Albertus. "Death took him, leaving this final vision unfinished. He did not tell us how your journey vould end, or the fate of your parents."

Rowanbole patted Tom's arm.

"Something dark and dangerous and wonderful is happening," said the old gnoman. "The balance of the forest is shifting. No one knows where it will settle. But you were *meant* to be here; you, your sister and even poor Professor Perkins, you were all meant to take this journey. It is the *outcome* that remains unknown to us."

Tom stared at the parchment.

"I've never done anything like this before," he said quietly.

"The Yellowcap army will travel with you," said Holligold.

"They will help you reach the tree and they will battle alongside you. Too long have we ignored Von Rippenbaum and his poison. Too long has he divided the gnomen. Let this be the cause that unites us."

"Did you say 'battle'?" interrupted Tom.

"Don't be alarmed," said Holligold. "See. *Your* battle lies elsewhere. The prophecy shows you moving in a different direction." She pointed to a block of writing in which Tom's symbol appeared for a third time, and Holligold translated the words for him. "Here, Theocrastus speaks of the grassy mound on which the Ringwood Tree grows and of Von Rippenbaum's workshop deep inside it. A giant gourd grows there, extracting the living essence from the tree like a horrible, bloated tick. Theocrastus speaks of a boy who will attempt to destroy the gourd."

"I'm a boy!" cried Tom. "Does the gourd *really* grow there? Has anyone seen it? Has anyone tried to destroy it?"

Captain Jussell shook his head.

"We gnomen cannot travel overland by day," he said. "Sunlight burns our skin and robs us of our sight. Nor can we tunnel under the mound or dig beyond the borders of autumn. Spring gnomen live at the centre and Von Rippenbaum's lies have turned them against us. Even the summer gnomen, who lie between us and spring, are weak and unprincipled and are ruled by a foolish–"

"Captain!" warned Rowanbole. "Lord Furrowfox may be weak and unprincipled but he is no fool. He is young and easily distracted and displays none of his father's great insight. I am hopeful he might change... when the right moment comes."

Captain Jussell bowed deeply.

"Forgive me. I meant no disrespect to the summer gnomen. I only meant to say that Lord Furrowfox prefers to remain neutral on matters of... importance."

"Won't the winter gnomen help us?" asked Tom.

A gloomy silence settled on the group.

"The winter gnomen were warlike and difficult," said Holligold. "Many years ago they chose to fight Von Rippenbaum alone, refusing all offers of help. Many were killed and the creeping decay appears to have scattered the rest."

She handed Tom a square of old leather on which a faded image appeared. It showed chambers and rooms hidden beneath the mound.

"*Where did you get this?!*" gasped Tom, suddenly aware that he was seeing Von Rippenbaum's lair beneath the tree.

"My husband," said Holligold quietly. "As a young warrior, he travelled to the centre and crept inside the mound. He travelled by night and succeeded in his mission, but on his return he was captured by a band of marauding mechanicals."

"How did the map get back here?" asked Tom.

"I was travelling with him. I managed to escape."

Tom stared at the frail gnoman.

"Did your husband escape with you?" he asked.

Holligold looked away.

"I was destined never to see my husband again," she whispered, "nor anything else. After the ambush, I ran in terror and quite forgot the hour. I stood, transfixed, as beautiful colours filled the night sky. I turned and looked and saw that it was dawn, and felt the great eye of the morning sun burn into me."

Holligold's blind, unseeing eyes filled with tears.

CHAPTER 41

The Long Gallery

The single lantern cast restless shadows against the walls of the storeroom. Cassie blinked and rubbed her eyes, and stumbled over to the wooden shelving. Overturned boxes lay scattered across the floor. The man-bird was slumped in the corner, its crane's neck resting on the forehead of the man's head. Crane and head were both fast asleep.

"Hisst!" whispered Cassie, tugging the crane's wing.

The crane opened a beady eye.

"Oh!" it exclaimed, clacking its beak in surprise. It rose on its pencil-thin legs and roused its sleeping body.

"What is it? What is it?" blustered the head.

"What happened?" asked Cassie, staring at the boxes.

"A minor disagreement, nothing more," explained the crane, stretching its wings. "But I am pleased to say that we finally came to a decision. Would you open your bag, please?"

It bobbed its head up and down with excitement as Cassie lifted the flap of the shoulder-bag. Inside, Cassie discovered

179

a beautifully crafted bird's foot and feather, both made out of gold. "You are holding what is left of Von Rippenbaum's first raven," said the crane sadly. "It is rumoured that the poor creature failed its master and that its eyes now gaze from a glass window in the boar's head. Duman's fondness for this golden bird was great. He would trade anything to own its remains."

"Why don't you display them in your museum?" asked Cassie.

"Why not indeed!" muttered the head.

"No," insisted the crane. "We would attract too much attention. Questions would be asked and a good collector never reveals his sources."

"Well, if you're sure," said Cassie, overwhelmed by the man-bird's generosity. "Thank you. You've been so kind and helpful."

The head scowled but the crane bowed, before striding towards the door. "It is almost sunrise," the crane announced. "Do your species indulge in regular acts of preening? If so, there is a chamber of convenience just through there." It pointed to an archway on the far side of the room. "Join us in the gallery when you are finished and we will take breakfast together."

It turned and flapped away.

Cassie smiled and tucked the golden items inside the shoulder-bag.

She wandered through the archway and found herself in a circular room whose floor sloped towards a circle of wood. Cassie lifted the wooden lid, and the smell of dung and pine needles filled the air.

"Toilet!" whispered Cassie, dropping the wooden circle quickly.

She wandered over to a water trough and picked up a block of soap. She was about to scrub herself clean, when a sinister face made her jump in surprise. Cassie almost turned and ran when she suddenly noticed that she was standing in front of a large mirror. She peered at her reflection and gasped. Her face was pale beneath streaks of dark mud, her hair was lank and greasy, while her eyes stared back at her from two dark circles.

Cassie plunged her hands into the icy water, determined to be clean again, when she suddenly remembered her disguise. She sighed and contented herself with a quick neck wash before returning to the long gallery. The museum was still and silent.

"Hello?" cried Cassie.

The sound of splintering wood shattered the silence and echoed down the long gallery. A bright shaft of daylight pierced the darkness and was quickly filled by the ragged silhouettes of dozens of marauding mechanicals.

Cassie turned and ran, suddenly aware that she had left her gatherer's helmet in the storeroom. The gibbering devices raced nearer.

Cassie leapt into an alcove and hid beneath a table.

CHAPTER 42

A Gift

"hat you did was really brave," whispered Tom.

"It did not feel very brave," said Holligold. "What *you* have achieved, however, has taken true bravery for you have endured many terrors far beyond your age. Would you accept a small gift?"

Holligold reached beneath the table and produced a leather scabbard. She handed it to Tom. "It fell from my husband's side during our ambush. It would please me greatly if you would take it."

"Careful," warned Rowanbole as Tom slid the blade from its sheath. "That weapon was forged by our most skilful craftsmen and probably has the sharpest blade in the kingdom."

"A dagger!" said Tom.

"Dagger?!" laughed Holligold. "To us it is almost a sword, but whatever you call it, it will serve you well... should you decide to help us."

Lord Rowanbole walked around the table and stood next to Tom. "This prophecy, Thomas: we do not bind you to any of its truths. You are free to go at any time. We would only part as friends."

"No!" exclaimed Tom. "No, I *want* to help you. I have to help the forest. I have to stab that gourd."

A ripple of relief spread through the gnomen.

"Then it is decided," said Captain Jussell. "Our army will travel with you overland by night and will meet you at a pre-arranged location near the centre of the forest."

"You mean you're not travelling with me?" asked Tom.

Captain Jussell smiled.

"Your friend was most insistent that you and he travel alone. Given his size, I did not feel inclined to disagree."

"Bearskin!" said Tom. "You've spoken to Bearskin?! Where is he?"

"He waits for you at the Table of the Feasting Kings and knows of the prophecy and the battle to come. He means to help us. He is a stout companion, Thomas. You would do well to stay close to him."

"I will," said Tom, eager to see his friend once again. "Was he all right? Was he safe?"

"Come and see for yourself!"

Captain Jussell saluted and marched out of the room. Doctor Albertus waved his birch twig in an elaborate figure of eight before handing Tom a leather pouch.

"Keep safe," he whispered, hanging the pouch around Tom's neck and tucking it inside his shirt. "Keep safe. *Safe!*" he insisted.

Tom nodded nervously and watched the little doctor scuttle away. Then he picked up his sword and started to tie it around his waist.

"Embedded within the hilt," explained Holligold, "is a splinter of wood taken from the bark of the Ringwood Tree."

Tom studied the handle and saw a clear ball of glass set into its end. Inside, a splinter of wood turned lazily, as if floating in water. "The painted tip always points towards the Ringwood Tree," added Holligold. "You will never be lost."

Tom thanked her and escorted her from the room.

The great feasting pit rang with applause the moment Tom stepped into it, and Tom knew that his decision to help the gnomen had spread throughout the crowd. Flower petals filled the air and the gnomen pressed forwards to congratulate him. Gnomen warriors appeared and cleared a path.

"Goodbye!" shouted Holligold over the cheering crowd. "May the light of the forest protect you!"

"Goodbye, Holligold. I'll try my best. I promise."

Holligold nodded tearfully as Tom reached his sleigh. Then he was gone, and a hundred Yellowcap voices sang in farewell.

Tom raced through undecorated tunnels that rose in a dizzying spiral. The air became colder and the scent of pine resin and tree bark suggested that he was nearing the "upperlands". The sleighs came to an abrupt halt and Tom sat upright.

The walls of the tunnel were rough with tree root and stone, and a murky light filled the narrow opening. Rowanbole climbed from his sleigh and whispered,

"Don't stand up! You will catch your head on the ceiling. We are near the surface, Thomas. Crawl forwards now, up towards the light."

"Thank you, Lord Rowanbole," said Tom. "Will I see you at the centre?"

The old gnoman gripped Tom's sleeve.

"You may depend upon it." The old gnoman's grip suddenly tightened and he added, "Do not risk your life unnecessarily, Thomas. Promise me that you will take the *very greatest* care."

Tom remembered Cassie's mocking words: how scared she thought Tom was of everything, how terrified he was to move. Here was his chance to prove her wrong.

"*Promise me you'll be careful,*" insisted Rowanbole.

"I promise that I'll try," said Tom.

He scrambled from his sleigh and crawled towards the light.

Chapter 43

The Owl of Minerva

The howling figures had almost reached the alcove when a tapestry next to where Cassie was hiding suddenly parted. The crane's head appeared and grabbed Cassie by the scruff of her coat and hauled her, backwards, through the doorway. The crane locked the door behind it and listened as the patrol thundered past.

"If any more of those damned mechanicals pass through our museum, we'll be down to *one* surprising thing: me, staying here!" The head scowled furiously.

The man-bird flapped up a staircase that had been skilfully carved into the inside of the tree trunk and brought Cassie to another long gallery.

A wooden table and several wooden benches glowed beneath the light of seven circular windows. Cassie peered through the nearest window and saw the forest far below her, nodding restlessly.

"We gather our own ingredients," said the crane, inviting

Cassie to sit next to an old cooking range. Cassie drew close to the oven's warmth and stared hungrily at a plate of fresh pancakes. The crane poured a jug of fruit and syrup over the sweet-smelling food and invited Cassie to eat her fill.

Cassie spent the morning listening to the crane as it told her of its life in the forest. She tried to relax but her thoughts kept returning to what lay ahead of her and to the creature she had killed in the pine grove. Suddenly, Cassie jumped up and said,

"Have you seen my guide? That skeleton-creature that brought me here."

The crane shook its head and its body, and Cassie jumped to her feet and returned to the lower gallery, hoping that Horse-head hadn't joined the patrol.

She ran the length of the museum, peering into every alcove. The man-bird flapped after her, gasping at the new trail of destruction. When they reached the end of the gallery, the circular door lay in splinters.

"Miserable wretches!" cried the head. "Why do they torment us so?"

Cassie looked outside and saw the skeleton, kneeling at the base of a tree and scrabbling at the earth with its claws.

"Journey in peace," said the crane, handing Cassie her gatherer's helmet and shoulder-bag. Cassie blinked in surprise and realised that it was time for her to go.

"Thank you," she said, pulling on her disguise. "Do either of you know what a forest gatherer is?"

The crane and the head looked at her in astonishment. "You mean you do not know?! You did not choose these clothes on purpose? What a surprising thing you are!" The head and the crane both laughed. "Gatherers are collectors," explained the crane, "but not of curios or of jewellery. They collect broken mechanicals; figures who have come to the end of their essence or the end of their usefulness, depending upon Von Rippenbaum's whim. Gatherers wander the forest and are feared and despised by all who meet them."

"You are *death*, my dear!" laughed the head. "To those mechanical ghouls, you are the living embodiment of those nightmares' nightmares!"

Cassie thought of the gatherer whose clothes she had taken at the tea house, and remembered how its chest, and the bottle of essence within it, had been smashed.

"Not all mechanicals are scared of them," said Cassie, remembering her encounter in the pine grove. "Some of them fight back."

"Which is why you must be careful," insisted the crane. "Now please. Accept this: a small token of our friendship. We sell them in our gift shop… what is left of it." It dropped something into Cassie's hand.

It was a miniature carving of the man-bird, standing on a wooden plinth. The word "Curator" was written underneath it.

"Thank you… curator," said Cassie, leaning forwards and wrapping her arms around the crane's neck.

The crane clacked its beak in surprise but the head grumbled, "Never mind all that. We want those surprising things you promised us. And don't try and deceive us or we will enter your world and will hunt you down!"

The crane gasped at the head's rudeness and pinched it on its nose. The head jerked backwards, sending both it and the crane tumbling into the museum.

"Goodbye!" said Cassie, wincing at the sound of breaking glass. She turned and stepped into the bright morning sunlight.

"Gatherer!" cried Horse-head. "Gatherer, come. Eat! Eat!" It held up a knot of slimy worms.

"*No!*" cried Cassie in disgust, making the little skeleton jump. "I mean, I'm not hungry."

"But gatherers always hungry," said Horse-head, staring

at her with a puzzled expression.

"Will we reach the Turk's Head today?" asked Cassie briskly.

"This day. To-day. Yes!" sang Horse-head. It jumped to its feet and rattled off into the forest. Cassie sighed with relief and ran after it.

It was a crisp autumn morning, the sort Cassie enjoyed walking to school in. The sun had risen above the forest canopy, and its warmth was a welcome tonic. The memory of school and of sharp, frosty mornings made Cassie long for home, and she cursed Von Rippenbaum. She became so angry, that when Horse-head brought her to a place where oversized bracken grew in huge, curling fronds, Cassie almost walked into them. Horse-head lunged at the ferns, toppling them easily, and Cassie followed, trying not to trip on the cable-thick stalks.

Occasionally, Horse-head would run ahead of her and would return with a dead bird, which it would place at Cassie's feet as an offering. It would kneel, as if waiting for a blessing, but Cassie would step around it, shivering with disgust. The little skeleton stared at her in confusion.

When they finally emerged from the over-sized thicket, Cassie gasped in astonishment for the forest ahead of her had been transformed into metal. The floor was now a slab of solid bronze, while the crackling leaf-litter had been transformed into sheets of fused metal. Forest breezes whistled eerily through unmoving branches, and no animals or birds moved within them.

Cassie's boots clanked over the dead landscape. Horse-head scurried ahead of her, rattling noisily.

A series of grooves, like miniature tramlines, ran in all directions, and curved mysteriously into the trees. A large, ornamental key stuck up from the ground, and as Cassie passed it, she couldn't resist giving the key a little twist. The moment she did, the sides of several trees sprang open to reveal dozens of mechanical figures. The figures trundled along the tramlines, spinning and dancing in time to a strange, fluting music. Cassie scrambled up a steep bank of metal to where Horse-head was waiting for her.

The little skeleton pointed to the metallic forest far below and cackled.

"And how are we supposed to get down there?" panted Cassie.

Horse-head threw itself into a shallow trough that snaked the length of the hillside. It fell quickly, rattling like an upturned toolbox, and Cassie knew that the trough was the only way down.

She shuffled forwards, clutching her shoulder-bag, and felt herself drop. Cassie plunged to earth, her back barely touching the metal, when the twists and turns softened and Cassie felt herself slowing to a halt.

She sat up and saw that she had arrived at the base of a tall pine tree. It was made of bronze and its needles and pinecones had been expertly cast. An opening in its trunk revealed that the tree was hollow, with a spiral staircase twisting up through its centre.

Horse-head emerged from the tree clutching a square of card. Cassie noticed a sign hanging next to the arched opening. It read,

THE OWL OF MINERVA.
A QUESTION
ASKED.
AN ANSWER
GIVEN.

"What's an Owl of Minerva?" asked Cassie.
"One who speaks truth," snapped the skeleton.
It shredded its card and glared at Cassie.

CHAPTER 44

At the Table of the Feasting Kings

om pushed his head between the roots of an old oak tree and was blinded for a moment by the bright, morning sunlight. He had emerged at the edge of an overgrown clearing in which an enormous tree stump grew. A table had been carved out of the wood of the stump and on it was a carved, wooden feast. Six wooden noblemen sat in high-backed chairs. Their forms were old and rotten, and straggling lengths of ivy bound them to the forest floor. Tom wriggled out of the hole and saw Bearskin kneeling in front of the figures, his head bowed as if in prayer. Tom smiled and was about to creep over and surprise him, when Bearskin turned and gestured for Tom to join him. Tom sighed and wondered if anyone had ever sneaked up on the giant.

"I did it!" whispered Tom excitedly, sitting next to Bearskin on a log. "I found the gnomen! They thought I was a spy and they were going to kill me but when they saw the button – which I sort of, erm, dropped – they changed their mind. You should have seen it down there. There were taverns and caverns and mines and everything! They even had sleighs."

Bearskin remained silent, his gaze fixed upon the tree stump.

"The gnomen said they'd help us," continued Tom, wondering why his friend seemed quieter than usual. "There's a giant gourd growing under the Ringwood Tree that's killing the forest. I've been asked to destroy it. Lord Rowanbole said you'd help me. He said you knew the plan."

"Aye," sighed Bearskin wearily. "I know the plan. But I also know this forest an' the mechanicals 'oo live in it an' what they do to a person if they catch 'em. Those gnomen talk of battle an' of glory as if they were jewels to be plucked from the earth. Well, they're not! Prophecies an' promises! Prophecies an' promises! They've filled yer head wi' nonsense!"

"Are you still going to help me?" asked Tom.

The giant straightened, as if he had come to a decision.

"I've sworn to protect you," he said. "I've promised to tek you to the centre, an' I will. But I'm sendin' you straight home the minute danger gets too near, an' the devil can tek their prophecies!"

"But the gourd!" insisted Tom. "I have to try and destroy it."

"Those're my terms. Favour 'em or not."

Tom stared into Bearskin's eyes and saw something he had never seen in them before: fear.

"All right," mumbled Tom. "You can send me home if things get too dangerous. But you have to let me have a proper go."

Bearskin nodded and reached behind the log. "Littlebeards left yer this," he said gruffly, handing Tom a leather backpack. "It's filled wi' food an' other bits o' tackle. Yer can bring it along if yer can carry it."

The backpack felt no heavier than his schoolbag, and Tom lifted it easily. He silently thanked the gnomen for the gift.

"Who are those statues of?" he asked, nodding at the stump.

Bearskin rose.

"They're not statues," he rumbled. "They're six innocent men, lured to their deaths by Bristlebeard."

"You mean they used to be...?"

"Aye, flesh 'n blood. Bristlebeard transformed 'em into wood, laughin' an' dancin' as 'e did it."

Tom saw that he had mistaken the figures' open mouths and raised arms for merrymaking, and he stared in horror when he realised that the men were fighting for their lives.

"Bearskin," he whispered. "How do you know all this? Were you here when it happened?"

"Was I 'ere?!" laughed Bearskin bitterly. "I were the bloody fool 'oo caused it!"

CHAPTER 45

Question and Answer

assie climbed the metal staircase, pausing at every turn.
Horse-head had been unwilling or unable to explain
the "Owl of Minerva" to her, and the little skeleton had
sat on the ground and had scowled at her moodily. So Cassie
had entered the bronze pine tree alone, determined to ask the
owl her own questions.

The staircase spiralled higher until Cassie doubted
whether there was any tree left to climb. She was about
to turn back, when a final bend brought her to a circular
opening. Beyond it lay a dimly lit chamber.

The chamber was small and had been scooped out of the
tree's metal core; its curving walls like the inside of a hollow
egg. As her eyes grew accustomed to the light, Cassie noticed
something large sitting on the floor. She called down to it
and clapped her hands but the shape didn't move.

There were no steps or footholds leading into the chamber,
so Cassie slid down the wall on her back and came skidding

to a halt in front of a pair of fierce talons. The talons merged into the metal of the floor and supported the imposing statue of an owl. Cassie jumped when the statue's eyes suddenly flickered into life, and she gasped when its pupils became two bright circles of amber. The chamber filled with golden light, and a voice, unfamiliar and distant, suddenly asked, "Will I ever see my family again?"

Cassie frowned, aware that she had just asked her question, but uncertain whether she had spoken the words aloud or had thought them. She tried to clear her mind of an unpleasant fuzziness, when the owl's head started to turn. It completed a full circle, and from somewhere inside its chest a bell "pinged". Cassie jumped, as if waking up from a dream, and sensed that her meeting with the owl was now over.

A card tumbled into an opening in the owl's chest and Cassie picked it up and angled it towards the light. The card read,

> TWO LIVES, YES.
> TWO LIVES, NO.
> THOSE ABOVE,
> WATCH BELOW.

"What does *that* mean?!" shouted Cassie, glaring at the owl. "*Who's* watching above? *Who won't I see again?*"

But the owl had returned to its former state: a cold, unmoving lump of metal.

Cassie scrambled from the chamber and clattered down the stairs, frightened by the owl's mysterious answer.

"The Turk's Head!" she snapped, running into the forest, her eyes shining with tears. Horse-head scurried after her.

"Owl good?" it croaked. "*Owl wise?*" Its tone was mocking and sarcastic.

Cassie ignored it and slid the card inside her waistcoat,

annoyed that she had allowed yet another forest mechanical upset her. *Of course* she would see her family again, she told herself, *and* she would lead them all to safety.

Horse-head sped past her, jabbering away in its own peculiar language. It danced and pranced and pointed and laughed and seemed filled with a new and sinister purpose.

After a while, the metallic forest ended, and the soft, living colours of autumn returned. Sunlight, soil and rich forest scents surrounded them and Cassie was relieved to be amongst the living forest again.

They walked all day, Horse-head jabbering and pointing while Cassie tried her best to ignore it. As the afternoon drew to a close, Cassie discovered a seed cake tucked inside the shoulder-bag. It was a gift from the museum curator and Cassie smiled and nibbled at it gratefully. Suddenly, a raven flapped to the ground in front of her. It cawed twice and Cassie tossed it some cake crumbs. The raven gobbled the offering and cawed again. Cassie edged backwards and didn't respond. The bird was about to raise an alarm when Horse-head burst from the undergrowth and launched itself at the creature. The raven flew into the air, screeching in terror.

"Th-thank you," stammered Cassie.

"Raven think you not gatherer!" Horse-head laughed. "Raven think you not *real!*"

Cassie looked away.

"Raven want you for itself!" Horse-head added. "But I chase away! I keep safe!"

It ran into the forest, giggling slyly, and Cassie pulled her helmet and goggles lower.

The setting sun bathed the Ringwood in a blood-red light, and Cassie kept her gaze fixed upon the path ahead of her, not realising that Horse-head had stopped beneath an oak tree. It was pointing at something just ahead of them and Cassie followed the bones of its outstretched claw.

"The Turk's head!" Cassie whispered softly. "We're here, but The Turk's Head…is a Turk's Head!"

The building had been carved into the shape of an enormous head, with a pumpkin-shaped turban for a roof. A gap between the teeth of its grinning mouth served as a doorway, while the "eyes" were two semi-circular windows that blazed with light. Wooden timbers had been varnished to a coppery sheen and a timber moustache gave the head a rascally appearance. The building was old, and it had settled into the ground where it rested on one cheek, as if using the forest as a pillow.

Suddenly, a voice echoed through the twilight, and Horse-head jumped with excitement.

"Gatherer stay!" it babbled. "Gatherer stay! I go!"

It ran towards a figure that emerged from the building.

"Hey!" shouted Cassie. "Hey, where are you going?"

"Duman!" laughed the skeleton. "Duman is here! Duman will help!"

CHAPTER 46

Patrol and Encounter

earskin plunged through the undergrowth, Tom drifting behind him like a cork in the wake of a ship. Tom tried to discover more about the figures on the tree stump but Bearskin had refused to speak of them and had stalked away. Uneventful mile followed uneventful mile, and the forest stirred restlessly around them. Eventually, they came to a forest pool where Bearskin stopped for a drink. He was about to suggest that they rest for a few hours when Bearskin's guide Chiffchaff appeared and flew around his head, chirruping loudly.

"Quick!" ordered Bearskin, rushing to his feet. Drumbeats rumbled through the forest.

Bearskin swung Tom onto his shoulders and carried him across the river. He scrambled onto the bank and tunnelled inside a thick patch of bramble where he ordered Tom to hide under him. Bearskin covered them both in a tangle of undergrowth.

The drumbeats grew louder and Tom peered from his shaggy shelter. A metal pole slammed into the water beside him, followed by another and another. Tom stared up at a towering creature as it strode past and jumped when it gave a piercing whistle.

Dozens of mechanicals burst from the forest and hopped, limped and slunk along the riverbank. Tom edged forwards, hoping to see more of the creatures, but Bearskin pushed him back.

The air vibrated with the sound of drums, and a mechanical toad-thing slithered closer. It blinked, confused by the tangle of bramble and fur, and moved on.

As quickly as they had come, the patrol had swept by, but Bearskin remained hidden. Chiffchaff signalled the all clear and the giant scrambled from the bank, hoisted Tom onto his back, and ran on all fours. Tom clung to Bearskin's fur and bounced up and down like a frightened jockey. He was just beginning to enjoy his wild ride when he suddenly noticed something standing in the bushes ahead of them.

"Wait!" cried Tom. "Wait, Bearskin! Look out!"

But his warning came too late.

An enormous forest spider towered over them. It leaned backwards, as if readying itself to pounce, but started rocking sideways at a peculiar angle. Bearskin lowered Tom to the ground and strolled beneath the spider's belly. He tapped the enormous abdomen with his staff, then tapped it again and roared. A terrified squeak sounded from inside.

"*It's a mechanical!*" cried Tom, suddenly noticing wooden peg-joints dotted all over the spider's massive frame.

"Aye, it's stuck," grunted Bearskin, pointing to its legs that were wedged between tree trunks. Bearskin scaled the wooden spider easily and clambered onto its head. He threw open a hatch, reached inside, and pulled out a skinny animal.

"Got any rope?" shouted Bearskin, nodding at Tom's backpack. Tom found a sturdy loop and threw it up to his friend. Bearskin bound the creature and lowered it back inside the spider, then jumped in after it. He reappeared in an opening in the spider's abdomen and clambered to the ground using a rope ladder.

"Was it part of that patrol?" wondered Tom, staring up at the eight-legged contraption.

Bearskin nodded and angled his staff against the logs, freeing the spider's legs.

"Now it's ours!" Bearskin panted. "Shall we travel to the centre, lad, and pass undetected?"

"You mean we can drive this thing?" gasped Tom.

For the first time since they had met, Tom thought he saw a smile soften Bearskin's features.

CHAPTER 47

At the Turk's Head

orse-head introduced itself to Duman by bowing flamboyantly and dancing in little circles around him. It rubbed its claws together and pointed to the oak tree where Cassie was hiding.

Suddenly, there was a rush of warm air, and Cassie smiled when a familiar presence enveloped her. She turned and saw the white deer, and was about to rush forwards and embrace them, when a terrible fear gripped her. The deer fixed Cassie with a piercing gaze and Cassie fell against the oak tree, suddenly aware that her life depended on hiding the golden feather. She saw an opening in the side of the oak tree and hid the feather in a bed of leaves. The moment she did, her fear left her. Cassie spun round and saw that the deer had vanished.

Suddenly tired of waiting, Cassie stepped from her hiding place and strode towards the Turk's Head. Duman, Cassie noticed, had been carved from a single block of wood. His wooden clothing resembled billowing robes while his shoes were pointed and curled at the ends. But it was Duman's head that held Cassie's attention for it was a smaller version of the building he was standing in front of.

"A grateful forest gatherer thanks you," said Cassie, addressing her skeleton guide. "Go now and never return."

Horse-head didn't move until Duman spoke to it in its own language. The little skeleton slunk away.

"Merhaba," said Duman, bowing politely.

Cassie nodded.

Suddenly, the front of Duman's chest sprang open to reveal a shelf filled with jars and pouches.

"My specials today are Serdor Turmac, Emperor's Blend and some very, very fresh Velvetfire."

His voice was rich and exotic, and when he smiled his wooden face creaked like an old galleon. Cassie hesitated, uncertain what he was selling. "You seem undecided," said Duman. "May I suggest the Velvetfire… ah, but forgive me. Your journey has been long and you must be exhausted. Come. Join me in the Turk's Head. One should always conduct business in comfort. Such a handsome building, don't you think?"

He smiled broadly and revealed a gap in his teeth. Then he turned and led Cassie into the larger gap that was the entrance to the tavern.

The air was thick with the scent of coffee and tobacco, and clouds of incense swirled about the room. Cassie stared and saw several mechanicals lounging on silk cushions, smoking and talking. They were bizarre combinations of humans and animals and wood and bone, and none of them seemed to notice or care that a gatherer was amongst them. A mechanical musician played a melancholy tune by drawing a bow across the strings of its body.

Between the music's hypnotic rhythm and the drone of

conversation, Cassie started to relax, and she joined Duman at a dimly lit table.

"Pin!" shouted Duman. A mechanical boy appeared. He was wearing carved wooden breeches, a shirt and a waistcoat. He ran on pegged ankle joints that creaked like old leather while his head was made out of porcelain. The top of his head was missing, and sticking out from his hollow skull was a bristling selection of needles and pins and several long-handled instruments.

Duman spoke in the language of the forest and the wooden boy scurried away. He returned with an enormous coffee pot and a colourful glass vase, out of which a tube protruded. He offered the tube to Cassie, who refused, uncertain what she was meant to do with it.

"A forest gatherer resisting a water-pipe?" said Duman in surprise. He took the tube and inhaled deeply, and made the liquid in the vase bubble and roll. Smoke streamed from every split in Duman's wooden body, and Cassie grabbed the tube and tried to copy her host. The sudden taste of tobacco made her cough and splutter, and she fell forwards, gasping for air.

"A little coffee for the gatherer!" smiled Duman, handing Cassie a glass. The coffee was bitter and it made Cassie cough even more. "Some Wine of Life for the gatherer!" smiled Duman, helping Cassie again. Cassie nearly choked on the foul-tasting liquid.

"I... I think I need some air," gasped Cassie, rising to leave.

"I think you need to tell me who you really are and why you have risked so much to come here."

Duman's cold, wooden hand grabbed Cassie's wrist.

CHAPTER 48

An Unsteady Start

om and Bearskin squeezed inside the spider's head; Bearskin curled into a furry ball while Tom sat at a wide control panel that curved around the eight glass balls of the spider's eyes. They both had an excellent view of the forest below.

A circular opening led into the spider's abdomen in which their prisoner had been tied. The creature stared as Tom examined all the levers and pedals.

"Well?" said Bearskin. "Can yer make it work, lad? Can yer make the beast move?"

Tom pulled a lever and the spider juddered forwards.

"I think so," said Tom.

"Yer don't sound sure."

"I need more practice – but I think there's a better way."

Tom pointed to a ball set into the ceiling above them. "That ball's filled with living oil," he said. "Cassie and I found some in a gourd on the path."

Bearskin peered suspiciously as the oil slithered back and forth. "This lever's painted red," continued Tom. "It's larger than all the others and it's the only one connected to that ball. Every time I've gone near it, our prisoner's gone mad. Look."

Tom gripped the lever and pretended to pull it. Behind him, in the abdomen, the creature struggled and moaned. "I think this lever releases the living oil. The oil makes the spider move and lets the spider drive itself - like automatic pilot in an aeroplane."

Bearskin frowned at Tom's modern words.

"Why would yer let spider drive itself?" he asked gruffly.

"It'd walk more smoothly, for one thing," said Tom. "It'd travel more quickly, too; more quickly than I could ever drive it. But I'm only guessing, Bearskin. I don't really know for sure."

"How'd we get to the centre if spider were drivin' itself?"

Tom smiled.

"Those legs you freed, the ones that were trapped. They looked quite damaged. With the living oil running through it, maybe the spider would be in pain. Maybe it'd *have* to head back to the place it was built, where it knows it would get repaired."

"The centre!" whispered Bearskin. "Bristlebeard's workshop! Aye, maybe it would!"

"I'm only guessing, Bearskin. I don't know for sure."

"Could yer seize back control if beast ran astray?"

"The lever moves both ways," said Tom.

Bearskin rubbed his muzzle and thought.

"Let's try it," he said. "But be ready to jump if damned thing teks off – or teks against us."

Tom held his breath and drew the lever towards him. The mechanical spider creaked and buckled and sank to the ground. It rose slowly, turned in a circle, and flexed each leg as if it were waking from sleep. Then it limped forwards and moved without guidance. Tom slid Holligold's sword from its sheath and placed it on the control panel, watching as the sliver of wood in its handle spun round and round.

"The needle!" whispered Tom. "Look, Bearskin, it's working! The spider's walking home!"

In the hemisphere of the ball, the peculiar, living essence bubbled and rolled.

CHAPTER 49

A Trader's Agreement

"It was your bony guide who betrayed you," said Duman, drawing smoke through his pipe and smiling.

A pair of dog-headed mechanicals stood in the doorway, blocking Cassie's escape.

"Its suspicions were aroused when you failed to kill with sufficient relish," continued Duman. "And when a certain forest owl shared its wisdom with it, why, your horse-headed guide realised you were not what you claimed to be."

"If Horse-head knew I wasn't a forest gatherer, why didn't it just hand me over to a patrol?" asked Cassie miserably, removing her helmet.

"His slyness is matched only by his greed. He knew that delivering you to a patrol would win him a shiny medal. Delivering you to me, however, wins him this!" Duman held up a bottle filled with life-giving essence.

"My friend said you'd help me, not trade me like a… like a sack of coffee beans!" said Cassie.

"Oh? And what is the name of this friend of yours who claims to know my mind so well?"

"Perkins. Professor Perkins."

Duman thought for a moment then opened the drawer in his chest. He rummaged amongst trinkets and jewellery and produced a circle of silver.

"Perkins. I remember Perkins. Such an irritable fellow! He paid for his bed and his board with this pocket watch then complained about the music, the food and the comfort of his bed. We did, however, share a fondness for tobacco, and we spoke of many things. But that was long ago. Surely he has not been wandering the Ringwood all this time?"

"Yes," said Cassie. "He was caught by…by something horrible and was turned into a monkey."

Duman's eyes rattled in their sockets and his jaw clacked up and down. He placed the professor's watch back inside his chest and offered Cassie a glass of coffee. Cassie took the drink and added several cubes of sugar to it.

"I need to get to the centre," Cassie pleaded. "Will you help me?"

"A forest patrol has already been sent for. It is they who will take you to the centre. Oh, my reward for your capture will be great! And no mere medal, either!"

Cassie suddenly remembered that she had come to trade, and she thrust her hand inside her pocket.

"Will your reward be as great as this?" She placed the golden bird's foot on the table and Duman's jaw fell open.

"By all the leaves, it is true!" he cried. "You have the raven's claw! Do you have the golden feather?"

"I do," smiled Cassie. "But it's safely hidden."

Cassie suddenly realised that the deer had been guiding her movements at the oak tree, and had probably saved her from capture.

"Pin!" shouted Duman, turning towards the door. The

spiky-headed boy appeared and listened attentively as Duman babbled orders at him. Pin scuttled away and Duman sprang to his feet.

"Follow me!" he said, gesturing at Cassie. "The patrol will be here shortly and they *must not* find you. It seems we will be trading after all."

He swirled from the building and Cassie ran to keep up with him.

The cresting rim of the giant moon illuminated the forest. Deep within its shadows, a lantern flickered softly. Pin crouched at the bottom of a rocky embankment, hidden amongst tree roots and gorse. He pulled a curtain of ivy to one side to reveal a deep crevice. Duman passed through it and Cassie squeezed after him, glad to be out of the forest.

The path twisted and turned like a subterranean snake and ran between ancient rock pools and chasms. Cassie stayed close to the flickering lantern light, her goggles illuminating the shadows of the tunnel in peculiar shades of green.

They stopped in front of a tall, iron gate that was scaly with rust. Pin leant forwards and presented his head to his master, who selected a key from the boy's spiky crown. Duman unlocked a leaf-shaped padlock and invited Cassie inside.

Instead of the vast treasure house she had expected see, Cassie was surprised to find herself surrounded by sculptures and carvings and strange, wooden cabinets.

"They are the forbidden wonders from the old times, before Von Rippenbaum arrived," explained Duman, seeing Cassie's expression. "Do not touch them. You would be surprised and alarmed at what they can do."

"Did you say, 'before Von Rippenbaum arrived'?" said Cassie. "I was told Von Rippenbaum invented the forest and everything in it."

Duman laughed and hurried Cassie over to a second

chamber where five wooden spheres rested on stilt-like supports. The spheres were large and hollow, and were a criss-cross weave of wood and metal. Some of the spheres resembled spiky sea-urchins while others resembled lumpy fruit. An opening in the side of each one revealed a seat suspended at the centre, while an anchor secured the spheres to the ground.

"I've seen these shapes before," said Cassie, approaching the nearest ball.

"Impossible!" snapped Duman.

"No, I have. They're pollen! They're huge grains of pollen! There's a poster at school about hay fever with a picture of a pollen grain magnified hundreds of times."

Duman frowned, not understanding Cassie's words.

"These are aerial craft," he insisted. "They catch forest breezes and fly above the treetops, then spiral to the centre. They are forbidden now as Von Rippenbaum insists on being master of the air. That is why you must travel at night. Quickly, now. Choose your device."

Cassie pointed to the spikiest sphere, deciding it looked the sturdiest.

"How long will it take?" she asked, clambering into the seat.

"You will land before dawn," replied Duman, securing a harness around her. "Forest breezes are capricious and I guarantee nothing. If you are caught, I will deny all knowledge of you and your mission. Duman knows nothing and sees nothing, yet Duman knows all and sees all!"

He smiled through the weave of the ball.

"How does this thing land?" asked Cassie, worried that there were no levers or pedals.

"As softly as a rose petal," smiled Duman, closing the hatch.

He secured the anchor to the side of the ball and stepped

backwards. "Now to complete our transaction. The golden feather. Where is it?"

"Not until I'm up there!" said Cassie, pointing at the ceiling.

Duman clacked his mouth in frustration.

"If you trick me I will report you."

"You're probably going to report me anyway," said Cassie.

Duman gasped in horror.

"By all the leaves, I am not! I am Duman the Trader, and traders never betray a sacred trust."

He snapped his fingers and Pin opened a pair of wooden shutters set into the ceiling. Moonlight flooded the chamber and bathed the sphere in delicate light. The spiky ball began to rise.

"May your arms and your wings never be broken," said Duman, bowing politely.

"And may yours, er… never drop off," said Cassie, gripping the edge of the seat.

"If you see your friend again, please give him this," Duman threw Professor Perkins' silver pocket watch up onto Cassie's lap. "A dis-satisfied customer must never over-pay."

Cassie smiled and felt an unexpected wave of gratitude towards the mechanical rogue who had nearly betrayed her.

"What do you want the golden feather for?" she asked, rising quickly.

"Duman has his reasons. I may tell you them one day."

Rocky walls flashed by as the sphere entered a channel in the ceiling. Far below her, Cassie heard Duman cry out, "The feather. Tell me where you have hidden the feather."

"Look in the oak tree!" shouted Cassie.

Duman's laughter rang through the forest as the ball burst from the ground. It hovered for a moment then started to rise up into the trees.

A figure leapt from the undergrowth and jumped onto

the ball. It clung desperately, hidden beneath Cassie's feet, then scrambled higher until it perched on top of the ball. It glared down at the top of Cassie's head and waited.

The ball was climbing faster now, and Cassie gasped when in a sudden, dizzying rush, the sphere burst through the forest canopy and raced into the sky.

The Ringwood lay below her, shimmering like a field of moonlit broccoli. Cassie gasped at the view and at the colourful images of Von Rippenbaum as they flickered across the moon's ghostly surface.

Suddenly, the ball slowed and stopped, as if sensing the night air. It caught a night breeze and bobbed forwards on it like a boat on a river. Cassie sighed and drew her gatherer's coat around her, glad to be drifting so high above the dangers of the Ringwood.

Above her in the dark, a pair of eye sockets glared at her hatefully and started to plot its revenge.

CHAPTER 50

A Surprise Picnic

Bearskin studied the forest carefully, trying to guess when the spider was going make a sudden turn or a plunging dive into the undergrowth. Whenever it did, he would warn Tom and they would both take hold of wooden handles carved into the walls of the control room, waiting for the spider to right itself.

Their prisoner was wedged between the timbers of the abdomen. It lay, bound and gagged, pretending to be asleep.

The view of the forest was hypnotic, and Tom stared as the spider strode through mysterious rivers and passed curiously shaped rocks. Tom suddenly remembered the gnoman's gift and he lifted the knapsack onto his knees and rummaged inside. He discovered a loaf of bread and a slab of cheese, and he divided the food carefully, giving Bearskin the largest pieces. Tom rummaged again and discovered a long-necked bottle.

"Yer really did make friends wi' them littlebeards, didn't

yer!" gasped Bearskin, peering at the bottle and the label that showed a fireball blazing across a starry sky. Bearskin removed the cork with his claw and sniffed the contents.

"Comet Wine!" he said. "The finest in the forest!" He offered Tom the first swig.

"I can't!" said Tom. "I'm not allowed to drink."

"'Oo says?!"

"Everyone! I'm too young. Anyway, I don't like the taste. I tried some once at Christmas and it was horrible."

"There might be some ale," said Bearskin, nodding at the knapsack.

"Beer's *worse!*"

"I were raised on ale," grunted Bearskin. "Water were bad. People died."

"Water's safe now. It comes out of taps in people's houses, hot and cold."

Bearskin snorted in disbelief.

"It's true!" insisted Tom. "Lots of things have changed. Men have even walked on the moon!"

"Now yer take me for a fool," snorted Bearskin, gulping the wine.

When Bearskin saw how earnestly Tom was staring at him, his curiosity got the better of him and he asked, "Yer mean the *real* moon? The one that's fair and silvery in the real world?"

"Yes!" laughed Tom.

"And were those great explorers Englishmen?"

"No, they were American," said Tom.

Bearskin grunted.

"Yer *do* take me for a fool. I've been to the colonies. I've fought in 'em too. I saw no explorers, only farmers an' politicians."

"So you *were* a soldier!" said Tom triumphantly. "I knew you were!"

"More like a fool wi' a head full of nonsense."

The wine had loosened Bearskin's tongue and Tom decided to find out as much as he could about his mysterious friend before the giant's mood changed.

"How long have you been trapped in the forest?" he asked casually. Bearskin took another drink and considered the question.

"A year? A century? I really cannot tell. But I arrived a man; a foot soldier an' guard to a British diplomat of the government of 'is Britannic Majesty King George the Third."

Tom tried to remember when King George the Third had been on the throne but quickly gave up when Bearskin continued, "The ambassador an' 'is men were travellin' through Germany when a terrible thunderstorm drove us from the forest path. A little man appeared an' offered us shelter but the villain led us through the disc an' into this strange forest. That villain were Bristlebeard, an' 'e brought us to a feast sat upon a tree stump. That's when 'is sorcery began. My men were transformed into wood. The ambassador became a toad. Bristlebeard's final spell turned me into the creature you see before you."

Bearskin thumped the bottle on the floor.

"That wasn't your fault!" cried Tom. "You didn't know what Von Rippenbaum was going to do."

"It were my *place* to know!" grumbled Bearskin. "I were a guard 'oo failed in 'is duty."

The giant curled into a ball and said no more, and Tom stared at his furry back, wondering how to comfort his unhappy friend.

Behind him, in the abdomen, the rat-headed prisoner started its escape.

CHAPTER 51

Trapped Landing

The centre of the forest lay hidden behind mist and shadow. Cassie studied the sky, relieved that Von Rippenbaum's hot-air balloon was nowhere to be seen. She settled back in her seat and listened to the night, and between the rocking of the sphere and the wind's gentle rushing, Cassie was soon lulled to sleep.

Above her on the ball, the stowaway cackled with glee. It decided to strike at daybreak when there would be more of its kind to help, and it pressed itself against the sphere and waited.

Circular winds drew the sphere on, every gusting breeze drawing Cassie past autumn and summer to where the green shoots of spring shimmered in the distance.

A keen rush of air blasted through the ball, waking Cassie with a start. She squinted against the bright, morning sunlight and stared in disbelief at what she and the sphere were now circling.

The Ringwood Tree rose from the mist like a prehistoric beast. Its leaves were withered, its branches misshapen, and bark hung off it like rags on a witch. The tree grew at the top of a giant mound that was choked with the tree's snaking roots, and Cassie stared at it in horror and doubted she would ever return home.

Suddenly, the sphere wobbled and started to descend, and Cassie gripped the seat as the forest rushed towards her. Above her, a familiar voice suddenly rasped,

"Hello, *forest gatherer!* No escape now!"

Cassie looked up into the empty eye sockets of Horse-head.

"*You!*" she cried. "*Wh-what are you doing here?! What do you want?*"

"*You!*" cried the skeleton, thrusting its claws through the ball and grabbing Cassie's hair.

The sphere bobbed over a forest meadow that was filled with sinister mechanicals. They stood around a fire, unaware of what was passing over them, until Horse-head reached for the anchor that was attached to the side of the ball.

"Put that back or I'll shoot!" shouted Cassie, grabbing the revolver.

Horse-head cackled and dropped the anchor into the treetops.

The explosion of twigs and branches echoed across the meadow, and every mechanical turned to face the sky.

"*What have you done?!*" screamed Cassie, seeing the commotion below. "*I'm only trying to get home! I'm only trying to escape!*"

"My friends see you now!" shouted Horse-head. "My friends get you now!"

The sphere came to a juddering halt when its anchor-line suddenly caught in a tree. The sphere pulled against its unexpected mooring and tried to tug itself free, when the anchor-line snapped, catapulting the ball high into the air. The sphere rose like a rocket then plunged into the forest, sending Cassie tumbling over and over like laundry in a dryer. The forest roared past her outside.

The sphere stopped in mid-fall, and Cassie sat up, confused by the unexpected silence. Twigs and pinecones poked in at her through the ball, and far below, on the forest floor, Cassie saw Horse-head lying on the ground, silent and unmoving.

Drums sounded in the distance and bloodthirsty voices took up the cry of the hunt. The sphere was caught in the branches of a fir tree where it hung like a peculiar Christmas bauble, dangling at the end of a long branch.

CHAPTER 52

In the Night Forest

The bubbling essence coursed through the mechanical spider, powering every splinter in its wooden frame. The creature crept from shadow to shadow, avoiding the moonlight with predatory caution and feeling its way with the tips of its legs. Seated within the spider's head was Tom, who stared, intrigued, by glimpses of the forest's otherworldly creatures.

He saw ferry boats carrying animal-headed passengers to an island where leaves and branches glittered like stars. He passed burning caves where bird-headed monsters ran back and forth carrying tools of red fire. He saw enormous berries dripping juice into the mouths of robed figures. Tom even thought he saw a shoal of wooden fish flickering through the forest. He leant against the control panel, his mind reeling, and rubbed his eyes. Intending to rest for just a moment, Tom soon joined Bearskin in sleep.

The rat-headed prisoner smiled, knowing that its

219

moment had come. It sliced through the final strands of rope and crept into the cabin. Holligold's sword glinted invitingly on the control panel and the creature held it at Tom's throat. It stared at Bearskin, wondering if it had the speed and the agility to murder both the boy *and* the giant, when it suddenly remembered its master's command: the bloodlings were to be captured, not killed, and anyone disobeying this order would be taken apart peg by peg.

It returned the sword to the control panel and scrambled through the hatch. It launched itself at a passing branch and watched as the spider stalked away. Then it turned and ran, wondering where it should go to raise the alarm.

♦ ♦ ♦   ♦ ♦ ♦   ♦ ♦ ♦

"How long's it been missing?" mumbled Tom, blinded by the morning sunlight.

"Long enough," grumbled Bearskin, studying the frayed rope.

Tom rubbed his neck and groaned. He stared into the forest and saw that the spider was stalking through a forest of wild flowers.

"Spring!" he shouted, checking the sword. "We must've travelled *miles* last night."

"Aye, but rat-'ed's doubtless raised the alarm by now. Gather yer things, lad. I'll not risk capture now."

Tom reached for his knapsack, and was about to throw it over his shoulder when he heard a familiar noise.

"Drums!" he whispered.

The spider crested a bank and emerged onto a wide and cultivated path. Tom recognised the path at once.

"Look!" he whispered. "It's the ceremonial path."

Ahead of them, in the distance, a group of mechanicals swarmed around the base of a fir tree. They were bellowing and pointing at a spiky ball that dangled high above them, and they were piling fresh wood onto a bonfire.

"Get us off this path!" shouted Bearskin as the spider stalked forwards.

"But I think there's someone in that ball!" shouted Tom, glimpsing a shadowy figure.

"They're beyond our 'elp," shouted Bearskin. "Now get us off this path, lad. Quickly!"

Tom hesitated, wishing he could help. He pulled the red lever and felt the spider sink and rise, creaking as the living essence returned to Tom's control. Tom drove the wooden spider back into the forest.

Chapter 53

Out of the Frying Pan

A rock struck the side of the sphere, making it sway. The mechanicals roared with laughter.

Cassie lay inside it, clutching the shoulder-bag and remembering Professor Perkins complimenting her on her resourcefulness. She wondered what the professor would think of her now, alone, afraid and unable to escape. She saw Horse-head below, laughing as it danced around a bonfire.

Tom drove the spider deeper into the forest when a bright ball of light suddenly zigzagged in front of him.

"What's that?" he cried.

"Them drums 'ave got yer bewitched," muttered Bearskin. "I see only flowers."

The light bounded up a hill and formed itself into the outline of a magnificent white stag. The stag pawed at the earth, and Tom felt his fingers curl around the steering handle. A voice echoed strangely in his mind telling him to return to the path.

The spider burst from the brambles and squatted next to the bonfire. The mechanicals cheered with delight, pleased that one of their own had joined in the hunt.

Tom stared ahead of him, too terrified to look at Bearskin. Instead of harsh words and a lecture on the dangers of disobeying him, Tom was amazed when Bearskin threw open the hatch and roared loudly. The cheering mechanicals fell silent.

High above them, Cassie screamed at the sight of the giant spider and almost fainted when a giant bear-man burst from its head.

The bear-man opened his arms and gestured for Cassie to fall into them. Cassie scrambled for the revolver, intending to frighten the beast away, when she suddenly became aware of a familiar presence surrounding her. The white deer were staring up at her, their love, strength and kindness filling her with courage. Cassie put the gun away and suddenly understood that she was meant to trust the fierce-looking bear creature.

Cassie unlatched the door of the sphere and sat on the edge of the opening. The mechanicals rushed forward. The bear-man raised his arms again, and Cassie stifled a scream as she let herself drop.

Sky, trees, mechanicals and forest tumbled wildly as she fell. The bear grew larger as Cassie raced faster, when all of a sudden, Cassie became aware of a second object racing up to meet her. Pain seared across her forehead and Cassie tumbled into unconsciousness as she fell into Bearskin's arms.

Horse-head cackled with glee. Its aim had been true - the rock it had thrown had struck its target – and that pleased the little skeleton.

Bearskin dropped into the cabin and slammed the hatch behind him. He tucked Cassie's body deep inside his sash and shouted,

"Go!"

Tom rammed the lever forward and sent the spider scuttling up the path. The mechanicals ran beneath it. Tom was about to turn and ask Bearskin who they had rescued when smoke began to curl around his feet. Flames flickered between the floorboards and the wooden casing began to crackle.

"I must've got too close to that bonfire!" he shouted. "I think we're on fire!"

"Quick!" bellowed Bearskin. "Tek us into the forest, lad! Get us off this path!"

CHAPTER 54

The Nest

A plume of smoke billowed from the spider as it staggered through the trees. Horse-head raced after it, determined not to let his prize escape him for a second time.

"Out yer come!" shouted Bearskin, hauling Tom clear of the cabin. They stood on the spider's wooden head, swaying wildly.

"Tek 'old!" shouted Bearskin, half-pushing, half-lifting Tom onto an approaching tree branch. Tom clung to it desperately, uncertain of the drop beneath him. Bearskin dangled next to him, watching as the spider staggered away.

"I gave it back control," panted Tom. "It must be in terrible pain. What if it burns to death?"

Bearskin hoisted Tom into the tree.

"I'll track it later," said the giant. "There's water nearby. Reckon it's headin' there."

They watched in silence as the mechanicals passed beneath them.

"Good thing that smoke 'id us," muttered Bearskin.

"The figure in the ball!" cried Tom, suddenly remembering their rescue. Bearskin patted the bulge in his sash and clambered to the ground. Tom scrambled after him as Bearskin recovered his staff, which he had thrown from the spider moments earlier. Chiffchaff fluttered nervously around them before disappearing into the trees. Bearskin chased after it.

They eventually came to a wide forest stream were Bearskin paused and crouched upon a rock. He moistened a cloth, parted his sash, and started to wash the blood from Cassie's wound.

Tom stood on tip-toe, trying to see in.

"Who did we rescue?" he wondered, too small to see anything.

"Some kind o' gatherer," said Bearskin uncertainly, pressing a leaf to Cassie's cut.

"What's a gatherer?"

"They collect old an' damaged unnaturals an' haul 'em off to the centre. No wonder the others were tryin' to kill it."

"Will it be all right?"

"Aside from an artilleryman's 'eadache; aye, it'll live. But why did yer go back, lad? Why did yer return to the path?"

"I'm sorry," said Tom. "There was a weird deer glowing with light. It ran out in front of the spider and I…I just felt that I had to follow it. Now I've lost the spider *and* Holligold's sword."

"Littlebeards'll find you another sword. As fer the deer, 'oo knows what dark influences surround us at the centre. The Ringwood Tree crackles wi' energy, thick enough ter spread on bread. No one's ter blame when spells are the enemy."

"But you blame yourself for the death of your friends," said Tom, remembering the figures on the tree stump.

"Th-that were different," rumbled Bearskin. "I were a

soldier then, 'oo failed in 'is duty."

"But spells were the enemy."

"It weren't the same," growled Bearskin.

"Grown-ups always say one thing and then do another," muttered Tom. "It's not fair. I can't fight spells any more than you can, but you tell me not to feel bad about it! What's the difference?"

Bearskin fell silent and didn't speak again until he had brought Tom to the edge of a wide and circular plain. Rising at its centre stood the mound and the Ringwood Tree.

"Bristlebeard's lair," whispered Bearskin.

Tom stared at the mound and at the path that spiralled around it, and started to wonder whether he was brave enough to even approach it. He stepped back into the forest, trembling with fear.

Bearskin turned away and brought Tom to a rock that was hidden beneath a curtain of ivy. Bearskin drew the tangling leaves to one side to reveal a dark and jagged opening. The sound of clanking metal and faint snoring could be heard.

"Gnomen warriors," whispered Bearskin. "The entire Yellowcap army are scattered 'ereabouts. We meet at moonrise."

"Is the battle tonight?" asked Tom nervously.

"Aye."

Bearskin wandered over a group of pine trees and scrambled up the tallest of them. He sat on a sturdy bough and plaited several branches together until he had formed a broad and ragged nest. Then he reached above him and built a shaggy roof. Tom joined him.

"Spread the gnomen blanket out," said the giant.

Tom pulled the blanket from his backpack and gasped in disbelief when Holligold's sword tumbled into his lap. The sword's jewelled hilt glinted in the sunlight.

"I left this in the spider!" gasped Tom. "There wasn't

time to pack it."

"Littlebeard magic," sniffed Bearskin suspiciously. "Now move aside while I lay out our patient."

Bearskin opened his sash and lifted Cassie onto the blanket. A sliver of sunlight fell across her face and Tom grabbed hold of a branch and stopped himself falling out of the tree. The gnomen prophecies, he realised, were beginning to come true.

CHAPTER 55

Revolution!

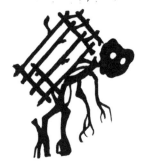

Two add two add two, then add another two… no, add *four!*" said the mechanical, whose wooden head was a collection of several carved vegetables. The creature squealed at its own cleverness and stared through the cage with its sprouty eyes.

The figure in the cage looked away in disgust. "It doesn't know the answer!" the mechanical sang. "I win! I win!" It rattled its parsnips with excitement.

"Of course I know the answer!" snapped the figure. "I am Professor Augustus Perkins; classicist, scholar, man of science… and miserable fairground attraction."

The witch, who was sitting nearby, was watching him closely.

"Go away," sighed the professor. "Go and boil your head in water, remembering to save the juices for soup."

The wooden bars of the cage suddenly sprang into life and several snaking tendrils wrapped themselves around the professor's legs and dangled him upside down.

"Ten! *Ten!*" gasped the professor. "The answer is ten! Now release me! This instant!"

The tendrils withdrew and the professor slumped to the floor. His tormentors laughed and wandered away.

The professor's journey through the forest had been long and difficult, with the witch parading him through a variety of fairgrounds and taverns. The witch itself was wary of the professor now and would rarely let him out of the cage – or out if its sight.

The witch had travelled quickly, leaping from tree branch to tree branch like an oversized squirrel. It had stopped on the edge of the summer forest where the oppressive heat made the professor faint with thirst. At night, he would think about Cassie; how shamelessly he had lied to her, how foolishly he had risked her life and how intolerant he had been of her youthful high-spiritedness. He prayed that she had heard the message in his song, had reached the centre of the forest and was now safely home.

A sudden noise announced the arrival of yet another forest patrol. The witch jumped up on its stumpy legs and advertised the professor's talents in the rickety language of the Ringwood. The patrol stopped and peered into the cage, and the witch decided that her pet would give a rare outdoor performance. It unfastened the cage and backed away as Professor Perkins tumbled out, a sprouting tendril wrapping itself around his tail.

The mechanicals sat in a semi-circle and waited.

Instead of the usual verses from Shakespeare or the low, comic songs his audience always preferred, Professor Perkins decided to try something different. He would list Von Rippenbaum's crimes and would unsettle the creatures. Arguments would begin, and once his audience was distracted, the professor would slip into the forest.

He raised his arms and shouted, "Tyranny, like hell, is not easily conquered!"

The mechanicals gasped.

"But even the most unassailable empires crumble and fall!"

The mechanicals were transfixed.

"Observe the humble ant," continued the professor, trembling with excitement. "Individually they are weak and vulnerable, but when they join together even the mightiest forest beast may be overthrown!"

"Ants attacking beasts?" shouted a voice. "I've never seen that."

"Couldn't happen," said the skeleton of a toad.

Murmurs of agreement rippled through the audience.

"Of course it could!" snapped the professor. "Driver ants of the genus *Dorylus* are predatory and aggressive, and will, on occasion, fell a sick or unwary cow."

"Sing us a song!" croaked a voice. "A funny song!"

"No. Listen to me!" snapped the professor. "I have something important to tell you."

He noticed that the witch's sightless head had turned towards him, and he suddenly shouted,

"Rise like lions after slumber
In unvanquishable number,
Shake your chains to earth like dew
Which in sleep have fallen on you
You are many —
He is few!"

The creatures clapped politely.

"No, no, no! This is not a poetry recital!" cried the professor. "Can you not hear the fire of revolution in my words? Rise up and fight!"

"Against the ants?" asked the toad.

"Against *Von Rippenbaum!*" shouted Professor Perkins.

"Rise up and fight! Strike the tyrant down!"

The tendril around the professor's tail suddenly hoisted him off the ground. The mechanicals threw sticks, stones and pinecones.

The witch cackled with pleasure.

"I-I spoke in jest!" cried the professor. "You – *Ow!* – misunderstood me. I was merely *–Ow!* – acting – *Ow!* – the fool. Please, let me finish! You will be amused by my witty ending."

"Yes, let him finish," said a voice quietly.

A gasp of astonishment spread through the crowd, and the hail of missiles stopped. From his upside-down view of the world, Professor Perkins saw a pair of leather boots come striding towards him, and he turned to thank the mysterious stranger. He froze in terror when he found himself staring up into the dark and bristling features of a smiling Hans Von Rippenbaum.

Chapter 56

Two Adventures

Tom stared in amazement, determined to tell Cassie how much he had missed her – if only he could find the right words.

"Tom?" croaked Cassie, her eyelids fluttering open.

"Careful," he warned her. "You might have a bit of a headache."

Cassie squeezed Tom's hand, then squeezed it some more, then squeezed it again until Tom cried out with pain.

"It really *is* you!" smiled Cassie, peering into his face. "You're real! I'm not dreaming! And you're not made of wood! *Oh, Tom! Tom! It really is you!*" She fell forwards and threw her arms around him. Tom hugged her back, suddenly aware that his stumbling words of affection wouldn't be needed.

They stayed like that for a while, each drawing strength from the other's presence, until Tom suggested they should eat. He emptied the contents of the gnomen knapsack onto the woollen blanket, and discovered a leather pouch filled with fresh water. He also found some apples, another block of cheese and a bunch of chewy Burgoroot. Tom spread the food and started to recount his adventures in the forest. Cassie smiled, pressing Bearskin's leaf to her forehead. She dropped it when Tom passed her the handwritten note Bearskin had delivered to him, the note written by their real grandfather.

"*So the Grandfather you met at his house was...?*" she whispered.

Tom nodded.

"But Tom, you had tea with a mechanical. Couldn't you tell it wasn't Grandfather?"

"I-I just thought he looked ill or was tired. It sounded just like him. It gave me tea and cake."

"Oh, the perfect distraction," groaned Cassie.

She rubbed her eyes and sighed. "I'm sorry. I'm not blaming you. Some of those things do look almost human." She shivered at the memory of the "boy" Professor Perkins had examined in the tea house, and suddenly noticed the branches of the Ringwood Tree in the distance. "Is that where Grandfather is now – under that tree with Mum and Dad?"

"Von Rippenbaum's lair, yes," said Tom, deciding not to mention the essence or the fact that Von Rippenbaum needed blood to make his creatures live.

"Is Professor Perkins with you?" asked Tom suddenly. "Is he still–"

"Alive?" interrupted Cassie. "I haven't strangled him if that's what you mean, although I should have after I discovered what he was up to."

Cassie closed her eyes and asked Tom to open the shoulder-bag. She reached inside it and removed the bandages from the bottle, before handing it to Tom. The tea-coloured image of the Victorian gentleman swam to the surface, the image glowing as it moved. Tom stared, and listened as Cassie told him about the stick creature and how it had captured the professor, and how she had found the bottle shortly afterwards.

"If only he'd told me what he was up to," said Cassie. "I would've helped him."

"You still can," said Tom. "Keep the bottle safe and give it to him when you see him."

"I don't think the professor'll be seeing anyone ever again. No one *human*, anyway."

"No, he will!" said Tom. "His symbol appeared on the parchment at the centre. Yours was there too. That's how I knew I'd see you again."

"Parchment? Symbol? What're you on about?"

Tom smiled, suddenly aware that he hadn't finished telling Cassie of his adventures underground. He told her of the gnomen's prophecy, how it spoke of a boy journeying into the mound in an attempt to destroy the giant gourd.

"We're going straight home, Tom, not hunting for gourds," said Cassie. "What if one of those creatures catches you?"

"But I promised, Cassie. I promised I'd help the gnomen."

"Let them do it themselves!"

"Their prophecy said it would be me!"

Cassie suddenly realised how much Tom had changed, how the frightened little boy she had lost near the edge of the forest was now filled with courage and determination and an all too familiar stubbornness that Cassie recognised only too well.

"All right," she sighed. "We can hunt for this gourd thing, but only if it's safe. And only if I come with you. *And only after we've found Mum and Dad.* Agreed?"

"Agreed," mumbled Tom, remembering how his symbol was the only one that appeared inside the mound.

CHAPTER 57

To the Centre

on Rippenbaum rode upon a mechanical skeleton, steering it expertly from a saddle with stirrups and reins. He had constructed the beast himself and had built it to resemble the skeleton of a giant chicken. Rods and wires clicked noisily, and nestling in its ribcage was a tube filled with the life-giving oil.

Professor Perkins dangled upside-down from the rooster's neck bones, bound by his hands and his feet. The professor replayed the events of the last few minutes and wondered why the witch had acted so foolishly.

The witch had insisted on payment for the professor, and Von Rippenbaum had poured several drops of essence into the witch's claw. The witch had gestured for more and had held out its other claw. Von Rippenbaum had reached inside a second pouch and had hurled a handful of dust into the witch's face. The witch had screamed and had dissolved in a bubbling puddle, while the terrified mechanicals had

236

stampeded in all directions.

"Where are the children?" asked Von Rippenbaum calmly.

"Water!" gasped the professor. "I must have water!"

Von Rippenbaum laughed.

"If you do not tell me where the children are, I will take you to my workshop and fix your head upon a spike."

"Then I choose the spike and welcome death as a friend!" shouted Professor Perkins.

Von Rippenbaum laughed again.

"Oh, but the spike is mechanical and is attached to something quite monstrous! You would live forever, my dear little monkey, or for as long as it amused me. Death would remain a stranger to you."

Professor Perkins stared in horror but said no more, so Von Rippenbaum tugged on the reins and guided the giant rooster home.

The skeleton leapt over ditches and gullies, its bones rattling rhythmically as it ran. Pain and exhaustion quickly sent Professor Perkins tumbling into unconsciousness, and when he next became aware of his surroundings he was astonished to see that the day was almost over. The Ringwood Tree loomed ahead of him, its jagged outline as ugly as he remembered it. He pleaded for mercy and tried to wriggle free but Von Rippenbaum laughed and urged his diabolical beast on.

The rooster burst from the forest and sped across the plain. The patrolling mechanicals parted noisily and let their master through. Monstrous fish-eyes, telescopic lenses and other sinister sockets crowded in to see what Von Rippenbaum had captured. The rooster climbed the spiral path and trotted beneath giant tree roots that grew like twisted sticks of liquorice. The creature ran higher until it came to an opening in the side of the hill, which it entered without pausing.

The rooster ran until Von Rippenbaum heaved on its reins and jumped from the saddle. He cut the professor's bonds and dragged him by a rope into a large and spacious chamber.

"Wh-where are we?" gasped the professor, blinking at the walls of a domed ceiling that was filled with mummified bodies.

"You stand at the heart of the forest!" smiled Von Rippenbaum. "Come, re-acquaint yourself with an old friend."

He dragged Professor Perkins over to the far wall and stopped in front of an alcove in which a figure stood. Tree shoots grew from the figure's head and ran along the wall until they merged with the stalk of a giant gourd.

"No!" cried Professor Perkins, recognising the figure immediately. "This really cannot be! This really *shouldn't* be!"

CHAPTER 58

Hidden Scent

The mechanical creature circled the tree, its lantern eyes and dagger teeth glinting viciously in the sun. It resembled a bizarre crocodile and its jointed tail swished noisily before the creature clanked away.

Birdsong returned to the forest.

Tom and Cassie remained in the tree all day, Cassie dozing in her gatherer's coat while Tom memorised Holligold's drawing of the chambers within the mound. The forest stirred restlessly, as if it knew of the battle to come, and its fretful murmuring eventually woke Cassie.

"My headache's gone!" she announced, sitting up and stretching. "When's your friend coming back, that bear-man? It's almost dark."

"Soon," said Tom. "And his name's Bearskin."

Cassie frowned.

"Is he really on our side?" she asked cautiously. "He looked so fierce."

239

"He used to be a soldier and he fought in America when George the Third was on the throne. I don't know when that was so I can't work out how long he's been trapped here."

"George the Third!" spluttered Cassie. "He lived *centuries* ago, back in the seventeen-hundred and somethings. Has Bearskin been wandering the forest all that time?"

"I suppose so. But he can hide almost anywhere and he can slip past almost anyone, and he's really strong and clever. He must have been a good soldier."

"He'll have to be good to get past those things guarding the mound. There are hundreds of them going round and round and round."

"One hundred an' twenty-seven, if yer count the patrols," rumbled a voice near Cassie's head.

Cassie froze and saw a dark pair of eyes gazing at her through the branches of the nest. Their owner began removing the shelter one stalk at a time.

Tom spent the next few moments telling Cassie not to be afraid when she saw Bearskin close up. But his warning came too late. Bearskin's head and shoulders were looming over her. Cassie stared at him, open-mouthed.

"Th-this is my sister," said Tom, praying Cassie wouldn't scream or jump from the tree. "Her name's Cassie. Cassie Trenham."

"Aye, I recognised 'er scent," said Bearskin.

"My *scent*?!" said Cassie. "Well you're no walking perfume counter."

Bearskin's eyes narrowed.

"I meant yer *hidden* scent, given off by ev'ry livin' thing - the scent that's as clear as a footprint. That's why I left yer in this pine tree. The resin hides yer smell."

"Oh," said Cassie. "I see. I'm sorry. I didn't mean... Anyway, thanks for rescuing me. I thought I was going to die."

Bearskin grunted.

"The gnomen are gatherin'," he said. "It's time to go. Follow me."

Bearskin turned and clambered to the ground.

"Why did you say he smelled?!" hissed Tom.

"I thought he was saying I did!" whispered Cassie. "Anyway, he *does* smell. Like a leafy old bonfire. And there was something moving about in his fur."

"That's Chiffchaff, his lookout. It's also his pet."

Tom tied Holligold's sword around his waist and scrambled out of the tree. Cassie climbed after him.

They followed Bearskin into a complex of muddy ditches that were deep and gloomy, and overgrown with gorse. As they walked, Bearskin explained that they had entered the ancient defences of the winter Bluecaps, dug when they had fought Von Rippenbaum centuries earlier. The area was cursed, Bearskin told them, the soil still tainted with the blood of their dead.

Mist drifted lazily out of derelict shelters and swirled curiously about their feet. Fire-blackened stones lay scattered across the floor. Rusting cooking pots hung from hooks, ready for use. The atmosphere was heavy and oppressive and the shadows seemed filled with a mournful presence.

Tom and Cassie broke into a trot, and sighed with relief when Bearskin led them out of the ditches and back into the forest. Bearskin parted the undergrowth with his staff and revealed a finger-like buttress of rock that pointed into the trees. The giant told Tom and Cassie to stay where they were while he shambled over to the outcrop. He gave three long whistles, and a Yellowcap warrior appeared and bowed graciously. Cassie jumped in surprise.

"Tom!" she whispered. "I've seen one of those little men before. It was in that museum I told you about. The man I saw was dead."

"Only one Yellowcap's ever been captured," said Tom. "And that was Holligold's husband. This is his sword."

"Well I'm sure the museum curator didn't kill him," said Cassie. "And I know he'll be happy to return the body to the gnomen."

Tom nodded sadly and thought of Holligold.

Bearskin turned and gestured for Tom and Cassie. They ran forwards and the gnoman warrior bowed and led them beneath the rock. Bearskin remained outside, too large to scramble after them.

"Thomas Trenham!" cried Captain Jussell as Tom and Cassie tumbled beneath the rock. "How good it is to see you! Lord Rowanbole sends his greetings."

A leafy crest glowed on Captain Jussell's armour.

"And I see that the forest fates have returned your sister to you."

He bowed at Cassie, who lay on her hands and knees, her back pressed uncomfortably against the low ceiling. "We must move swiftly," said the captain. "The moon is rising and we must prepare for battle. Do you have the leaves?"

Tom frowned.

"For the tea," added the captain. "Without them we are lost."

"I-I don't understand," said Tom. "What leaves? I don't have any leaves. There weren't any in the knapsack."

"But the brew!" cried Captain Jussell. "The alchemical brew! You were entrusted with its safekeeping. You promised you'd keep it safe."

"Did I?" said Tom.

CHAPTER 59

Von Rippenbaum's Lair

"What is this trickery?!" cried Professor Perkins, staring in horror at the figure in the alcove. "I bade farewell to this gentleman not five days ago, yet here he stands at the centre of the forest!"

"What you bade farewell to was my finest creation: a copy of this fool made out of wire, wax and wood!"

Professor Perkins reeled in horror.

"Then the man I took to be Professor Trenham, the figure whose hand I clasped shortly before entering the disc, was...?"

"A mechanical? Yes!" crowed the toymaker. "Quite magnificent, don't you think? I achieved new heights of realism with that one!"

Von Rippenbaum dragged Professor Perkins over to a circular table that stood beneath the gourd and tied the little monkey to one of its bowed legs. "I do not usually honour my ingredients an explanation," he said, "but as you seem to be an intelligent specimen, I offer you that privilege."

Professor Perkins slumped to the ground as the toymaker continued, "Too long has my genius gone unrecognised, my entry into your world blocked by intolerance and hatred."

"And several feet of soil," muttered the professor.

"Recently, I met two bloodlings, newly arrived specimens who were so sad and so desperate to return home."

"The children's parents!" cried the professor. "So you *did* meet them! What have you done with them, you fiend? Where are they? Tell me this instant!"

"I befriended them," smiled Von Rippenbaum, slyly. "That friendliness was rewarded when I learned that the disc had been uncovered and was now hanging upon the door of an elderly English gentleman. The children's mother even showed me paintings of the disc's new owner. And what magnificent paintings they were! Such brightness of colour! Such depth of tone! I had never seen the like. They proved extremely useful."

Professor Perkins began to understand what had happened and he finished Von Rippenbaum's story for him.

"Those 'magnificent paintings' you admired are called *photographs*," the monkey explained. "From them you were able to create an astonishing likeness of Professor Trenham, which you sent through into our world, forcing the real professor into the Ringwood."

"How clever you are!" smiled Von Rippenbaum. "Though perhaps not clever enough. You spent an entire week in the company of my mechanical, whose every thought and movement was controlled by me!"

Professor Perkins suddenly remembered how Professor Trenham's mood had changed during the second week of their acquaintance, something he assumed was due to illness or exhaustion.

"What are your intentions towards the children?" he

snapped. "What evil do you intend to inflict upon them?"

Von Rippenbaum patted the giant gourd.

"My forest needs life. My mechanicals need life. The blood of living things provides it. Human blood is best but children's blood is better, while the blood of an entire family is... oh, it is beyond price. Imagine my fury when the children escaped the ceremonial path. They must and they will be purified!"

"Murderer!" shouted Professor Perkins, tugging at his ropes. "Insane, black-hearted murderer!"

"When you witness the procedure for yourself, my genius will be revealed to you. I may even allow you to help. Yes! You can restrain the children once the transference begins. There is usually some tiresome struggling at the beginning but it does not last very long."

"I would rather *die* than help you!"

"No, you will live, my dear little monkey, in one form or another. You will live to witness a new generation of my magnificent mechanicals spreading far beyond the confines of the Ringwood!"

A wild boar suddenly burst into the room. It was wooden and held together by scraps of armour and leather. Its hooves clacked noisily as it walked upright across the floor.

"Gnomen, sir!" it grunted. "Hundreds of 'em! Yellowcaps, gatherin' for battle."

The boar's marble eyes swivelled nervously between Von Rippenbaum and the floor.

"*Gnomen?*" spat the toymaker. "Haven't those miserable little soil-scrapers tasted enough death?"

"Don't know, sir, but they're hidin' in the shadows and shoutin'."

"Shouting?! What are they shouting?"

"Insults, sir. Directed at you."

"And how do they insult me?!"

The creature hesitated and stepped backwards, its eyes now fixed upon the floor.

"Th-they say that your time has come, and that you enjoy the company of pigs and that you often smell like one. I wrote the rest of the insults on here."

It handed its master a long list of paper.

"Idiot!" shouted the toymaker, ripping the list into shreds.

Von Rippenbaum placed his hands on the belly of the gourd, and a three-dimensional image of the plain, the mound and the Ringwood Tree appeared on the surface of the table. Professor Perkins studied the miniature landscape in amazement and stared as the mechanical army circled the mound.

"Draw back every patrol," snapped Von Rippenbaum, jumping from the table. "Draw them back to here and put them into attack formation." He pointed to the mound. "Position the fireworks here, the big ones, and blast those soil-scrapers out into the open. Tell the orchestra to gather on the mound. I want the gnomen to enjoy their final moments."

The boar bowed awkwardly and left the room.

"We must end our pleasant discussion," smiled Von Rippenbaum. "Watch the map closely, for you are about to witness yet another of my triumphs. When I return, you will tell me where the children are."

A dog suddenly bounded into the room. It was small and mechanical and appeared quite ordinary apart from one horrible feature: Von Rippenbaum had given it the head of an old man. A crown perched on its head, and almost fell off when the creature greeted its master.

"Emperor Joseph!" laughed Von Rippenbaum. "Down, emperor! I want you to guard this prisoner when I am gone. His mind is teeming with thoughts of escape."

The man-headed dog snarled at the professor.

"My mind is teeming with the horror of your grotesquery," snapped Professor Perkins, staring at the dog.

"Emperor Joseph, grotesque? Perhaps, but it is remarkably satisfying to be able to kick the likeness of the man who once ordered the destruction of my forest workshop all those years ago."

"So the emperor *did* order your death!" gasped the professor. "Why, Von Rippenbaum? History did not tell us."

The toymaker's smile faded.

"The emperor took me for a common thief and accused me of stealing a valuable artefact from the royal treasury. I never steal. I merely encourage the habit in others. Besides, the disc was a marvel too wondrous for those fools. It was my sacred duty to recover it."

Von Rippenbaum walked towards the door. "Speaking of fools," he added, "you asked me about the welfare of the bloodlings' parents."

He smiled and pointed at the ceiling, and Professor Perkins gazed above him.

High above him, standing side by side between the roots of the Ringwood Tree, were the mummified remains of Mr and Mrs Trenham.

Chapter 60

A Strange Brew

om's hands trembled nervously as he searched his pockets. He shook his head miserably.

"Then we have lost," said Captain Jussell.

"Wait!" said Cassie. "What's that, Tom, dangling round your neck?"

She pointed to a bulge in Tom's shirt.

"Dr Albertus!" cried Tom. "He *did* give me something, when we said goodbye. I'd completely forgotten!"

Tom opened his shirt and removed a leather pouch. He handed it to Captain Jussell, who grasped it joyfully.

"What is it?" asked Tom.

"I suppose Doctor Albertus was right not to tell you, in case you were captured and interrogated," explained the gnomen. "This pouch contains the doctor's most recent and most remarkable discovery: a compound of roots and herbs and other, more mysterious elements, which the doctor has called 'Shadow Tea'. It briefly transforms those who drink it into pale and ghostly outlines, and is the magical subterfuge we will use to cross the plain."

"But why did he give it to me?" wondered Tom. "I usually end up losing things."

Cassie nodded.

"Was it not predicted that you would arrive at the centre? Who better, then, to carry such precious cargo?"

Tom smiled proudly but Cassie wriggled uncomfortably against the low, rocky ceiling. Captain Jussell sensed her discomfort and said,

"Perhaps we should wait outside. The warriors will be gathering."

They emerged into a forest of glinting swords, spears and arrow heads. Standing at the edge of the gathering was Bearskin. He was leaning against a tree and was staring at the moon, lost in thought.

"Moon's up," he rumbled quietly as Tom approached him. Tom knew straightaway that something was wrong. "I 'ave to leave yer, lad," Bearskin said quietly. "The gnomen'll fetch yer to yer gran'father now."

"*Leave me?*" cried Tom. "Why, Bearskin? We're almost at the centre."

Bearskin ignored Tom's questions and continued, "Keep to the left when crossin' the plain. You'll avoid the wet ground. An' don't get drawn into any fightin'. Battlefield's no place for children. They stand when they shouldn't an' run when they oughtn't an' find themselves takin' musket shot meant fer others…"

He fell silent and stared at the moon.

"But you're the best soldier we've got!" cried Tom, "The best I've ever seen!"

"Oh? An' what is it you've seen? The dead and the dyin' an' the fiery weapons of war? I can tek yer no further, lad. I'm sorry. "

The giant turned and slipped into the night.

"I think he's shell-shocked," said Cassie, placing a hand on Tom's arm, "or cannon-shocked or whatever kind of shock they had in his day."

"What do you mean? He said he was going to help me. I thought he was my friend."

"He *is* your friend. That's why he waited to say goodbye."

"But Bearskin isn't frightened of anything. Why would he leave me now?"

"Because he knows you're in safe hands."

"But how am I going to get inside the mound? *I'm* the frightened one!"

"Funny sort of fear that got you this far," said Cassie.

"That was Bearskin. He made me feel brave."

"No, that was you, Tom, standing up for yourself at last."

"I still feel scared."

"Brave people do."

"*You* never do!"

"I hide it well," said Cassie. "Sometimes you have to if there's something that needs to be done – like getting out of this place."

A gnoman appeared and handed them some Shadow Tea. It glistened like tar and smelt of the forest, and Cassie wrinkled her nose. "Watch me hide my fear," she said, downing the drink in a single gulp.

A rush of warmth spread through her body and Cassie fell against a tree.

"Cassie!" cried Tom, jumping forwards. "Cassie! Where are you? Are you all right?"

An invisible finger tapped him on his forehead and Tom leapt backwards in surprise.

"No, *hide* your fear," laughed Cassie's voice from the empty space in which she had been standing.

CHAPTER 61

Shadow and Flame

A note sounded deep in the forest and it was followed by another and another. Torchlight circled the plain and a bloodthirsty cry filled the air. The gnomen rushed forwards, their pale, transparent bodies shimmering like fish. Tom went to run with them but Captain Jussell caught him by his coat-tails.

"Wait!" he shouted. "Let the warriors draw the mechanicals away from the mound."

Tom returned to the hiding place.

"Is Lord Rowanbole here?" asked Tom, staring across the plain.

"Lord Rowanbole went to seek the help of the summer gnomen," said Captain Jussell, "though they will not offer any. What need have we of their help? See how my warriors advance!"

To the mechanicals watching from the mound it seemed as if a low, creeping mist was rolling towards them. They remained unconcerned and unaware that the gnomen's attack had already begun, and their lenses remained fixed upon the shadows of the forest.

High above them, in the shadow of the Ringwood Tree, Hans Von Rippenbaum assembled his orchestra. He had made the instruments himself and had carved them into the shapes of real and imaginary animals. The instruments snapped and snarled, and limped along on limbs of bone and metal. Von Rippenbaum stepped between them, raised his arms and commanded,

"Play *fortissimo* and fill every heart with terror!"

He lowered his arms and the mound erupted in noise.

The gnomen warriors hesitated, unprepared for the demonic sound. But the quick, stabbing rhythm and the hurrying swirl of notes turned their terror into rage, and they raced towards their goal.

Invisible gnomen passed beneath a mechanical crane-fly and unwound a coil of rope. The long-legged mechanical flailed against the gnomen's hammer blows before toppling over. The other mechanicals bellowed in confusion.

"Devilry, sir!" shouted the boar commander over the sounds of battle. "The gnomen are here. They're runnin' amongst us! But they're as clear as glass!"

Von Rippenbaum stared with fury and skidded down the mound to a line of tubes that ringed the hill like a collar. Filling each tube with powder, he muttered darkly into each one, then stood back and ordered the tubes to be lit.

Sheep-skulled creatures held glowing tapers to short fuses, and a colourful ring of lights shot into the air. The lights burst open like hundreds of deadly flower-heads and covered the running gnomen with hot, burning paint.

"Finish them!" screamed Von Rippenbaum. "*Finish them all and bring me their heads!*"

The Yellowcap army stood revealed.

CHAPTER 62

A Summons to War

The terrified warriors ran for the safety of the tree line, when several enormous shapes loomed out at them.

"Battle badgers!" gasped an astonished Captain Jussell. "Von Rippenbaum has summoned battle badgers. My warriors are trapped. It is over."

The creatures trundled forwards, felling trees as they walked. Spears bristled from their sides like porcupine quills and a pagoda-shaped tower rose from each back. Shadowy figures rushed back and forth inside the towers, driving the devices on.

"Run!" yelled Captain Jussell as the mechanicals trundled nearer. "Run into the forest! Flee! Flee!"

"But the prophecy!" shouted Tom.

"The prophecy must be wrong! Return to the rock and wait under it. Whoever survives this will find you there. If no one survives… then may the forest gods protect you."

Captain Jussell unsheathed his sword and was about to

join his men on the plain when Cassie screamed.

A battle badger had seen them and it came trundling towards them, its horns herding them back against a tree.

"I think it's going to kill us!" whispered Tom, staring at the enormous, blunt snout. "It's going to run forwards and squash us!"

Cassie stared into the creature's eyes and saw that they were two iron braziers filled with burning coals. She darted forwards and raced between the creature's legs.

"*What are you doing?!*" cried Tom.

"Escaping, what do you think? Now run, Tom. Hide your fear and *run beneath its legs!*"

But before Tom could move, a bright beam of light illuminated Cassie and she jumped and stood still.

"Would any of you fearsome warriors like a lift?" cried a familiar voice, laughing down at them mischievously.

♦ ♦ ♦　　♦ ♦ ♦　　♦ ♦ ♦

Up on the mound, the wooden boar stood at its master's side.

"They're runnin' away, sir!" it snorted happily. "We've got 'em on the run!"

Von Rippenbaum swept his spyglass over the plain.

"I don't remember summoning battle badgers," he murmured. "But they are welcome."

The toymaker's brow suddenly creased. "*No!*" he breathed angrily, refocusing the lens. "*Those badgers attack us!*"

Von Rippenbaum scuttled into the mound and entered a sordid chamber filled with books, manuscripts and a giant, bubbling still whose glass was cracked and mouldy. Glass eyeballs, wax noses and wire fingers lay on every surface, while carved, wooden limbs dangled from the ceiling. Von Rippenbaum set the limbs swinging as he stalked over to the fireplace, where a bubbling cauldron hissed and smoked. He peered into the foul liquid and mumbled,

"Twisting roots and lumpen clay,

Form the shoots of your decay.

Nightshades darken, spirits pall,

Creatures harken to my call!"

He drew two mud-soaked fingers across his forehead and leant closer.

"Eyes of serpent, count of three,

Master's servants… *return to me!*"

A bundle of twigs floating in the filthy water suddenly twitched into life. "Return to me and *fight!*" shouted the toymaker. "Return to me and *fight!* Return to me and *fiiiight!*"

The powerful spell radiated throughout the forest, and every creature filled with the magical essence, whether it had been built for amusement or for terror, suddenly felt itself being drawn towards the battle. Screws, wire, limbs and wax – anything touched by the life-giving oil in Von Rippenbaum's workshop – sprang into life, and a line of miniature debris skittered across the floor.

CHAPTER 63

A Surprising Meeting

Captain Jussell grasped the rope-ladder and scaled up the side of the battle badger. Tom and Cassie climbed after him.

They scrambled onto the badger's broad, wooden head and followed a metal handrail to the decorative tower that stood silhouetted against the moonlight. A figure hobbled towards them.

"Lord Rowanbole!" gasped Captain Jussell, lowering his sword.

The old gnoman smiled, his beard glowing like silver candyfloss.

"Welcome, my friends. How good it is to see you. How lucky it was that we *did* see you, for the effects of the Shadow Tea still cling about you."

He gestured them towards the tower as another round of fireworks burst above the plain.

"This is my sister," said Tom. "We found each other in

the forest."

"As intended, as intended," smiled Rowanbole, bowing as Cassie passed him. "Now, hurry along," he insisted, shooing them into the tower and a spiral staircase that twisted down into the badger's wooden belly.

Tom and Cassie walked carefully, the Shadow Tea making their view of the world ripple strangely. They ducked beneath ropes and pulleys, and enormous, trundling cogwheels, when Captain Jussell suddenly sank to his knees.

"The attack is over, my lord," he said miserably. "The sorcerer's fire revealed my warriors, killing many as they ran. I offer you my sword."

"And what would we do without our finest commander?" Rowanbole sighed. "Headstrong you may be but you are no incompetent. The battle is only just *beginning*. Now go below and help rescue our injured."

Captain Jussell hesitated.

"These battle badgers," he asked, "they come from the jousting fields of summer. How did you come by them?"

"The summer gnomen!" smiled Rowanbole. "They have been repairing them in secret for many years and have been putting them to work in their mines. When the summer gnomen learned of our plan to attack Von Rippenbaum, they persuaded Lord Furrowfox to lend me these devices. Even his Redcap warriors have joined us in battle."

Captain Jussell blinked in surprise, then sprang to his feet and disappeared below. Rowanbole faced Tom and Cassie.

"Are you two ready for one more adventure?" he asked. Tom and Cassie nodded, and the old gnoman led them to a second flight of stairs.

' ' '   ' ' '   ' ' '

Von Rippenbaum emerged into the moonlight.

"The battle badgers, sir," announced the boar commander nervously. "They're stampin' on our men. Why did you order them to do that?"

"I didn't!" screamed Von Rippenbaum. "Unleash the fire-bombs! All of them! *Now!*"

"None left, sir," said the boar, stepping backwards.

"There is a chamber full of them!"

"We used 'em on your birthday, when we blazed your name across the sky – like you ordered."

Von Rippenbaum's scream could be heard above the music of the orchestra, and he sank to his knees and raised his fists.

"I am summoning spirits from the west!" he bellowed. "I am summoning spirits from the east! Rains, rains, give from your skies. Burst water upon them! Bring fire upon them! Blast death upon them!"

An ominous rumble echoed in the distance and clouds gathered from every direction, devouring the moon and the stars. Flickering thunderheads bubbled and rolled, and a heavy silence fell upon the plain. An ear-splitting explosion announced the arrival of the storm and a finger of electricity punctured the earth, flinging gnomen and mechanicals high into the air. A second bolt threw others even higher and drenching sheets of rain fell in sudden torrents. The plain filled with water, and the sure-footed tread of the battle badgers started to falter.

CHAPTER 64

The Battle Turns

ater trickled between armour plating and soaked into timbers and cogwheels. The gnomen ran back and forth, tightening ropes and securing pulleys and shouting as they steered the badger on towards the mound.

The air was thick with the smell of battle as the gnomen warriors loaded shot into cannons that poked from the badger's sides. Rowanbole weaved a skilful path between weaponry and men, and led Tom and Cassie towards a small triangular room.

"We stand at the breastbone of the beast," he explained, closing the door against the noise. "Here you may see what lies ahead of you."

Tom and Cassie stared through thick circles of glass and were astonished to see how close to the mound they now were. Jagged lightning illuminated an odd figure that stood beneath the boughs of the Ringwood Tree, its tubby body and bristling beard so comically different to the image they had seen projected on the moon that Tom and Cassie both laughed.

"Keep watching!" said Rowanbole.

A shape swept from the darkness and sent the toymaker sprawling backwards into the mud.

"An owl's attacking Von Rippenbaum!" cried Tom.

"A gnomen owler to be precise," said Rowanbole, pointing to a helmeted gnoman that rode the bird, guiding it with harness and reins. The owl turned sharply and tried to seize Von Rippenbaum in its talons but it was beaten away by a mechanical guard.

Owl and rider glided back into the night.

Hans Von Rippenbaum wiped the mud from his eyes and stared furiously across the plain. The gnomen were streaming from the forest now, unafraid and emboldened by the presence of the battle badgers. A sea of Redcaps and Yellowcaps swarmed towards the centre, and Von Rippenbaum shrieked and was about to return to the safety of the mound when the earth began to tremble. A jagged opening appeared in the mud, and out of it burst an army of spring Greencaps.

Von Rippenbaum jumped to his feet. He had corrupted these gnomen well and knew that they would defend him with their lives. The Greencaps lifted their weapons and were about to dash forwards when dozens of gnomen owlers swept from the forest and lifted the Greencaps off into the forest. A great cheer filled the air and the fighting turned back towards the mound.

Von Rippenbaum sank to his knees, aware that the tide of battle was turning against him. He lifted his spyglass and studied the nearest battle badger, and saw two little faces staring up at him.

"*Bloodlings!*" he whispered, trembling with fury. "So this battle is for them! They hope to return home. Let them try!"

Inside the mound, the man-headed dog lay fast asleep,

bored by its well-behaved prisoner, who was watching the miniature battle rage across the table top.

Professor Perkins cheered when Von Rippenbaum fell into the mud and cheered again when the gnomen owlers lifted the Greencaps off into the forest. Wet, slapping footsteps suddenly announced the arrival of the toymaker, and Professor Perkins squeaked in alarm and dived under the table.

"Useless mongrel!" shouted Von Rippenbaum, kicking Emperor Joseph awake. The dog howled in terror and scuttled away. Von Rippenbaum jumped onto the table and placed his hands on the belly of the enormous gourd.

"Arise!" he whispered. "Arise! Arise! *My aerial voice revive!*"

On the far side of the chamber, in the root-infested alcove, Tom and Cassie's grandfather stood to attention. The old man's eyes flickered open but they were pale and unseeing.

"Carry the disc," ordered Von Rippenbaum. "Carry the disc and bury it deep within the earth. *Quickly now! Obey me!*"

"*Von Rippenbaum!*" shouted Professor Perkins, jumping out from under the table. "If you bury the disc you will trap us here forever!"

Von Rippenbaum laughed and kicked the little monkey in the face.

♦ ♦ ♦   ♦ ♦ ♦   ♦ ♦ ♦

Between the world of the Ringwood Tree and the world Tom and Cassie had left behind, Von Rippenbaum's order drifted restlessly until it reached the ears of his distant mechanical. The device nodded and entered the hallway.

It headed to the front door, removed the peculiar disc of metal that still hung there, and stepped onto the driveway.

CHAPTER 65

Return to Battle

Inside the badger, two rows of gnomen guarded a hatch that led directly onto the battlefield. The sounds of fighting grew louder and Tom gripped his sword. Cassie unfolded her gatherer's helmet and put it on.

"Please," said Rowanbole, handing Cassie his walking stick. "Please, take this. A modest weapon, perhaps, but it may prove useful."

Cassie stared at the feeble stick and accepted it politely, deciding she would swap it for a sword or an axe the moment she found one. "Remember to stay close to Captain Jussell," added Rowanbole, fixing them both with his keen eyes. "Return home should your attempt to destroy the giant gourd prove too perilous. Enough blood has been spilled this evening."

"Don't worry, we won't do anything stupid, will we Tom?" said Cassie.

"No," said Tom, quietly.

The timbers of the battle badger quivered, and its vaulted spaces rang with the screams of the mechanicals.

"We are nearing the mound!" shouted Rowanbole. "Their struggle becomes desperate! Stand ready to fight. It is almost time."

Iron bolts slid across the hatch and the gnomen warriors lifted their weapons.

"Thomas," said Rowanbole urgently. "There is one other who wishes to fight alongside you. We found him wandering the forest this very evening, alone and in great torment. He insisted on travelling with us."

At Rowanbole's signal, the warriors fell back and an enormous shape appeared at the end of the gallery. The shape filled the corridor, and somewhere near the top if it, a pair of eyes glistened brightly.

"*Bearskin!*" shouted Tom, rushing forwards. The tower of fur swept Tom off the floor. "I *knew* you'd come back," cried Tom. "I knew you'd come back and help me!"

"He cannot hear you," shouted Rowanbole. "He asked us to stop up his ears with cloth and wax so that the sounds of battle would not reach him. His fear is deep but his heart remains strong. Above all, he wishes to protect you."

The cogwheels and pulleys fell silent as the battle badger shuddered to a halt. "And so we come to it!" shouted Rowanbole. "May the spirit of the forest protect us. Open the hatch!"

The gnomen warriors surged forwards.

◆ ◆ ◆   ◆ ◆ ◆   ◆ ◆ ◆

Deep inside the mound, Professor Perkins grew desperate.

"*Please, Von Rippenbaum,*" he insisted. "Do not bury the disc. You would trap us here forever."

"*You* will be trapped!" laughed the toymaker. "I still have time to escape."

"But you cannot return to the world you once knew. Much has changed. Much is unfamiliar. Where will you go? What will you do?"

The toymaker paused.

"I will journey to Paris and to Germany and to Vienna and will visit the descendents of all those learned gentlemen who once mocked my work."

"What on earth for?"

"I will need fresh ingredients. How else am I to begin my new work?"

"No, Von Rippenbaum!" squeaked the professor, tugging on his ropes. "You would be caught in an instant. Men have developed new and terrible weapons, far beyond your imagining."

"Have they, indeed?" said the toymaker with a smile.

. . .   .

Captain Jussell and his men leapt into a sea of nightmarish creatures and cleared a space large enough for Bearskin to jump into.

Bearskin's staff sent a ring of bone and wire flying in every direction, and his terrible roar sent many other mechanicals fleeing in terror.

"I've never killed anything before!" gasped Tom, standing in the doorway and staring as the battle swirled beneath him.

"Just keep the sharp end of your sword away from you!" shouted Cassie. "And remember - those things aren't really alive. They're just wood and metal."

"But their essence is alive. It's fuelled by…" Tom paused, remembering he had decided not to tell Cassie about Von

Rippenbaum's use of blood. He stared at the mound and at the path that spiralled up it, and wondered whether he really would be able to hide his fear long to do anything.

Suddenly, Tom heard Cassie yelling at him and felt her nudge him forwards. Tom flew through the air and landed on Bearskin's shoulders. He blinked in surprise and turned round and saw Cassie jump after him. Suddenly, she stopped and appeared to be hovering in mid-air.

A bird-headed knight sat upon the skeleton of a horse and squawked shrilly at its prize. It had caught Cassie at the end of its lance and had pierced the collar of her gatherer's coat. Cassie kicked and squirmed but couldn't wriggle free, and Tom watched in horror as she was lifted clear of the battle and carried off into the night.

"*No!*" yelled Tom over the noise of the orchestra. "*Casssie!*" he wailed. "*Casssiiieeee!*"

CHAPTER 66

Across the Plain

"D on't worry, lad!" shouted Bearskin. "The gnomen are after 'er."

A wooden box, carved into the shape of an over-sized flea, suddenly sprang up at Bearskin, and its sharp, drilling mouth stabbed at him viciously. Bearskin drove his staff into the mechanical's innards and leapt towards the mound, smashing more of the fleas as he went.

"I can see her!" shouted Tom as they scrambled up the path. "The creature's taking Cassie to the forest."

Tom watched as Captain Jussell and his men raced after the skeleton horse. "I've got to find that gourd," whispered Tom. "I've got to destroy it and stop this."

Bearskin ran on all fours and came to a sudden halt. Tom leapt from his back and ran to an opening in the side of the mound. Chiffchaff suddenly appeared and flew around Bearskin's head, and the giant tensed and noticed a figure scrambling above him between the roots of the

Ringwood Tree.

"*Bristlebeard!*" Bearskin whispered before bounding up the slope.

Tom spun round and saw that he was alone.

˙ ' ˙   ' ˙ '   ˙ ' ˙

"*Let me go!*" shouted Cassie, swinging like a pendulum at the end of the lance. "Let me go! *Let me go!*"

The bird-headed knight squawked with amusement and guided its bony horse on towards the forest.

The ground sped beneath her, and Cassie stared as the mound and the battlefield faded into the distance. Furious with herself for being captured in such a ridiculous fashion, she kicked the air but saw that she was caught fast.

Cassie suddenly noticed that she was still clutching Rowanbole's walking stick and she decided to use it to unseat her ghoulish kidnapper. She raised the stick carefully and aimed for the creature's eyes, when the twisted length of wood began to tingle and glow. A peculiar warmth spread through Cassie's hand and a bright ball of flame suddenly erupted from the stick. The fire blew the mechanical horse apart in a shower of wire and dust, and the knight was flung into the air.

The moon shone like a great, watchful eye, and Cassie found its presence strangely comforting as she lay in the mud staring up at it. Its light was suddenly dimmed when a dark silhouette stepped in front of her; the bird-headed knight had survived its fall. Cassie lashed out with her foot and struck the creature's kneecap, and the knight reeled backwards in agony.

Cassie found the remarkable walking stick, splintered and broken by the force of the blast. The knight lunged after her, dragging its damaged leg behind it, and Cassie turned and ran. A ragged line of mechanicals burst from the forest and quickly surrounded her.

٠ ٠ ٠   ٠ ٠ ٠   ٠ ٠ ٠

Tom and Cassie's grandfather saw nothing of the chamber in front of him, nothing of Professor Perkins, or of the man-headed dog that sat trembling next to him. His eyes saw only what the eyes of his mechanical double saw: his deserted driveway on a cold, December evening in the world he had been forced to leave.

Tucked beneath his mechanical double's arm was the disc.

Professor Trenham's legs rose and fell, powering the legs of his look-a-like, compelled by the power of Von Rippenbaum's spell to bury his only chance of escape. He watched in horror as the creature stepped onto the lawn. He willed it to stop, to drop the disc and run, but could only stare as the creature fell onto its knees and started clawing at the earth.

CHAPTER 67

The Gourd

Tom hadn't gone far inside the mound when a sharp, stabbing pain made him leap into the air. He stared at his foot and saw a group of screws trying to drill themselves into his shoe. Tom yelped and kicked them away and grabbed a torch from a wall bracket. Its flickering light revealed wire, eyeballs, latch-hooks and pliers, and other pieces of scrap, all crawling towards the battlefield in a long, jagged river. Tom scrambled up the wall and clung on to a tree root as the living debris swarmed under him.

The eerie silence returned and Tom lowered himself to the ground. He crept forwards and soon came to the crossing point of several narrow passages. He studied Holligold's map carefully.

"Take the narrowest tunnel," he muttered, peering left and right. Tom raised his sword and continued.

The path sloped sharply and the air grew stale. Tom groped forwards, pausing whenever the noise of battle made earth shake from the ceiling.

"Hide my fear, hide my fear," whispered Tom, wishing he could persuade his hands to stop trembling.

Light spilled from an opening just ahead of him, and the splinter embedded within the handle of Holligold's sword spun wildly. Tom checked the map and saw that he had reached the entrance to Hans von Rippenbaum's secret lair.

Professor Perkins lay beneath the table, sobbing quietly to himself as he imagined a lifetime spent trapped inside the Ringwood. He pulled at his ropes, wondering if he could bring himself to chew through them, when the sound of creeping footsteps made him pause. The legs of a stranger appeared in the doorway, and the professor slunk into the shadows and watched them draw near.

Tom leapt onto the table and stared at the enormous gourd that grew above him. He placed the tip of his sword against the gourd's leathery surface and saw the giant vegetable quiver as if it knew what Tom meant to do.

Filaments of light suddenly flickered across the gourd's even surface, the lights' eerie glow filling the entire chamber. Images of Tom appeared, jumping from scene to scene like a speeded-up film, and Tom stared in confusion and lowered his sword.

The images flickered faster and drew Tom nearer, and the gourd pulsed excitedly and extended web-like threads. The threads brushed gently across Tom's forehead and the images were immediately transformed into every troubling nightmare that Tom had ever had. He watched shadowy figures chase him through unfamiliar rooms, angry dogs chase him through unfamiliar streets, and he saw himself, frightened and alone, roaming through an abandoned, haunted house. Then came the most terrible nightmare of all: the gourd showed him his parents lying between the roots of a tree, dead and unburied.

"*No!*" croaked Tom. "*Help me, Cassie! Help me!*"

Hide your fear! Tom imagined his sister shouting. *Hide your fear and fight!*

Tom tore the threads from his face and raised his sword. "Stop it!" he shouted. "Stop all these lies! Mum and dad aren't dead! They aren't!"

The gourd magnified the image of his parents until they filled its entire surface. Tom almost ran from the chamber. "*N-no!*" he gasped. "*You're lying! You're lying!*" He closed his eyes and thrust the sword as far as it would go. The gourd bucked and heaved and quivered strangely.

"You!" cried a voice near Tom's feet. "You! Thomas Trenham! What the devil are you doing here? Quickly, my boy! Jump from the table before…"

But Professor Perkins' warning came too late.

The hot, cascading contents of Von Rippenbaum's sinister gourd burst all over him, dashing Tom to the ground.

CHAPTER 68

Truth and Tragedy

A lump of wood flew from the shadows and struck Cassie across her chest. She fell on her back, winded and unable to move, and watched in horror as the knight and its companions loomed over her.

The knight raised its sword and held it over Cassie's heart. The other mechanicals crowded closer, keen to see the blade do its work.

Captain Jussell shouted in alarm, but from the faintness of his voice and the distant replies of his men, Cassie knew that she was beyond their help.

She tried to wriggle free, but the mechanicals pinned her where she lay.

Cassie knew that her struggle was over.

She stared at the moon and decided to fill her final moments with the happiest thoughts she could imagine.

She pictured Tom and her parents and her grandfather returning home…

The knight raised its sword…

She pictured them in her grandfather's study, drinking tea and eating toast and cake…

The tip of the knight's sword quivered…

She pictured her grandfather burying the disc and promising that he would never to use it again.

The sword plunged down…

… and Cassie jumped when the blade tumbled into the mud next to her. The knight and the mechanicals were staggering backwards and were flailing their arms about as if they were on fire.

Across the plain, every mechanical device was reeling about in the same peculiar manner. Suddenly, the air filled with a sinister rumble that turned into a deafening roar. Cassie rolled onto her stomach, desperate to reach the mound and safety, when four pairs of white hooves started trotting around her.

♦ ♦ ♦   ♦ ♦ ♦   ♦ ♦ ♦

"*Bristlebeard!*" roared Bearskin, leaping up the mound. "*Ogerhunch! Devil spit! Thief!*"

He jumped from tree root to tree root, bounding towards his prey who stood silhouetted next to the Ringwood Tree. The toymaker was surveying his kingdom for the last time.

Bearskin sent his staff arcing viciously towards him, but Von Rippenbaum ducked and let it clatter past him. The toymaker laughed and was about to enter the tree, when the menacing rumble became a deafening roar.

The mound quivered, the air shook, and the twisted body of the Ringwood Tree exploded into a million jagged pieces.

♦ ♦ ♦   ♦ ♦ ♦   ♦ ♦ ♦

The deer were more vividly real than Cassie had seen them; their bodies shone with a new and dazzling intensity. They cantered around her then stopped when Captain Jussell and his men lifted Cassie onto the stag's back. Cassie nodded gratefully, her movements slow and tranquil as if she was underwater.

"You are safe," she heard the deer comfort her.

"That rumbling noise," mumbled Cassie, uncertain whether she was dreaming or awake. "What is that rumbling noise?"

"It is the end of Von Rippenbaum's influence. Look."

The stag turned and faced the battle, and Cassie gasped when the jagged silhouette of the mighty Ringwood Tree exploded into a million fragments.

"It's...*gone!*" cried Cassie. "How will we get home?"

"Watch," said the deer.

Far in the distance, a tiny shoot swayed back and forth at the top of the mound. It rose in the air, unfurling branches as it grew, and surged higher, stretching in all directions. Thousands of leaves suddenly filled its spreading form, and a magnificent new tree stood gleaming in the moonlight.

"It is over," said the stag. "The Ringwood is free. It is time for you to go."

The deer circled slowly then raced towards the mound.

CHAPTER 69

In the Professor's Garden

The mechanical scraped at the frozen earth, its wooden fingers worn away to the metal stubs of its framework.

The disc lay next to it.

It had reeled backwards when Tom's sword had pierced the gourd and it had fallen onto its belly when the Ringwood Tree had exploded. Now it lay on the grass, struggling to complete its final task as Von Rippenbaum's influence ebbed out of it.

‧ ‧ ‧   ‧ ‧ ‧   ‧ ‧ ‧

Deep inside the mound, a little voice echoed through the chamber.

"Thomas Trenham? Are you 'O' and 'K'?"

The chamber had rocked violently, sending roots and soil and mummified bodies crashing to the floor.

Thomas lay on his stomach, covered in a dark, foul-smelling ooze. He coughed and choked, then lifted his head.

"*Professor!*" he cried, wiping slime from his eyes. He wobbled to his feet and went to hug the little monkey, but Professor Perkins backed away.

"Perhaps after a little soap and water," said the professor. "And even then, a firm handshake only."

"I knew I'd see you again!" laughed Tom. "The gnomen were right! Your symbol *was* at the centre!"

"Symbol? Gnomen? How mysterious you are. But your story will have to wait, for we are both in grave peril. The disc is being re-buried, even as we speak. That villainous wretch is about to escape but there may yet be time to stop him. Your sword, Thomas. Quickly. Cut my bonds."

Tom sliced through the professor's ropes and the little monkey rubbed his wrists gratefully. "Well done," he said. "Oh, very well done, my dear, dear fellow. You may save us all yet!" Professor Perkins scampered over to the alcove in which Tom's grandfather stood.

For the first time since entering the chamber, Tom noticed the mummified bodies.

"Are they all…?" he wondered, staring around the room.

"Yes, quite dead," sighed the professor. "Now, I want you to be strong, Thomas, and remember that you are an Englishman. I have some grave news, some astonishing news – news that is both grave and astonishing. The figure in this alcove is none other than your…"

"*Grandfather!*" cried Tom, rushing over to the alcove. "So *that's* how Von Rippenbaum controlled his mechanical double!"

"*You know of your grandfather's presence in the Ringwood?!*" gasped the professor.

"He sent me a note. Can hear us?" wondered Tom.

"I do not think so," replied the professor, studying Professor Trenham carefully.

"Why are his hands twitching like that?" asked Tom.

"Your grandfather is steering his mechanical double and is quite helpless to resist. I hoped the destruction of the gourd would have severed the link between them, but that does not appear to be the case. The mechanical is attempting to bury the disc in the garden. From your grandfather's movements, it has not yet completed its task. That is good. That is very good! There may yet be time for us to escape."

Professor Perkins scrambled up the wall and dangled over the alcove. He studied the shoots protruding from Tom's grandfather's head carefully and tutted.

"Your sword," he snapped, "Stand ready to catch your grandfather. I am about to indulge in some vigorous pruning."

♦ ♦ ♦   ♦ ♦ ♦   ♦ ♦ ♦

At first, Bearskin thought that one of the forest owls had lifted him off the ground. But Bearskin remembered that there were no birds large enough or strong enough or foolish enough that would dare try and lift him, and he watched in confusion as tree roots, branches and bark spun around him. Bearskin curled into a ball, grunting as he bumped, bounced and skidded to a halt in a deep trough of mud. He struggled to his feet and roared defiantly, and several dazed mechanicals fled in terror. Bearskin turned and faced the mound, and stared in mute fascination as a new and unfamiliar shoot rose into the air. A sudden movement near the base of the mound made the giant spring forwards. Von Rippenbaum had survived the explosion.

The toymaker ran quickly over the remains of his mechanical army, kicking them aside as they turned to him for help. His ears rang and his vision was blurry but he reached the spiral path unharmed. He was about to race up it when an enormous shape loomed out in front of him.

"*Bristlebeard!*" growled the figure. Von Rippenbaum shrieked and threw a handful of powder in Bearskin's face. Bearskin's eyes streamed with tears and he plunged his muzzle in a pool of freezing rainwater. Bearskin blinked and cursed, and turned in time to see Von Rippenbaum running towards a cable of rope and an iron hoop spiked into the ground.

Von Rippenbaum climbed the rope as nimbly like a rat. Bearskin leapt after him, determined to stop his bearded tormentor reaching the safety of the hot-air balloon that floated above the plain.

Chapter 70

An Unexpected Truce

Cassie clung to the stag's neck as it galloped up the spiral path and skidded to a halt in front of a dark opening.

"Your friends are near," she heard it say. "Run inside and help them."

Cassie raced inside the mound, trembling at the thought that she was about to see her parents again. An imposing figure appeared from the darkness and gazed down at her tearfully.

"*Grandfather?!*" cried Cassie, rushing forwards to hug him. The old man blinked and said nothing.

"You!" cried a second figure, jumping out from behind Professor Trenham.

Girl and monkey stared at one another in silence, Professor Perkins wondering whether Cassie had forgiven him for his deceitfulness while Cassie wondered whether the professor had forgiven her for her short-temper.

"You are Professor Perkins," said Cassie slowly. The little

monkey frowned, not understanding her meaning. "You are Professor Perkins," Cassie repeated. "Classicist, scholar…"

"… *man of science!*" whispered the professor, suddenly aware that this troublesome girl, this maddening, argumentative and perplexing young lady, who had doubted him for so long and with such ill temper, finally believed him to be human.

"And you," he replied guiltily, "you are a strong-willed adventurer whose trust I betrayed and whose life I imperilled for the sake of my vanity. Can you ever forgive me?"

Cassie pulled the bandaged witch's bottle from the shoulder-bag and handed it to the professor. She took her grandfather's arm and stared at Tom.

"Is Grandfather all right?" she asked nervously.

"It's nervous exhaustion," said Tom, relieved that Cassie was unharmed. "That's what Professor Perkins called it. He said he needs lots of bed rest." Tom suddenly noticed Cassie's clothes. "Ergh! You're covered in mud!"

"And you're covered in slime," said Cassie.

"It was the gourd. It burst all over me. It wasn't very nice. But you were right, Cassie. I hid my fear just like you told me, and it worked."

"Conquered it, more like!" said Cassie, squeezing Tom's hand. "You saved my life again, Tom. That doesn't make me your slave, though!"

Tom suddenly remembered Von Rippenbaum and the disc, and he shouted, "Hey, we have to hurry! The disc's being re-buried. We might become trapped!"

"Your brother is right!" gasped Professor Perkins, deciding to unwrap his mysterious present later. "There is very little time and we have yet to reach the top of the mound."

"It's all right," smiled Cassie. "We have a lift."

◆ ▾   ◆ ▾   ◆ ▾

Down upon the plain, the living remains of Von Rippenbaum's army were being herded into groups by gnomen warriors. The rest of the gnomen were gathering their dead and their injured to the edge of the forest where pine-beamed sledges ferried them underground.

The forest echoed with a grieving lament.

"That's what I saw!" gasped Tom, staring in wonder as he approached the white stag. "It ran out in front of me when I was driving the spider. Is it real?"

"I'm not sure," said Cassie softly. "But they've been watching us from the very beginning, Tom, and they've been helping us – whenever they could."

The deer sat on the ground, and Tom and Cassie guided their grandfather onto the stag's back. Tom sat behind him and wrapped his arms around his grandfather's waist. Professor Perkins jumped onto the back of the hind and waited for Cassie to join him. But Cassie turned and ran towards the mound.

"Where are you going?" snapped the professor.

"I still have to find mum and dad!" shouted Cassie.

"We will become trapped!" cried the professor.

"Go without me. I'll see you all later."

"There may not *be* any 'later' in which we may be seen!"

Suddenly, Cassie heard the hind's soft voice echo in her mind.

"Do as the professor asks, Cassie. Run for the tree. Run and return home."

Cassie fell to her knees and stared at the deer. It had spoken to her not as the wise and kindly stranger, but with the voice of someone Cassie had sensed had been with her from the very beginning.

Cassie started to cry.

CHAPTER 71

Found and Lost

Frozen earth skittered across the disc's icy surface as the mechanical arm moved back and forth across the hole.

• • •   • • •   • • •

Mum?! cried Cassie, not wanting to speak the word aloud and appear foolish – or worse – in front of the others.

She had obeyed her mother's request and now sat with Professor Perkins as the deer raced towards the tree.

"I'm here with your father," Cassie heard her mother's voice tell her. "We've been with you all the time."

I don't understand! thought Cassie. *Where are you?*

The voice of her father suddenly filled Cassie's mind.

"Cassie, my love. Our essence, ourselves – everything we are; they're all part of the Ringwood now. We're in the trees and in the wind and in the leaves that cover the earth. We were even in the water that washed the blood from your face. We can go anywhere, Cassie, and can influence any animal, but only for a short while."

You mean… you're dead?!

"No!" said her mother. "Not exactly. It doesn't feel bad or scary any more. You've been so brave and clever. And you've looked after Tom so well."

Cassie fell against the hind's neck.

"Don't cry, Cassie," said her mother. "Please. Don't cry. We love you and Tom so much."

But Cassie couldn't stop, aware that the very thing she had sensed from the beginning of her journey, but had refused to accept, was true.

Come with us! she thought, wiping the tears from her eyes. *Run through the tree and come home!*

"We can't," said her father. "We only exist in the Ringwood now."

As deer?

"As anything we wish to influence. And that influence is stronger, now that you and Tom have lifted Von Rippenbaum's curse. You have helped so many, Cassie: every lost soul and forest traveller Von Rippenbaum has ever tormented. They're free."

"How am I going to explain this to Tom?" sniffed Cassie.

"You'll find a way. You always do. Look after him, Cassie. And let him look after you."

"We love you," said her mother. "We love you both so very much. Come back soon. Come back soon."

Their voices faded as the stag and the hind galloped for the tree.

Cassie rummaged in her pockets for a handkerchief, when a little square of card slipped between her fingers. Its message glinted in the moonlight and Cassie smiled bitterly as she finally understood the owl's cryptic words,

**TWO LIVES, YES
TWO LIVES, NO
THOSE ABOVE
WATCH BELOW.**

Cassie flung the card into the air and watched it spin away as the deer raced beneath the boughs of the new Ringwood Tree.

Like the rising orb of a second moon, Von Rippenbaum's hot-air balloon suddenly appeared in front of them. The boar's-head undercarriage turned slowly, trailing a length of rope to which a shaggy figure was clinging.

"*Bearskin!*" cried Tom, almost falling off the stag. Bearskin roared as if he had heard him.

A second figure appeared in a window high above him.

"It's Von Rippenbaum!" cried Tom. "He's got a knife!"

"Look away, Thomas!" shouted Professor Perkins. "There is nothing we can do for him."

"He's going to cut the rope!" shouted Tom. "He's going to murder Bearskin!"

Cassie closed her eyes.

Please, she thought. *Please, mum and dad. If there's anything you can do, please help our friend.*

Bearskin grew smaller as the balloon raced higher, when a soft rush of air made Cassie turn.

Far away, on the distant horizon, a darker shade of night came rippling towards them.

One by one, the stars began to vanish.

CHAPTER 72

Death of a Friend

"Goodbye, filthy stinkbeast!" laughed Von Rippenbaum, holding the knife against the rope. He paused and added, "Let us wait a little longer and rise a little higher. I want those bones of yours to *shatter*, not break!"

Bearskin inched up the rope, his rage focused on the toymaker. Chiffchaff suddenly appeared and launched itself at his tormentor, who laughed and fell back inside the boar's head, batting the little bird aside as if it were a fly.

Bearskin stared in horror when a dark shadow flew inside the open window. It was Risratch, Von Rippenbaum's raven, who had been hiding in the forest, determined to win its master's respect.

Bearskin climbed faster but froze when Chiffchaff suddenly reappeared. The little bird flew down to him, fluttering like a rag doll, until it fell against Bearskin's chest. High above them, Von Rippenbaum cut the rope, sending Bearskin plummeting to the plain below.

Bearskin hardly noticed. He held the lifeless body of his friend in his paws and saw that the raven's beak had done its work: Chiffchaff's neck had been snapped in two, his wings were broken and bent.

Bearskin curled into a ball and wept.

♦ ♦ ♦   ♦ ♦ ♦   ♦ ♦ ♦

"*Owls!*" shouted Cassie. "Owls and ravens and crows and rooks and all the birds of the forest! Look, Tom! It's incredible!"

The enormous flock swept over them and swarmed beneath Bearskin, gripping his fur and his sash in their beaks and claws and lowering him to the ground.

The deer bounded to a halt in front of the Ringwood Tree, and Tom leapt from the stag. He stared across the plain and saw Bearskin standing near the edge of the forest. Tom waved, uncertain whether his friend could see him, but Bearskin turned and looked.

"Goodbye!" shouted Tom. "I'll come back and see you, I promise!"

Bearskin raised a paw then vanished into the night, the body of his guide tucked inside his sash.

"*Tom!*" shouted Cassie. "Come and help me with Grandfather."

"Will the birds catch Von Rippenbaum?" asked Tom, running over to help.

The balloon and the boar's head passed in front of the moon, tiny against the giant ring of light.

"May we continue this discussion in a more familiar realm?" cried Professor Perkins, urging them towards an opening in the side of the Ringwood Tree. The opening was smooth and narrow, and it curved in on itself like a seashell. Tom entered first, leading his grandfather by the hand.

Professor Perkins followed, making certain that the old man didn't stumble backwards. Cassie hesitated at the entrance.

Thank you, she thought, uncertain whether her parents still influencing the deer. The deer bowed gracefully.

"Thank *you*," she heard them reply, their voices now a chorus of hundreds of people. "The forest lives in you and around you and because of you, and you will always be welcome to walk within its beauty."

The deer bowed again then turned and galloped away, and Cassie smiled and ran inside the tree.

"My fur is beginning to bristle!" announced Professor Perkins as he stumbled through the darkness. "Press forwards, Thomas. Time is flying that cannot be recalled."

But Tom had gone, snatched away by the magical process that was already returning him to an overgrown garden on a cold December evening.

Professor Trenham was next, and the old man gave a startled little cry before vanishing abruptly.

"And so it begins!" cried Professor Perkins, turning to tell Cassie the good news. Another voice suddenly sounded in the darkness.

"Hello," it croaked. "Go without me?"

The figure reached down and grabbed Cassie's hair.

CHAPTER 73

A Noble Gesture

The transparent outlines of Tom and his grandfather hovered above the disc, rippling like smoke. Nerves, veins, tendons and arteries clung to the framework of their bones, each layer visible beneath the next, until their forms gradually became full and solid. The surface of the disc glowed fiercely beneath them.

Their images suddenly vanished, drawn back into the mysterious tree.

The mechanical's arm swept back and forth, pushing frozen earth down onto the disc.

•••   •••   •••

"*Let me go!*" cried Cassie, trying to wriggle free. The creature's grip remained firm.

"Release her, whoever you are!" demanded Professor Perkins, peering blindly into the darkness. "I warn you: I am armed!"

He reached inside his shoulder-bag and pulled out the little bundle Cassie had given him earlier, assuming it was the revolver. He started to unwrap the bandages.

"Duman not help you now!" hissed the creature. "No scuttling eight legs to carry you away. No little beards to stop me doing *this!*" It jabbed the blade of a knife against Cassie's throat.

"*Horse-head!*" whispered Cassie. "Wh-what are you doing here? What do you want?"

"Reward!" the little skeleton clicked angrily.

"Reward? What for?"

"For you! Duman promise me essence – but you escape – *twice!*"

Cassie wondered whether she could pull the creature off the wall, and was just about to try when a burst of light filled the passageway.

"No!" whispered Professor Perkins, staring in astonishment at the bottle, and at the familiar image that glowed within it.

"Drink it!" shouted Cassie. "Drink it or splash it or dance around it but just hurry up and get your real body back! This thing's got a knife!"

"The witch bottle!" gasped the professor. "You rescued the witch bottle. My dignity, my true, human self, encased within glass!"

His eyes filled with tears.

Frightened by the eerie light and the mention of a witch, Horse-head started dragging Cassie back towards the opening of the tree. Tom's voice suddenly rang through the darkness.

"The disc, professor! It's almost covered. We couldn't get through!"

Professor Perkins fell against the wall, his mind reeling. He tried to remember the things he had learned when he had researched the folklore of the forest.

"I believe I once read that a… a combined strength of purpose," he stammered, "a single, unifying will, could force forest travellers out of the disc if their exit was partially blocked. Yes! We must act as a single entity, children, and travel as one. Join hands and *think*. Let us *think* ourselves free."

But Cassie was almost outside, and she screamed.

"Release her!" shouted Professor Perkins, raising the glowing bottle. "I offer you no further warning!"

Horse-head froze and stared at him uncertainly.

"No!" shouted Cassie. "Don't throw it, professor. It's you, your body, your real, human body. Isn't that what you came back for?"

"I believe I have found something far more valuable," said the professor quietly. "Humility's triumph over pride."

He hurled the bottle at the skeleton, and the container and Horse-head both exploded with a bang. A misty vapour filled the tree and Cassie staggered forwards, her eyes streaming with tears.

"This way," shouted the professor, taking Cassie's hand. "Think only of home. Now children. Think!"

As soon as Cassie gripped the professor's paw, she felt herself being pulled, stretched and then, quite unexpectedly, dropped. There was a peculiar drop in the weight of everything around her and Cassie was plunged into a terrifying darkness.

Chapter 74

A Dark Winter Night

A column of earth blasted from the hole and sent the mechanical waxwork tumbling backwards. Moments later, Tom, Cassie, Professor Perkins and Professor Trenham were all thrown out of the disc. They lay face down in the frosty grass as smoke drifted over them.

Tom blinked and raised his head, and saw a figure limping past him.

"Grandfather?" he whispered. "Grandfather, is that you?"

"Tom?!" cried his grandfather joyfully. "Yes, it's me! My mind has cleared and I see that we are standing in my garden!"

Tom jumped to his feet and threw his arms around the old man, who laughed and hugged him warmly.

"Go and help your sister," said Tom's grandfather. "I want to make certain we are safe." He limped towards the hole.

The glowing disc of metal had cooled, and it lay, half-buried, in the soil.

"Nearly, Von Rippenbaum, nearly," whispered Tom's grandfather, stepping over it. He saw his mechanical lookalike and he wandered over to it cautiously.

The figure lay on its back, its eyes dim and unseeing. Professor Trenham prodded it with his foot and crouched next to it. He touched its waxy face.

"Careful, professor," said a voice behind him.

Professor Perkins jumped forwards and opened a door in the mechanical's chest. "Living essence," he whispered, handing Tom's grandfather a glass jar. "You know whose blood is mixed within?"

Professor Trenham nodded and stared at the undulating liquid.

"I *will* tell the children, Perkins, but not now, not tonight." He tucked the bottle inside his jacket. "Oh, and Perkins," he said sadly. "Will you ever be able to forgive me?"

"Forgive *you*, professor? Whatever for? You were not the one who constructed a forest of phantasmagoria and powered it with the blood of innocents."

"I know, Perkins, but the disc, the deception, the loss of your human body – the loss of everything you once knew!"

"There is only one whose repentance I seek, professor, though I hardly expect the fiend to offer it. Besides, there are others who bear a much heavier loss than mine."

Both professors watched as Tom helped Cassie to her feet. "However will they manage?" the little monkey wondered quietly.

"As they did in the forest," said Professor Trenham, "with courage, with fortitude and with the wise counsel of others to guide them."

"Do you intend to oversee their upbringing?" asked Professor Perkins.

"Not I, Perkins, *we*... assuming you choose to remain and live in my... I beg your pardon, *your* old house!"

Professor Perkins stared in astonishment.

"*Choose* to remain? You mean you would allow me to live here with you?"

"Why ever not?!"

"I would be a daily reminder of the forest, a living symbol of its torment."

"Nonsense!" laughed Professor Trenham. "You are an invaluable friend without whom none of us might have returned. Tom is as fond of you as you are of him and there is much that you could teach young Cassie… and she you. Will you stay and be their tutor, Perkins? Will you stay and share your knowledge?"

"Their tutor?!" gasped the professor. "Their knowledge of Latin *does* appear to be non-existent, whilst their enthusiasm for the sciences seems less than wholehearted. There would be so many lectures to prepare, so many subjects to discuss…"

The little monkey's face beamed with pleasure.

"Then is it agreed?"

"It is agreed, professor!" He shook Professor Trenham's hand joyfully.

Tom and Cassie stared at the disc. It lay, silent and still and as dark as the earth that had almost covered it. Wisps of smoke rose from its surface.

Cassie suddenly jumped over it and threw her arms around her grandfather, who lifted her clear of the ground.

"Oh, but you're freezing!" he exclaimed. "And you're covered in mud. And *you* are covered in something altogether more unpleasant, Tom. Inside, both of you, and let's build up a fire. Hot baths and warm towels as well. Perkins, would you carry the disc indoors with Tom?"

"Indoors?!" spluttered the professor. "Should we not bury it, more deeply than ever?"

"*No!*" shouted Cassie. "The disc must *never* be buried!" She stared at her grandfather, wondering if he knew of her parents' survival.

The old man smiled.

"Cassie is right," he said. "The disc must never be buried, nor must we ever lose it, for I've an idea that it hasn't quite finished with us yet. Now let's go indoors before we all turn into icicles."

Tom and the professor crouched by the hole and started to lift the disc.

"Thank you," whispered Cassie, taking her grandfather's hand.

"That's all right," smiled Professor Trenham. "I've always considered it rude to bury loved ones, especially when they remain quite well and open to visits!" He squeezed Cassie's hand and winked.

"Tom doesn't know yet," said Cassie. "Mum and Dad didn't speak to him. I don't think they wanted to frighten him. He *is* younger than me."

"A bonfire!" interrupted Professor Perkins, following Cassie and the professor across the lawn. "We must build a bonfire and consign your waxy look-a-like to the fiery flames of justice."

"Tomorrow, Perkins, after we have rested. Besides, we have more important matters to attend to."

"More important than burning that *abomination?!*"

"You mean you've forgotten?" asked Professor Trenham. "Was there not a tea-tray and a teapot and plate of warm toast? Was there not a large and rather succulent ginger cake waiting to be eaten?"

"There was!" cried Professor Perkins, suddenly realising just how hungry he was. "Tomorrow, then. I will build a good fire and dispose of that thing."

He lifted the disc and padded towards the house.

Epilogue

The shadows were the same. The trees and the plants and the bushes were just as Tom remembered them. But to his surprise, and relief, the shortcut through the park held none of their former terrors.

Professor Perkins wore the same baggy clothes he had first met Tom in, and he illuminated the ground with a torch, highlighting where it was safe for them to tread. They emerged from the bushes and entered the park, and Tom and Cassie paused under the light of a lamp-post.

"I miss my gatherer's coat," said Cassie, plucking at the baggy jumper her grandfather had given to her.

"I miss my Ringwood clothes," said Tom, wearing the school uniform Professor Perkins had used as a disguise to deliver the note.

A snowflake settled on Tom's shoe and the air filled with dots.

"Are you sure we haven't missed Christmas?" asked Tom,

staring into the sky.

"You *know* we haven't," groaned Cassie. "Grandfather checked all the clocks. We only spent six minutes in the Ringwood – six minutes of normal time."

Tom watched the snowflakes flutter through the lamp light.

"When can we go back?" he asked quietly. "I want to see Bearskin again. And Rowanbole. I want to find out what happened to Von Rippenbaum. But most of all, I want to see Mum and Dad."

Cassie spun round.

"*You mean you know they're still alive?!*"

Tom nodded.

"Why didn't you say anything, Tom?! I've been tying myself up in knots wondering how I was going to tell you. How did you find out?"

"It was after I'd stabbed the gourd. The mound trembled and shook. Tree roots and bodies fell from the ceiling. Mum and Dad were lying on the floor."

"But how did you find out about their spirits?"

"When the gourd split open, hundreds of people rushed past me: the spirits of everyone Von Rippenbaum had ever used. They moved slowly, like a river of ghosts, but I wasn't frightened. Mum and dad came to me and smiled. I didn't tell you in case you got upset."

"And I didn't tell you because I thought you were too young."

Cassie sighed.

"So when can we go back?" asked Tom.

"Soon, I promise. But we need to rest and think about everything that's happened. And I need to do some serious Christmas shopping." Cassie remembered the empty alcoves of a certain museum and a promise she had made to fill them.

"Fresh air and snowflakes!" shouted an irritated voice.

"Fresh air and snowflakes! That is all I have been guiding for the last few minutes. I turned around and saw that you had left me!"

"Sorry, professor," said Cassie, hiding a smile.

She reached inside her pocket.

"If it's not too early, Merry Christmas."

The professor cupped the object in his paws.

"M-my watch!" he stammered, his voice thick with emotion. "Thank you – both of you – so very much. Our journey has been long, its dangers considerable, yet here we stand, together and in safety, handing one another Christmas gifts! As the forest sun revealed the day to us, you, dear children, revealed the adults in you. I know that I am in excellent company."

He handed Tom the torch and asked him to light the path. Tom ran forwards and slid across the snow-speckled ground.

"If I may return the favour," said the professor, handing Cassie a dark square.

"The book of shame!" laughed Cassie, flicking through a notebook filled with the professor's notes.

"May we begin anew and 'wipe the slate clean'?" asked the monkey.

"All right" said Cassie.

"Excellent! Then let me give you another Christmas present: a rather splendid piece of news."

"Oh?"

"Your grandpapa has appointed me as your tutor. I am to assist you and Tom in your studies after school!"

"*What?!*" cried Cassie.

"I know," smiled Professor Perkins. "I am as elated as you appear to be."

"You can't!" cried Cassie. "I mean… you just can't!"

The professor looked startled.

"Your time," blurted Cassie. "It's much too valuable to waste on us!"

"Oh, on the contrary. I consider it an honour, a duty and a privilege. In return, I ask that you assist me in the ways of your twenty-first century. I find them most perplexing."

Cassie stared into the professor's bright little eyes and nodded reluctantly. She sauntered over to the park gates where Tom was waiting, and told him the news.

"Our *teacher?!*" cried Tom. "Cool!"

"No, it will be warm," insisted the professor. "I always light two fires in my lecture room: the fire of coal and the fire of knowledge!"

Cassie groaned.

"*Your* first lesson will be twenty-first century English: phrases and slang," she said.

"My English is exemplary!" snapped the monkey. "I have won awards for it."

"It's fine, professor," laughed Tom. "It's 'O' and 'K'!"

Tom handed Professor Perkins the torch and asked him to lead them home.

THE END